THE ROSE OF THE WEST

Books by Mark Bondurant

★ The Rose of the West
★ Max and Mrs. Stroud: A Tale of Love
  and Destruction

The Autobiography of Calista Antoine:
★ Red Jacket
★ A Bad Crossing
★ Paris!

THE ROSE OF THE WEST

MARK BONDURANT

DIG IT

Bongo Books, Camarillo, CA

*I dedicate this, my first published
book, to
Thomas, Benjamin, and Stacy*

CONTENTS

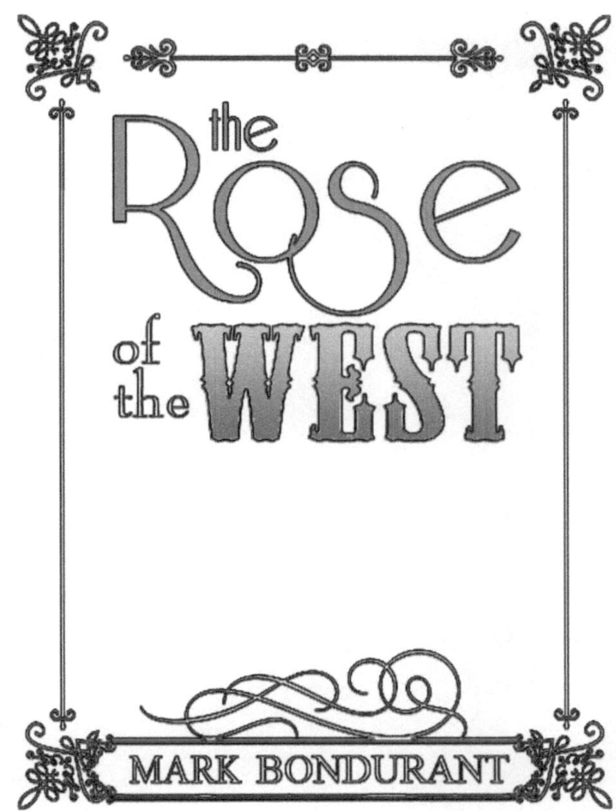
the
Rose
of
the WEST

MARK BONDURANT

INTRODUCTION

Now all of you I`m sure have heard about the Hayden gang and The Rose Mine, their daring exploits at Moon Ridge and Cripple Creek, at least as far as the dime novels tell it. But I don`t think many of you know a whole lot about Deke and Kay themselves, when they were young and alone, and that`s a story that should be told. For if it`s the blood of love that waters the West then this is a spring whose water should be tasted.

Deke Hayden grew up out on the plains during the Western Wars. Like many refugees, Deke's family was taken in by the Indians, Paiute, and fought by their side against Mexico and her allies. The loss of his family and their ranch, and just about everybody he knew to the war, left young Deke free to wonder the world and to come to terms with it as he chose. That was until the Great War came along.

Kay Mapleton, because that`s what she was before she was that Kay Hayden you read about, was a child alone in a sea of woe, something that wasn`t uncommon during the Great War. She had lost practically all her kin, having just about gotten back up from losing one, when another would keel over on top of her. It`s no wonder she learned early, like so many kids of her time, to stand on her own two feet and take matters into her own hands.

CHAPTER 1

Kay sat with her hat on her lap and her bag at her feet in a firmly padded chair with her aunt beside her, on a hot and stuffy summer morning in 1892, in Mr. Bayers the lawyer`s office on the second floor of a tall building in downtown Philadelphia. The interior was well appointed, with wood paneling and a lot of nice things like books and a globe. It had a window which let in sunlight stained yellow by coal smoke, and electricity, which he was proud of, having turned on the light over his desk even though he really didn`t need it.

Kay, whose real name was Catherine, named after some Russian queen and would have rolled her eyes if you mentioned it, did not want to be in that chair. She fidgeted appropriately. Her father had died when she was very young, she could barely remember him, her four brothers had all been killed in the war, which left her an only child, and her mother had died of fever two years ago. With the death of her grandma and the need to read the will, she had no choice but to sit in that seat again. Her grandma and she had lived in a cottage on the edge of the Philadelphia. She had moved there after they had sold her family`s house. Kay, being young and unmarried, couldn`t live there alone.

Her grandma`s house had been small, but Kay didn`t have much left, and she and her grandma had fit in nicely. What she had could fit in the large trunk at the foot of her bed, the blankets and linens being moved to the quilt rack by the window. There were some things of her parents, what they sent back of her brothers, and letters and pictures of relatives she never knew. Her aunt knew some of them, and with her Grandma`s death she realized her mistake, writing what she could still find out from her aunt in the corners and edges.

Neighbors had come by, bringing food, tisking as they thought of her now alone, eyeing the house wondering how much she was going to sell it for. Kay in return had been polite, even gracious, ignoring the soot they tracked in. The June summer was hot, but the rain kept the air as clean as it ever got, and she could open windows without worrying about things getting too dirty. This meant that there were occasional breezes through the house and the sounds of people in the streets. She could hear the neighbors as they walked up her doorstep.

The lawyer didn`t like summer and was clearly

over-dressed, but being as he was a lawyer and was charging for this, felt he needed to dress for the work. But he still had to mop his forehead with his handkerchief halfway through. He remembered most of what he was reading since he had helped to write it. The grandmother had not anticipated her relatively early death and had left the girl the house when she was clearly too young to own it. They would have to sell it. It was just a matter of getting this girl to realize the need. He did not relish what must come next.

Then of course, there was the matter of the envelope and the key. He could feel the key inside the envelope, could see its shape through the side. Things like this always left him with a certain amount of anticipation, a little mystery that made this work bearable. Sadly though, by its size he expected it to be a safe deposit box key, which meant he wouldn`t be around to see the contents. No he sighed, he would probably never know.

Kay saw that sigh at the end of the will, and mistook for weariness, like the reading had been a hard pull to get through. What would she do with a house? Where could she go? She had been through this before and knew she had to move on, but she couldn`t think of anywhere else she wanted to live.

The lawyer put down the page and looked up. "And so Miss Mapleton, do you have any preferences as to the disposition of the property?" He looked hopeful.

"No sir, I don`t. I`m not sure how I feel just now. You did say there was money. I`m not going to starve immediately?" She felt a little numb. The question had annoyed her for some reason.

"No, no, you`re fine for the time being," he said. "With your family`s money and your grandmothers, you`ll have no troubles for awhile. But you can`t live alone in that house. It just isn`t proper or safe."

Aunt Grace came to the rescue. "I will stay for a little while Hon. I don`t have to go immediately." She put her hand on Kay`s and said, "We`ll get things in order. There`s Mama`s things to go through and after that we`ll see."

"And then there`s this too," the lawyer said, sliding an envelope across the table. It was sealed with paste and on the side was the imprint of a key, like it had been stacked in a pile of paper for some time. "Your grandmother said you were to have this. You wouldn`t happen to know anything about it?" He looked hopefully at both women but received only blank stares. "No," he said. "I suppose not," weakly hiding his professional disappointment.

Kay took the envelope, flipped it over, but saw that it was entirely blank. With a frayed, annoyed frown she stuffed it in her bag next to her hated needlepoint.

"I`m afraid that`s it," he said. "This copy of the will is for you." He passed the sheets of paper across his desk. These she folded and stuffed in her bag next to the envelope.

Her aunt stood. After a moment`s hesitation Kay followed. Her aunt said, "We are thankful for your time." Kay felt like saying nothing and didn`t. She just wanted out of that office.

Outside in the street Aunt Grace turned to her with a bright expression, "Well? Aren`t you curious about the envelope?"

Kay blinked at her for a moment. Her cheek itched and she scratched it, finding that it was wet.

"Oh you poor dear! I`m so sorry, but you seemed to be holding up so well," Aunt Grace said. Kay just felt tired. "Come, we`ll go home and think about things later." And so they took the steam trolley home.

When she got to her room, she fell into bed and lay there, her shoes on and everything. She didn`t move when her aunt brought her soup. Later, when it got dark, Grace pulled off Kay's shoes and pulled a cover over her.

Late next morning she awoke. The world seemed strangely bright, like the sun was inside the house somewhere. Her bladder finally drove her out of bed.

Her aunt saw her on the way to the back of the house and said carefully, "Can I make you some breakfast?"

Kay didn`t feel hungry but said "yes" in a tiny voice and kept moving through the kitchen.

When she came back, she plunked herself down at the kitchen table and put her head down. She must have drifted in a daze for a bit, for the next thing she heard was the sound of a plate and fork. There were bacon, eggs, and new baked bread. They smelled good. And just like that, she was hungry.

After that she cried about her hunger because it didn`t seem right. She cried for her grandma. She cried for her brothers who had died in the war. She cried for her mom who had died of fever. She cried for her dad, even though he had died before she could remember, then she cried some more for no more reasons that could be told. Then she slept again and didn`t wake until dinner.

Deke awoke from a deep dreamless sleep. Even though the disturbance had been loud and had given his bed a good bounce, it made only a small dent in Deke`s fogged mind. His eyes, when he managed to open them, were sticky and his mouth dry. A ray of sunlight leaked through the window, crossing the dusty air above him. He moved his head and was quickly reminded of how much he had drunk the night before with those soldier boys. He had been staying in a room in a saloon in town and had finally decided last night to try out its wares. The bed creaked as he tried to move. He had to get up. Nothing was going to improve if he lay there. It had been a hell of a night, but right then what he needed was water; water to wash out the poison.

Edging his feet over the side of the bed, he brought his head upright, which sent it spinning. Looking down at his feet, he could see he was still wearing his boots and spurs, which wasn't like him. He could see the pitcher of water on the stand only a short six feet away. Deep inside he felt a desperate need for that water and was winding himself up to stand and get it, but something picked him up off the bed and tossed him against the wall instead.

Blinking away the dust, he noticed that the world was suddenly silent. People didn`t usually get picked up and tossed around for no apparent reason, but with his hangover he wasn`t in a condition to question things at that particular moment. The window was all over his lap and bed, with dust flying everywhere. The morning sunlight was shining through new holes in the wall and ceiling, making golden lines through the swirling air.

He looked at the drifting dust and thought, "That women hasn`t swept once in all the days since I checked in."

The window was gone, but the pitcher was still there. This made no sense to him, just like the tremors he felt bouncing occasionally through the floor.

But he surely needed that water, so he rolled over and tried to stand, only to fall forward to crawl towards the dresser. He couldn't help but notice that he floor wouldn't sit still. It gave an occasional bounce, which didn't fit with his general hung over dizziness. The water, when he finally made the difficult climb up the dresser, was layered with dust, but he didn't care and drank from the pitcher anyway. Then, breathing deeply as if that might rid him of the poison and choking on the dusty air, he stood unsteadily, staggering to the door with a sudden need to pee in the worst way. But the door was stuck.

Deke was contemplating the unfairness of it and thinking of something appropriate to say when there came another huge bang, and he and the door both were shoved into the hall. Lying there face down with the door under him, it finally became apparent to Deke that something was not right with the world. Rolling over and looking back through the door jamb, he could see where his room had been, only now it was the back alley and a tangle of splintered wood. And then, just as his hearing came back, he realized what was going on. "Lords alive, that was an explosion!" he said.

The crater in the street was suddenly blocked from view as the back of the saloon fell down with a crash. He rolled to his feet with a deep pounding in his head and made his way towards the front of the saloon, but it was empty of people. The windows were gone and there were more loud bangs out front and smoke in the air. So he staggered out the side door and leaned against the wall and relaxed, the steady stream of urine rolling down the dry, unpainted wood. It made him dizzy, faint, and nauseous, but felt good at the same time. He decided then and there that maybe whiskey wasn't for him.

Something took a bite out of the building across from the saloon and boards seemed to drift lazily down from the sky through the dusty air, some leaving smoky trails. Over the whine in his ears he heard a fluttering, buzzing drone. His eyes widened, and he looked up into the sky at the undercarriage of a Union zeppelin passing over his head some ways above. The doors in its belly were open, and it occurred to him that perhaps it was time to run.

He took time to button his fly though, because some things are important, and then lurched towards the street. It seemed the best choice was to run in the opposite direction than the zeppelin was going so he turned left past the wreckage of half a dozen buildings. Things kept on blowing up around him as he ran, but at the end of the street the stable was still there. Strangely so was Ned. He was about to credit his palomino with unbounding loyalty when he realized the stall the horse was bouncing around in was blocked by wreckage.

He could see the whites of Ned`s eyes, which is not something you generally see much of on a horse, and approaching him seemed a little more complicated than he was currently up to at that moment. But his saddle was still there on the rack a now that he thought about it, his gun was in his holster, which was damn nice of somebody not to steal it considering the state he was in last night. But half his gear was back at the saloon, probably gone with his room. He needed more water too. This was too much on a day after with a pounding head and ringing ears. Had he known that this morning would prove to be difficult, he would never have tried out the saloon.

Ned was trying to kick boards out of the stall, which was probably sensible from his point of view, but Deke was in no mood for it. He found that knot of anger that helped him do things he didn`t want to do, jumped up the side of the stall and grabbed his horse by the head, stared Ned in the eye and said, "Now you settle down." The horse stopped, its ears back, staring at Deke. Deke hopped down and leaned hard into the top board on the stall, which popped its rusty nails. He caught it before it fell and set it down carefully. Eyeing Ned a warning like he was some kind of trap waiting to pop, he edged back for his tack.

Despite his obvious opinions as to their situation, Ned took the bit and Deke edged the harness over the horse's ears. Ned clearly wanted to go and started dancing back and forth in the stall.

Once Ned was saddled, Deke popped a few more boards and Ned hopped and lurched over the remaining wood. Legging up and dropping heavily into the saddle, Deke stared at the ground far below. The height and waving motion was clearly not to his current taste, but if the horse bolted he wanted to bolt with him. The last thing Deke needed was to have to chase his horse across the prairie with no gear and a hangover. He made it through the door, past the blacksmith, into the street. It was then that he noticed that the droning was receding and that the explosions had stopped. Instead the air was filling with smoke. Things were starting to catch fire, and people, where there had been none before, were running in the street.

This seemed sensible to Deke and probably to Ned too, and he felt that it was probably time he did the same, but he needed his gear first, so he edged back along the side of the saloon, past the wet spot, to the back of the building. It was gone, along with the alley, probably because of the six-foot crater that cupped out the building in back. His bed was gone, but that pitcher was still where he left it. "Some things just clearly don`t know what to do when they've been blown up," he told Ned. The explosion had not done his clothes any good, not that anyone but Deke could tell. His bags were still there in the corner. Deke tied Ned to a big board that was sticking up for no reason and climbed over the creaking floor to drag out his stuff.

"SO, are you leavin?" said a familiar gravelly female voice from behind him. Mrs. Baker stood next to Ned, her hands on her ample hips, squinting at Deke`s wiry frame as he made teetering progress across the wreckage in the deep orange, smoke stained sunlight.

"Yes ma`am, I surely hope to," Deke said as he searched for bits of this and that, eyeing them for offense and stuffing them in his bags. Deke realized he had somehow acquired a set of splinters in his left hand and arm, and there under some boards he saw the brim of his hat.

"You still owe me for one night"

This struck Deke as being both odd and somewhat forthright. Ned snorted, Deke felt in agreement, but then maybe Ned was only smelling the smoke. "Ma`am, it`s not like I actually made it through the night, and you still haven`t made me breakfast. `Sides, I haven`t found my money yet," he said while straightening and dusting off his hat.

That wasn`t entirely true, of course. Deke kept some in his pockets, much of which was inexplicably missing, probably spent last night. Most of the motley assortment of Confederate and Union bills that most people passed for money both North and South was either under his heel in his boot or in a hidden pocket in his bags, under too much stuff to make its current retrieval appealing. Deke pulled his now full bags back across the wreckage of the building towards Ned. Wispy white flecks of ash danced by in the rising wind. Deke thought it looked like snow.

"I need that money now. I`ve still got stuff to move and my saloon is goin` to burn up."

"It surely is." Deke could see that she truly had need, so he said, "Can I help you move instead?"

Mrs. Baker, because that's what she was, even though all her husbands were dead, frowned like she'd rather have the money. But time was short so she just nodded. "I guess I could use the help too." Then coughed on some ash, turned and lumbering towards the alley to the front. "Come on!" she yelled. Deke tossed his bags over the saddle, untied Ned and followed.

Across town the steam lines in the ice-house blew, sending a low sharp thump echoing back around the town. Ned danced to the side ready to balk, but Deke whipped back and turned that clump of anger on him and stilled him. Ned and Deke generally had a certain understanding, but sometimes Ned just plain forgot.

In the front, Mrs. Baker was heading inside.

"Grab everything out in the street!" she yelled over her shoulder.

Deke tied up Ned and followed, only to bump into her at the door, her arms full of a stack of drawers hastily pulled from a dresser. Deke could hear the sound of burning.

"Don't just stand there, hurry!" she said.

"Yes, ma'am," he replied, because he had been well brought up. Deke let her by and then trotted in, blinking in the dimness. He thought of grabbing the whiskey, since it was surely valuable, but the thought of it made him sick. He frowned at the wreckage of the big mirror behind the bar. "Now that was just too bad," he said to himself. "It was nice." She kept a shotgun under the bar, which he laid on top just so she wouldn't forget it. Her shining new patented Incorruptible brand cash register was bolted down, and therefore immovable as well as being incorruptible, so he continued through the door behind the bar.

Inside he found clothes, sundries, books, a couple of pictures, and an odd box under the bed that Mrs.

Baker snatched from his grasp and with a red blush said, "I`ll take that." She couldn`t take the register, but she dumped its contents in a bag. It was too bad, because it was made in England, new and shiny from New Orleans, brought at great expense by train. She shook her head at it and sighed. He finally did help her out hauling the whiskey and an odd assortment of other bottles and glasses too. Deke tried not to breathe as he walked, as the smell of alcohol was more than his head could stand.

Mrs. Baker went to find something to help carry her things to safety, so Deke and Ned stayed to watch her stuff. The pictures were photographs, and although he knew none of the people in them, their grey faces stared back at him in a most familiar way, like they were his own relatives, which Deke had none of that were alive at the moment. There were several pictures of men; some of them were surely her husbands.

Things were really starting to catch, buildings burning all around them, and Deke hoped she wouldn`t take long. The sunlight was rippling orange and hot across the dirt, making the grey faces in the photographs seem almost blue.

When she arrived she came pushing a large wheelbarrow clearly too big for her. The hair on one side of her head had somehow gotten burned up, and it made her look a bit lopsided. They loaded in a panic, tied Ned to the back, and started pushing toward the railhead, each taking a handle. That was where the soldiers were and probably the best place to be safe, except perhaps of course out of town, maybe in Philadelphia, Deke thought. He`d never been there, but he had always enjoyed the name.

Things were burning all around them and it was hot. Ned was not pleased, and that made pushing the wheelbarrow a lot harder because Ned was not inclined to keep up. The closer to the train station they got, the more people they saw. Some were injured, and Deke promised himself that as soon as he planted Mrs. Baker somewhere he`d be back to help.

He figured that the soldiers would help, but they were nowhere to be seen and he soon found out why. They were all working on filling in the holes in the rail yard, their motley assortment of grey crawling over the gravel rail bed like ants across the dirt. They even had some teams of Negroes and a steam shovel working, although where they found them was beyond Deke.

Deke was just untying Ned when he heard a shout, and three soldiers in grey started marching towards him. He knew what this was and hopping up on Ned, he rode like the dickens. A shot buzzed by somewhere on his right, which sent the crowds scrambling in chaos. They were pressing men to work, and Deke knew that once the army had you, they never let go. They`d take Ned too. Ned charged through the crowd out of control, Deke holding on and keeping low. They headed up the rail line, past the perfectly intact telegraph office, which was probably the whole point of the bombardment. He looked longingly with his pale eyes at the post racks as he rode by. He sure would love to get a letter someday, but he really didn`t know anybody except for Ned, who of course couldn`t write.

Ned charged down the tracks like he was a train himself, and pretty soon they had outdistanced the attention span of the soldiers. But up ahead there were more. They were standing around a train that was parked at the end of the track, at the edge of a crater. In the distance another was chugging up behind, and up above an airship drifted down towards town. This one had a big red flag painted over the former owners' names and was clearly there to help.

Deke veered to the left around the outskirts of town, away from the tracks, past the cattle yards, slowing Ned, who was looking a bit overheated. They stopped in sight of the train but out of gunshot, amongst the scattered scrubby trees. He needed to check Ned. It'd been a bad morning for them both. Ned`s hooves were fine. The stable had apparently picked and cleaned them as promised. The horse was wet with sweat though, and they would both need water soon.

As he worked on Ned, Deke watched the airship glide lower over the train. It was a sight to see, a bright dusty white almost glowing against the dark blue sky. They dropped ropes to a flatcar and winched her down until the carriage was right on top of the stack of iron rails, some of which they chained to the bottom of the airship. Then they started shoveling dirt, sand, and rocks out the side doors until the big thing started to drift free back up into the air. The motors kicked over with a bang and the airship slid upwards and forwards towards town, taking the rails with it. Deke stared, watching it go, absently mindedly picking splinters from his arm. He had to head back to town. He and Ned needed supplies. It was a long way to anywhere from Abilene, in the summer, in Texas.

CHAPTER 2

Kay helped Grace pull down boxes and trunks from the attic and closets. Most of it was junk, some of it was strange, and some of it was precious. Precious, like the embroidery off her great grandpa`s Revolutionary War uniform. He had been in the cavalry, the First City Troop, and served under George Washington himself. Strange, like the small porcelain dog wrapped up in a box. Why hadn`t she put it out? It was very pretty. Kay felt that it had to have had a story, and she was sad that the story was lost now. Now, it was just a porcelain dog.

They stacked the clothes and many of her grandmother`s things to give to the church. The church sold things like this to help widows and returning veterans. Some of grandma`s old hats were fun, and Kay tried them on in front of the mirror. They reminded her of old times.

Some things smelled of cigar smoke and she wondered if that had been Grandpa. Grandma had saved his straight razor and spectacles. He was quite blind at the end. She labeled these by gluing looped strips of paper with notes around them.

There was a pocket watch and inside of the lid was a picture of a baby. Grace looked at it and tsked. "That was your father`s," she said. "That`s you when you were a baby. I remember when they had it taken, the year before he left to go out West. He must have left it with your mother." Kay slipped it into the pocket of her apron. Later that night, before bed, she wound it and listened to it tick as she went to sleep and thought of her father.

The next day, as they were eating breakfast, Grace brought up the problem of the house. There really was no avoiding it. "You can come and stay with us," she said. "We don`t have much room, but there`s always a way to find more space." Grace lived in Baltimore with her husband and three kids. Kay had never met them, but Grace was nice and it seemed the only option, at least until she was married.

"I do need to get back too. Bill and the landlady can`t be doing the kids any good," Grace said. Bill worked in a factory that stamped machine parts. "It`s good work, and since the war started, good money too." They had three rooms on the second floor of a tenement, which was so much better than the single room they had had before the war. Perhaps with Kay`s money, Grace felt that they could find a place with four rooms. This didn't sound like a very bright end to Kay, but she really had no other options.

Her grandma had some travelling trunks, which

had been emptied and sorted, and into these they packed the precious and some of the strange. She squeezed as much as she could of the really important into her own trunk. The rest would just have to go up for sale. The furniture would go with the house.

That day she walked alone to the bank. She could tell that Grace really wanted to go with her, but she felt that this was something she had to do alone. In the envelope she had found a key with a number stamped on it, along with a note. The note had the name of a downtown bank and the words, "Your mother wanted you to have this," in her grandmother's perfect handwriting. She left the house, walking across the high grass to the edge of the street, crossing the muddy ditch to the street itself over the old board that was laid across. She walked up to the boulevard at the top corner and onto its wood plank sidewalks lined with shops. A block up the street, in its center, was the steam trolley stop. When it arrived, she ducked between the wagons, carriages, and people to climb on, where she paid her nickel to roll downtown.

It had been awhile since the last rain, and the buildings were grey and black with coal soot. The windows of the shops, though, were clean and shiny, and she watched their contents as she rolled by. The dirt streets were full of traffic, especially people, walking to and fro, all with purpose but no apparent direction. The white trolley driver was constantly ringing his bell. She could hear the Negro coalman humming a tune as he shoveled coal and as she rode deeper into the city, the buildings grew taller. Steam trucks chugged along in the traffic, leaving trails of smoke and steam. Above, the strip of grey sky was suddenly crossed by a great airship. Its kerosene motors fluttered noisily as they crossed and then quieted as they passed behind the building tops.

She was so taken by the sight that she almost missed her stop.

Threading through the traffic, Kay had to hop around horse dung back and forth to the concrete sidewalk. Warm damp air gusted from the door of the shop in front of her. It was a laundry, and she could see the boilers in the back. The sidewalk stretched down the street, covered with a patchwork of canvas awnings. There were so many people. Behind some crates she saw a Negro woman with a child at her breast begging. Her wrists were scarred. Kay gave her a quarter, enough for a day's food. She hated what people did to each other.

She saw a shop selling pastry and almost stopped, but the crowds pushed her on by. "This won`t do, " she thought, so she ducked behind a newspaper stand. It would be stalling, but the smell had been heavenly, so she worked her way back to the bakery. Inside the floor was tiled and the ceiling was patterned in tin. She bought some tea and a flaky pastry shaped like a triangle, filled with apple! She took her tea and plate to a table with an empty seat. Also sitting at the table were a man in a bowler hat and suit reading the newspaper and two girls very nicely dressed. They were tittering between themselves clearly trying to get his attention, but he was having none of it.

On the front page of the paper was the headline, "Disaster at New Orleans, Farragut Repulsed!" Apparently there had been a battle and it had not gone well. She thought of her brothers, which spoiled her appetite halfway though her pastry. The man, having finished his food, got up and left, taking his newspaper with him. Kay sat staring at the traffic through the shop window sipping her tea.

One of the girls had apparently had said something to her and she hadn`t noticed.

"Is your man away at the war?" the one on the left asked again. Kay blinked for a moment and thought she had misunderstood the question.

"Pardon?" Kay replied

"Is your man away at the war?" she asked, looking at Kay encouragingly.

"No, no I`m unmarried"

"You`re not a war widow are you?" the one on the right asked, looking worried.

"No, I`m not."

"It`s just that you looked so sad. It`s awful the ones that get left with children."

"Yes, it is," replied Kay.

"So you`re like us!" she said, brightening up. "One of the unmarried!" and they both giggled. "There are no men."

"At least none that anyone would want. My father says the war will be over soon and then he will find me a husband, but I don`t want a broken man," the one on the left said.

"And they`ve been saying it will be over soon for years!" her friend added.

Kay had no father to arrange a marriage. Practically no family at all. So there she was, a spinster at 17. "I`m not worried. It can`t last forever," she said.

"We were down at the docks looking at the English sailors yesterday," said the one on the left, with a mischievous smile. She was immediately shushed by the one on the right.

"Don`t shush me, Tilly Sanders. We`re nowhere near home!" said the one on the left, frowning at her friend.

Tilly was clearly embarrassed. "You`ll get us in trouble."

Kay was a little embarrassed herself. "I`m sure they

are all very nice," she said. "I`m sorry, but I must go and finish my errand," and picked up her bag. The girls looked surprised and perhaps embarrassed as she left, but Kay wasn't interested in hearing about English sailors.

She was swept along the sidewalk toward the address of the bank. She saw it sitting like a block of stone flanked by tall buildings. Through the polished bronze doors, eyed by guards, she looked for someone who could help. Picking the first desk, she said to the balding man behind it, "I`m here to see a safe deposit box."

"That would be Mr. Dougherty, the Vault Manager," the man sitting there said, tipping his head back towards a large desk behind him. He was stamping pieces of paper with a large rubber stamp. She thanked him and made her way between the desks in front to Mr. Dougherty. He was old and fat, with a scowl, as he ran his finger down a ledger, fixated on the sums.

"Be with you in a moment," he said. When he reached the bottom of the page, he sighed and looked up at Kay like she was an unwanted chore. "What can I do for you, ma`am?"

"I`m here to see a safe deposit box, at least I think that`s what this key is for." She handed him the key.

He looked it over and nodded. "Yes, this is one of ours. And your name is?" He got up from his desk with a huff and went to the shelf in the wall behind him.

"Kay, Catherine Mapleton"

He pulled down a book and opened it, thumbing through pages, then finally running his finger down the lists. "Yes, here you are. And who is the owner of the box?" he said, scowling at her over his spectacles.

"Blanche Mapleton, only she`s dead."

"Oh, I`m sorry to hear that," he said, showing no

concern, scribbling a note in the book. And then he yelled, "Billings!"

An old thin man looked up from his work several desks away. "Yes, sir?" he said. The bank was full of old men.

"Take, Miss?" he looked at her with eyebrows raised. She nodded. "Miss Mapleton to her box." He closed the book with a thump and turned his back to her to return the book to the shelf. Mr. Dougherty then turned back to his desk and wrote her number on a slip of paper along with the time and handed it to Billings, who had managed to limp over to them. You might think it odd that Kay didn`t notice the limp, but there were a lot of men with limps in those days.

"This way, Miss," said Billings. He led her to a small enclosure. "Take a seat and I`ll be right back." She sat at the desk and Billings returned with a long narrow metal box. Sitting it on the desk in front of her, he said, "I`ll take my leave."

Kay thanked him and turned to the box. The key fit in the lock, and, with a bit of pulling, opened the box.

Deke had to head back into a burning town, despite it being full of soldiers. But the soldiers were busy in the rail yard, taking no notice of the town burning under great columns of black smoke. Deke found Mr. Fulkerson, of Fulkerson`s Feed and General Supplies, busy moving things out of his yet-to-burn store into a wagon. Young strong backs, especially ones with horses, being in short supply during wartimes left Deke in a high bargaining position, saving him the unpleasantness of pulling off his boot and fishing for money. Deke helped the old man move until the fire took his store that afternoon, stacking things to be kept dry in Fulkerson's tiny house, then in the shed after that, and then finally close to the house itself. In return Deke got the supplies he needed, even a can of peaches for a job well done. Mrs. Fulkerson fed them a nice dinner, which took the last of the edge off the hangover. Afterwards he cleaned his pistol and rifle and even got to wash some of his clothes, leaving them to dry overnight.

Deke had it in his mind to go north, mostly because he had never been that way. He had heard so many stories about northern cities that, even if a little of it were true, then they surely would be something he needed to see. Sticking around Abilene would certainly get him pressed or even drafted sooner or later.

Mr. Fulkerson asked him if he wouldn't mind staying for awhile. He certainly could use the help rebuilding and frankly, with their children gone in the army, Deke thought they looked just a little lonely. But Mr. Fulkerson could see the need in him to go and didn't press.

Deke saddled Ned. Poor Ned was a bit loaded down. What Deke really needed was a mule to help carry, but he might as well have wished for his own airship. Those were gone to war. No, he'd just have to spend a lot of time walking. There would be no taking the train with all the soldiers about and besides, he'd miss all the things in between.

They had to make a wide circle around the town to avoid all the trains and soldiers backed up waiting for the track to be repaired. The trees gave him cover as he and Ned walked through the scrub. With all the trains lined up in a row, he thought it would be a good time for the Union to come back with their airships, but the sky was a clear empty summer blue. He would have to steer wide of the river too, because of the fort north of town. "Fort Phantom Hill" the soldier boys had called it, when they were well and goodly soaked. But he didn`t expect trouble from them. They were busy filling holes and laying track.

It took an entire day before he got to one of what the town called rivers, such as it was. "More of a creek this time of year," he told Ned. The sun weighed heavily on his head and the air was thick. "But it`s got water, real trees, and it`s going north. Maybe I`ll take some time to fish. There will be game for me and green grass for you, Ned." The problem with that was that everybody else was thinking the same thing too. It wasn`t long before he saw someone`s camp. They could be cowhands, they could be deserters, or they could be bandits, so he gave it a wide berth, and they seemed to be inclined to let him alone as well.

Now there`s a problem with the land in that part of Texas mostly having to do with its flatness. Water flows this way and that. Sometimes it would be, judging by the sun, flowing south toward the ocean as it should. But then, just as often, it could be flowing east or west, and sometimes, it even flowed north! Deke realized pretty quickly that following Texas rivers would get him nowhere. So sun and heat be damned, he set off straight ahead across the hard scrubby ground. A day didn`t go by before he ran into another creek or river. Nevertheless he wished, not for the first or last time, that he had bought that compass last year in Dallas when he had the money. The flatness of the land left nothing on the horizon he could use to mark his direction. In fact, nothing even close by. So Deke`s path meandered in its progress north.

He was camped by a lake. Then again maybe it was a pond, depending on your sensibilities. He decided that he wanted some rabbit. He shot two and risked a fire, which made a nice change. Up until then, he had held off making fires for fear drawing attention to himself. He washed clothes and himself in the stream that fed the lake and felt relaxed as he watched the sun set. That was, of course, until he heard the pop of twigs in the brush and the click of a revolver hammer being pulled back.

Deke glanced around quickly, but he had nowhere to go. They had caught him flat-footed without his gun.

"Now you stay where you are, young man," said a deep voice behind him.

A short, wide cowboy with a big bushy beard, an overcoat, and a black domed bowler hat came out of the brush in front of Deke carrying a shotgun aimed right at him. He didn`t stop once as he was out either, but started to edge around Deke as smooth as a snake. Then Deke heard the brush behind him crackle as the man with the voice came out behind him. "Now keep your hands where I can see `em and just edge away from the fire," and away from his pistol as well, which was lying on top of some clean dry socks on a flat rock he was using as a table. He`d been oiling the leather of his holster to keep it from drying out, thinking that maybe it might look nice if he could work some kind of design into it.

"Take off your shirt. Let`s see what you are," the voice said. Deke knew what that meant. They were bounty hunters hunting for deserters. The army tattooed your unit on your shoulder. It was a sign of proud service and at the same time it also made it hard to leave. Deke unbuttoned and pulled down his shirt, leaving it still tucked into his belt. He had just washed it and didn`t like the idea of dropping it in the dirt.

"He`s clean, Jake," said the man in front of Deke.

Now, you see, the problem was that many bounty hunters caught unmarked men too. Sometimes they`d tattoo them themselves and sometimes recruiters took conscripts for bounty. Worse still, the law said everyone ages 18 to 35 had to join the army unless they had a planter exemption, which Deke would have had if he had stayed on a ranch, and it didn`t matter that Deke was only just 17 and wasn`t Southern at all. He had been born in the Paiute homeland. He had nobody to vouch for him.

The man with the deep voice walked over to where Deke could see him and picked up his pistol from the rock. He had a long handlebar mustache flecked with grey, a long nose, and a tall, wide-brimmed hat. His leather jacket stretched down to his calves and had seen a lot of sun and miles. "Put your shirt on, boy," he said. He looked the pistol over critically and then nodded ever so slightly, as if he approved. "And don`t worry, you ain`t going anywhere today."

He held out his hand to shake and said, "I`m Jake Hayes and this here is Bigfoot Wallace."

The big man in front relaxed a bit and lowered his shotgun. "Call me Big," he said.

"Texas rangers," Jake said. Jake holstered his gun, and then they paused like they were waiting for something.

Deke`s mind stopped blank for second, so unexpected was this turn. "I`m Deke. Deke Hayden." And he shook the ranger`s hand.

"Those rabbits sure smell good. We`ve got some onions and corn that would go real well with it, if you`re willing to share," Jake said, smiling.

Deke smiled too. "That sounds real good." And Jake handed him back his gun.

They cut up the half-cooked rabbit in the last of the day`s sun and boiled it into stew in a pot the rangers had, and then after that Deke shared his can of peaches.

They passed the can around and ate them out of their cups, cutting them into bite-sized chunks, then skewering them with their knives. The juice was sweet. It had been a long time since Deke had tasted anything so good. The men smoked, which Deke didn`t. He never had taken a liking to the smell, especially around food. He supposed it was because he`d been out in the open air most of his life.

The rangers were going northeast to join General Terry to scout for the army of Texas. A big battle brewing there, which was why the Union was bombing supply lines. Deke was dismayed to learn that northeast wasn`t exactly the direction he thought it was, and that he`d been drifting to the west, and was now northeast of Lubbock. He had covered a hundred miles, but he was about fifty miles away from where he thought he was.

The food and the fire were nice, and it was nice not to worry so much about being seen. They told stories to pass the time, and the rangers had a lot to tell. It seemed that a ranger`s life was one endless adventure. They fended off Indians, bandits, caught criminals, and now worked for the Army. Jake and Big had been west trying to recruit Indian tribes for the Confederacy. "There`re a lot of tribes fighting on both sides, although for them," Big said, "it seems more like a sport. Best light cavalry in the world though. Crack shots and nobody can cover ground like they can."

"I think they do it just because it gives them a chance to shoot at us," Jake said, and both Jake and Big laughed.

"You have an odd accent. Deke. Where`re you from?" Jake asked.

"Paiute Homeland," Deke replied.

Deke told them how he was born in the territories. His parents had ranched Kaibab Paiute land until they were killed in a Yavapai raid. The Yavapai lost a lot of territory in the Mexican American War. They`d been pushed down into Mexico along with the Mexican Army, and they aimed to get their land back. His parents had lost everything in that war, and the Paiute had taken them in. They fought beside the Paiutes against the Yavapai until they were burned out of their house. Young Deke had hid in the well while the house burned above him and had gone unnoticed when the Yavapai refilled their canteens and water bags. He got his rifle off the kid who had been left to watch the ruins of the ranch. The kid`s job had been to count the heads of any Paiute posses that might have been trying to chase after the Yavapai. Deke took Ned from a Yavapai scout he caught in a canyon three days later. Deke had nothing left to root him in any spot, and so he wandered, eventually drifting into Texas. For the last two years he`d been a ranch hand when he wasn`t travelling.

Then they turned to swapping news of the big war, which campfire talk always seemed to come around to in those days. Deke told them about the bombing of Abilene and they told him about the big battle that would start soon up north.

"The line stretches from the Mississippi across Arkansas and out into the plains," Jake said. Deke could see excitement and a distant look in the man`s eyes as he stroked his mustache.

"The North wants to cut off the Arkansas and Mississippi rivers, but we stopped `em!" Big said, being less reserved than Jake, slapping his knee and grinning. "And now there`s going to be a reckoning. They`re stretched down towards Memphis thinking that helps coming up the Mississippi, but we stopped it too. Our iron ships and air corps sent Farragut to the bottom of the Gulf. So now they`ve reached too far south!" and he whooped. "Their backs are to the Mississippi and their flank is wide open. And that's just where the battle is a-going to start."

"It'll extend clear across the Ozarks with mobile engagements all across the plains," Jake added.

It sounded to Deke like that battle was going to be right in his way, and it didn't bode well for his plans to go see the North. He was beginning to think that maybe he ought to have headed for Mexico instead. Deke was going to need advice if he was to get north of the lines, but he couldn't ask Jake and Big. They'd think he was a traitor. "Maybe," he thought, "maybe I ought to head west." But Deke was tired of wilderness. He wanted to see big cities. Besides, the Indian Nations didn't always take kindly to strangers, even if you could speak half their languages. And it sounded like the plains weren't going to be safe either.

CHAPTER 3

Inside the box Kay found a stack of paper folded lengthwise. There were documents, receipts, and letters. She pressed them flat on the desktop. On top she found the bill of sale for her family house. It had sold for $12,500 and had been deposited to this bank two years ago in her grandmother`s name. It seemed to her to be quite a sum. Next was a certificate from the State of Pennsylvania giving her grandmother custody. Folded together were birth certificates for her whole family, which brought tears, and almost made her stop before she saw the letters at the bottom of the stack.

The paper was cheap and yellow and varied in size, but the handwriting was her father`s left-handed scrawl. They were stacked by date.

"My Dearest Rose, I miss you so much," that brought more tears. "The train ride to Denver went well despite some delays. We were held for two days in Selina while they renegotiated passage with the Indian Nations. Something someday must be done about them." He had apparently sent this from Denver. "Equipment and goods are very dear in Denver. It`s good that I bought much back East."

Her father had gone west before the war, as had so many, to look for gold and land in the newly opened western territories. But her mother had never been inclined to speak of details or how he had died. With the defeat of Mexico, vast tracts of land lay open in the West, ceded by the Mexicans and Indians, and with the discovery of gold in the mountains every last man jack had hopped on a boat or wagon and had headed west. Then, when they built the railroad, even more went. That was, at least, until the Great War started.

As she read through the letters, her father`s story began to take form. She could tell that he was hiding his difficulties. He had joined an "expedition" to the Southern Rockies. She gathered as she read that expeditions were really a dozen or so men who travelled together for safety. And then it was a year before the next letter.

"The land was poor, but we saw trees there as wide as our house, but we had no way to cut them and they would be too big to move even if we could. Some of the fallen ones were hollow and made good houses that winter. No gold to speak of, despite there being thousands trying to find it. The Indians just laugh at us. I am very tired and disappointed."

But then, in the very next letter, he was excited again and ready to head further west, over the Rockies to California. "The passage over the mountains is very difficult we are told. We are camped at Fort Laramie, although some call it Bedlam, with about a thousand others, too many for the available supplies. It`s in a beautiful valley with good land. This would be perfect, but we must push on or starve. The soldiers will not allow us to stay because of the treaty. I hope this letter reaches you as I`m not sure I trust them with the mail."

"Our journey through the South Pass went well and was actually very beautiful, with many high waterfalls and meadows. Sacramento is quite big with its own sea-port. I`ve seen men from China! Their eyes and dress are very strange. They mostly keep to themselves in their own areas of town." Folded in was a newspaper clipping with a drawing of a Chinaman. He had a long thin mustache and a brimless square hat.

"There are so many languages spoken here. Half the army is Indian, with an Indian regiment stationed just to the north at Fort Sutter. They speak their own tongue, Maidu I think, and Spanish mostly. The land here is good, although there`re floods, mosquitoes, and it`s mostly settled or very expensive when not."

The next letter was six months later. "I`ve been forced to come out of the mountains for supplies. We have struck it rich Rose. We are rich! I have buried the claim and covered it as best as I can. There are men who follow those who find gold and kill them for their claim, but I`ve been careful. I`m sending you a map showing the location. Next to you, it`s the most beautiful thing I`ve ever seen. Rose quartz striped with gold. I`m going to name it after you, The Rose. I will send for you from Denver by telegraph. Be ready to sell everything. Love, James." And that was it. She thumbed through the pile again, but that was all. No telegram. Just that last letter and a piece torn from a map. She sat back in her chair with a frown.

Apparently she did have an account at the bank. Mr. Bayers had sent a letter to have her name added. She had $26,255.18. An amazing sum! And more when her grandma`s house sold. Since she was a woman of means she asked for $20, which seemed an incredible amount to her, more than she had ever had in her purse. It felt heavy. The coins were large and silver since all the gold coins had been recalled for the war effort.

It was past lunch and she was hungry. She needed to sit and think. In front of the bank she looked up and down the street, but there were no restaurants with indoor seats. Just thin brown sunlight and the rush and noise of the city. She had returned the box to the bank and taken all the papers with her, which now filled her bag.

"Excuse me," she asked one of the guards at the door.

"Hmm?" he started, apparently daydreaming. The other guard quietly chuckled. "Yes, ma`am?" he said, frowning sideways at the other guard.

"Is there some place where I can sit down for lunch nearby?"

He gave her a hard look, apparently classifying her by age and dress. "Well, ma`am, the missus and I like to eat in the Italian Market sometimes, and it`s only two blocks away, that is if you`re not the kind that minds folks not speaking much English." Perhaps he thought that young equated to adventurous? Perhaps it did.

She clutched her bag of papers close and with a look of determination said, "Which way is it?"

He nodded his head at the corner, and said, "Turn left at the corner."

"Thank you," she replied, stopping a curtsy. She was not a little girl anymore. Especially not with strangers.

The guard replied with a half-hidden smile, "Not a problem, ma`am." She turned before he could see her blush and headed up the street towards the corner.

The market started a block past her left turn, on the corners of the intersection under awnings with banners written in what must have been Italian. There were fruits and vegetables in tables sloping towards the street with prices on signs at the top. Next door they sold poultry with chickens and ducks in cages stacked to the sides of the shop. A boy had just dumped a bucket of water on the floor and was scraping a mixture of bird droppings and water across the sidewalk towards the gutter with a wide, long-handled brush. She stepped across quickly to avoid being splashed. He had dark curly hair and a tan face and looked to be about eight.

She could smell food and her stomach rumbled. A boy was selling loaves of bread from a basket by the curb, and women walked with baskets under their arms, their heads all wrapped in cloth, like shawls over their heads, only thick. She wondered if they were in mourning. Someone was playing some sort of stringed instrument, but it came from an upstairs window. Further down the street were carts, parked in the street, selling sundries. The sidewalk grew more crowded. She had to dodge around a man in a long coat down to his knees, a big mustache, and a pipe. He was talking to a friend in Italian!

Then she saw the restaurant, *Il Madonna*. It was open in the front with plain walls and round tables with white table-cloths. Inside she could see two other white women eating at a table and felt encouraged.

"Lei amerebbe sedere?" a waiter in a white apron said.

"Pardon?"

"Ah, would you like to eat?" His accent was very

thick, the words went up in the wrong places, but she was relieved that he spoke English.

"Yes, please," she replied, with a smile and a nod.

"Very good. Follow me," he said, and he led her to a table near the two other women.

She sat down and unpinned her hat, sitting it on the seat next to her. The waiter came back and handed her a card with the names of dishes on it. She didn`t recognize a thing. She sat staring, perplexed.

"Try the spaghetti," said one of the women, with a mischievous smile.

"Oh, here it is," she said, looking at the card. "What is it?"

"It`s like a kind of bread string with red sauce. It`s delicious!"

They were older and seemed to know their way here, and so she decided to take their advice. But bread string!

"It`s very good with wine," the woman`s friend added. They both had small cups of red wine. "I`m afraid it`s that, grappa, or coffee, which doesn`t sit well. Grappa is a hard liquor."

She had never had wine before but knew it was alcoholic. "Today -is- a day of adventure!" she said to herself. So when the waiter came back, she ordered spaghetti and wine.

The waiter smiled a big smile with his coffee-stained mustache, bowed and said, "of course!" retiring to the back.

"You can eat with us if you wish," the women said, smiling. Kay smiled back and moved over to their table, putting her hat on the empty seat.

"Do you live nearby?" the friend asked.

"No, I came into town on business."

"Oh, that`s nice. It must be cleaner there. Things

are always so sooty here," she said with a frown. "Oh! Pardon me. My name is Merrybell and this is Amanda. We have an apartment four blocks from here."

"Yes, we come down here to eat often," Amanda said. "That and there`s nice fish to be had near the docks."

"You can get used to variety in the city," Merrybell added.

"Oh yes, it makes it hard to go back, even with the trolleys," and Amanda giggled.

When her spaghetti arrived, Kay saw that it really was bread strings! They were slippery, and the ladies showed her how to wind them on her fork with her spoon so she could get more than only a strand or two. The red sauce was made with tomatoes, another first for her! It and the wine slipped by very easily. Her aunt would be so jealous!

The ladies were clearly done but seemed happy passing time with someone new. Their bill arrived, 50¢, a scandalous amount, and Kay was wondering how much she had just spent when she noticed the sound of someone beating a drum in the distance. She wondered if the soldiers were parading nearby.

Suddenly the waiter rushed into the restaurant in a fluster.

"Tutti. Correre al dorso!" He clearly wanted to say something to them, but in his fluster his English seemed to have fled him. The drums were closer, and she could hear chanting echoing down the street. "Rapidamente!" He clearly wanted to nudge them along to the back but was too polite to literally do so. Everyone else was heading back. She could hear screams and crashes in the distance. "Per favore, per favore," he was saying.

"We better go," Mabel said. She looked worried. They stood up from the table headed towards the door to the kitchen, following the others.

The waiter was constantly glancing towards the street. Kay heard people running past the front of the restaurant and then more crashes nearby. The chanting was growing closer. She could hear them saying, "Go home, go home," and there was breaking glass.

At the kitchen door, Kay suddenly turned back. "Oh, my hat," and started back towards the table.

"No!" cried the waiter and grabbed her wrist to stop her. Just then, three factory men with long clubs careened through the front of the restaurant, knocking over tables and breaking chairs. The waiter wailed, let go of her wrist and ran. The men ran after him, right at Kay.

"God damned Itie whore!" shouted one and pushed her back against a table, knocking her and it over. Silverware and food spilled over the front of her dress. More men came, and then the street was a sea of men, some with drums and flags, knocking over and breaking everything. Men were throwing themselves at the kitchen door, which thankfully wasn`t budging.

One of the men came over and grabbed her by her hair bun, pulling it loose from the pins, dragging her forward. "We know what to do with Itie whores don`t we boys?" he said, and threw her towards another table. Over it went and so did she, sitting there stunned beyond belief. And there, lying on the floor beside her, she saw her hat.

Deke had drifted a long way off path, and that worried him. Towns were far and few in the prairie, and he didn`t like the idea of living off of rabbit and tortoise. The rangers seemed to know where they were going, and

Deke thought that maybe perhaps there wouldn`t be much harm in following them for a few days, just to get a little more east, and besides, Jake and Big didn`t seem to mind. The problem with that was that it was towards the battle.

They were riding northeast over flat country crossed by streams and rivers going this way and that. At night they told stories and sang songs; Deke especially liked ghost stories. He could come up with whoppers just by changing Indian spirits to ghosts. During the day the sky was hot dark blue as they rode under the sun, except for the part when it rained, which it did with exceptional ferocity the night after. Big shelved clouds rolled down on them from the north, lit orange by the setting sun. They could see the flash of lightning underneath.

They debated as to whether it would be better to face it in the open or under the trees. The trees would attract the lightning and the stream might flood. Meanwhile, being in the open with the wind, which was rising fast, did not seem appealing either. What decided it was their collective memories of Texas hailstones over an inch across.

They pitched their tent halves in the trees as far from the water as they could. The horses were hobbled as well as tied, and Deke shoved everything he owned, except of course Ned, under his tent. It was angled towards the wind, burying the down side under dirt and trenching around the front. He knew the wind would pull the edge of the tent free before long, but sometimes the raised line of earth kept the water from blowing under. The trench upslope would channel the water coming down towards the stream around him. He climbed in on top of his pile, under his blanket and coat, and stared out into the twilight as the canvas whipped up and down on top of him. He could see Jake and Big sitting under their tents as well.

The last gold of the sun lit the trees in front of him before the clouds snuffed it out, leaving nothing but a strip of green and gold on the horizon stained by black falling rain. The air was thick and humid and smelled of lightning, and when the rain hit it came down like a stampede, making its own fog on the ground. His tarp stretched down over Deke from the weight of the pelting water. Lightning boomed all around them. It went on and on until the fear of its ferocity slowly ran out, being replaced by irritated resignation. Deke hoped Ned was OK.

The world went from grey to blue to black. Deke couldn`t see his own hand. The rain and lightning came and went, leaving nothing but after images, and just when it seemed like it was giving up, it would roar back. He must have slept because he was woken by the racket of hail. Deke stuck his hand out to try to collect some, but it seemed to melt before he could get a sense of its size. He heard the horses whine over the roar.

Then he woke up again. It was still black out, and he had a wicked need to pee. He shook his head, mumbling that this must be some kind of justice for his many wrongs. Happily, his tent half was still up and he was still kind of dry, so there were still good things he could count. His bladder, though, wouldn`t wait, so he decided to do it naked. It was warm – well to be truthful, at least it wasn`t cold – and he could see no reason in getting his clothes wet and then trying to sleep in them, especially his boots. He couldn`t pee out the side of a tent in the wind either, something he knew from experience. So he slipped his clothes off, leaving them as high as he could on the stack, and stumbled out into the rain, his toes squishing in the mud.

He knew Jake and Big were to his left and the wind

was at his back, so he walked carefully three steps downwind and let fly. The cool rain on his bare back felt great, and his hair whipped around his face. It was too bad he didn`t have a little light and his soap, he thought. Since he was drenched, he paused and took time to rub off the dirt as best as he could. Of course, doing this got him turned around, and if it wasn`t for the fact that he was between the two tent ropes, he would have been completely lost in the dark. But, feeling his way forward, he found a tent rope which led him back, at which point he rolled his wet self back up in his now damp blanket. He left his feet for last, letting them dangle out in the rain hoping to wash off some of the mud.

Morning woke with blue sky and no sign of the storm except the line of debris that showed how high the stream had risen. It had come quite close. The horses were still there, wet and miserable. Deke pulled on his pants and boots before he crawled out of his blanket and squished over to check Ned. Ned clearly needed consolation, which Deke was in short supply of, being as everything he had was piled under the tent. But, digging around in the pile, he found Ned`s brush and started working the damp burrs and muddy scarf out of Ned`s hide until Ned was dry and clean and staked in the center of green grass. Only then did Deke think about a fire and breakfast.

Jake woke with a snort. After a minute he batted the puddled water from the top of his tarp and rolled over until he could stick his head out. He saw what Deke was doing, took a deep breath of air, and emerged with grim determination to set to work on his horse as well. It was half an hour before Big`s snores stopped and he woke with a wail. He had rolled over his bowler hat and crushed it flat. Now normally this kind of thing was to be expected. Hats out on the prairie got crushed, stomped, blown off, twisted, rained on, and pushed into small places all the time, and bowler hats are not exactly rare. But Big`s hat wasn`t just any bowler. It had come all the way from England by boat, and he cared a great deal about it. So now its formerly smooth dome had creases, which Big worried with his fingers all day long, whenever he had the time.

Deke wore pretty much whatever came his way, currently a planter`s hat. He had punched down the center of the dome and stuck a feather in the band, which suited him fine. The brim was curled up at the sides to keep the front down when he was facing the wind. When you work on ranches, there`s really no point in trying to keep nice clothes.

After breakfast they sorted their stuff, cleaned and oiled their guns. They worked over the horse`s hooves, checked their ears and teeth. Stuff that was wet got set out on rocks to dry, and stuff that wasn`t got washed. They weren`t ready to ride until late afternoon. By then the creek was down and the mud dried and cracked.

Deke thought that maybe they ought to wait until the next day to start, but Jake and Big felt determined to push on, claiming that they were already overdue, so they saddled and rode on across crusty ground. Two hours out, they ran across horse tracks heading north of their path. Jake was of the opinion that they ought to check them out, being that was part of their job. Big and Deke could see no reason to object, so they started following them.

The tracks led on into the twilight until they could see the spark of a campfire in the distance. They dismounted and started closing the distance on foot, leading their horses, taking their time. It was almost dark before they could make out two figures sitting at the fire. Apparently the lone rider had met up with somebody.

Jake eyed the pair in the distance.

"I think we ought to take this one slow," Jake said to Big.

"It's probably nothing," Big replied.

"Maybe, but a little care won't hurt. Be a shame to get shot by a couple of pathetic deserters."

"Lead on then," Big replied.

"Deke, watch the horses," Jake said to Deke.

"I'm just as good at sneaking as any Indian," Deke said, with a frown.

"No doubts there boy, but we get paid for this," Big replied, with a smile. "Sides, this is probably just a boring crawl through the brush for nothing."

So Deke had to lead the horses back a ways until he could just see the fire. Jake and Big took off to each side.

He waited, and waited. A coyote trotted by, which unsettled the horses and led Deke to check his holster. The stars came out and lit the ground with black shapes and shimmering grey. It was dark, but he still could see the fire in the distance and no Jake and Big.

Finally, curiosity got the better of him, and he pulled up the stakes, and started walk the horses forward. The fire ruined his night vision and made it hard to be sure of the ground, stepping down into low spots occasionally to some surprise. He went close enough to see the fire properly. There were five figures around the fire! Why hadn't Jake or Big come to get him?

Deke turned and pulled the horses back and tied them up to a dead tree. Pulling his rifle from his saddle, he chambered a round and walked carefully back towards the fire.

There they were, Jake and Big, sitting butt flat on the ground, and three men standing about them. One of the men had his rifle out and another had a pistol, both pointed at Jake and Big! The third had a cup of coffee.

The one with the coffee was pacing and pointing at Jake, yelling something like he was some sort of damning judge. Deke could see no sign of either Jake`s or Big`s guns. The situation didn't look good.

Finally, the one with the coffee put his coffee down and was starting to reach for a rifle. Deke couldn't allow that until he knew what was going on. He picked a flat spot to lie on, cocked the hammer on his rifle, and picked a target.

The round went through the wood pile in the center of the fire, scattering it and sending up a burst of sparks. Jake and Big rolled and tackled the two gunmen standing beside them. Deke put a second round at the feet of the coffee man, his hand just resting on his gun. In the tangle of men rolling on the ground somebody`s gun went off, but Deke couldn`t tell if anyone had gotten themselves hurt.

There wasn`t much Deke could do, so he sat there. The standing man didn`t move. The men on the ground rolled around until Big managed to do something final. Standing up with a pistol he said something to the man standing, who pulled his hand back from his gun. Then they both watched Jake and the other man, Big with some apparent amusement. After a bit, Jake and the man realized that they had an audience and eased off, Jake laughing until he realized he was bleeding.

All four men were bleeding and bruised. Jake`s nose was bent, a red trail of blood had already made its way down to his shirt. Big`s man was out cold and would need stitching where his head had hit something hard. Big had used his knuckles too, and they were a mess.

Deke walked up, rifle aimed, and stood in the firelight, keeping the bushwhackers covered while Big worked on straightening out Jake`s nose, which was swelling. Big insisted that if they didn`t get it straight, it would stay bent, so Big stood behind Jake, tipped his head back between his knees and gave his nose a sharp push. Jake howled, turned white, and damn near fainted. The two strangers still standing looked smug.

"You done Big? I need to go get Ned," Deke said, not taking his eyes off the bushwackers.

"He`s done," Jake said, weakly pushing Big away.

Big found his shotgun and took over watching.

The horses were where he had left them, out in the dark, for which Deke was sincerely grateful. He had been worried by the coyote. When he got back, Jake had been trying to stop the unconscious man`s bleeding by pressing the wound, but the gash was deep and long. Deke could see bone under the blood. Jake fetched some needle and thread from his bags and started trying to sew the wound closed. "Might have to burn it," he said to Big. His fingers fumbled with the needle, but the stitching seemed to do the trick. They tied the men`s hands and feet, including the unconscious one, just in case he woke.

"Well, let`s see what we have here." Jake began pulling apart the men`s bags. "So why are you three out here in the middle of nowhere?" he asked.

"Could be, we could ask you the same," said one. He sounded like a Northerner.

"Hush, Jay," the other said.

"Could be you all are spies," said Jake, pulling a cloth-covered polished steel mirror out of a felt bag from one of the saddle bags. "Look at this, boy," he said handing it towards Deke.

Deke slipped off the cover. It seemed like a normal mirror, except that it had a little hole in the center and it was polished on both sides.

"That is a signal mirror. I bet they were scouting for the airships at Abilene," Jake said.

"Why would they need that? I bet those airships can see everything from up in the sky," Deke said.

"They can`t see anything that can`t see them. These men make sure there`s no anti-airship guns around," Jake said. "And to tell them about any nice targets before the attack starts."

There was a moment of quiet before Big looked over at Jake and said, "Probably be kindest to kill them now, Jake."

"No, somebody will want to talk to them for sure." Jake sounded tired. His nose was swelling and changing color. After that they cleaned their wounds and went through them men`s things looking for evidence, taking out any weapons, survival gear, and even their spurs. Anything that the spies might use should they manage to ride away.

It was an early night that night, since they`d need to get up and take turns guarding. The next day they rode out with only two prisoners tied to their saddles. The man with the head wound died that night. They covered his body with rocks. There wasn`t much more that could be done.

"You know, Deke, you probably should stay with us," Jake said, as they rode. His nose was no use and it made his voice sound odd. "This is going to get worse the closer we get to the lines. Even this far back you`ll be dodging deserters, bushwhackers, and scouts."

"I`m not going to join any armies!"

"You never did tell us why you`re going this way," Big said.

They'd been good about that so far, even though they were lawmen. Deke realized he`d been frowning, saying nothing. Jake had cocked his eyebrow as he stared at Deke, which set his swollen nose bleeding again. He dabbed it with his already bloody handkerchief, still looking at Deke. Deke couldn`t think of any other way through, so he decided to take a chance.

"I want to see the big cities," he said in a flat monotone.

Jake and Big looked at each other surprised. Even the union agent`s eyebrows went up.

"Ye haw, now that`s a big wish!" whooped Big.

"How did you think you were going to get north?" Jake said, with a frown of concern.

"Well, I didn`t expect things to be so unsettled when I started. I kinda had a mind to cut north around the Ozarks then pull in east towards the railroad."

"That won`t work," Jake said.

"That railroad will be gone as soon as the battle starts," Big said. "If it ain't gone already. "

"I didn`t know about the battle."

"Besides, the basin is crawling with Indians working for who knows who, and cavalry even when things are quiet," Big said.

"I can sneak as good as any Indian."

"No doubts," Big replied.

"You could go with us boy," said one of the Union agents.

"Now I thought you all were for keeping quiet," Jake said, with a threatening stare.

"Well, I was only trying to keep all possibilities in mind," the agent said, with mock hurt and innocence.

"I`m not runnin off with spies!"

"Well I hope not," Jake said, with finality. "This is going to need some thought."

So they rode on. That evening, Jake showed Deke how to use a signal mirror. It was simple, although Deke couldn`t quite figure out why it worked.

"You look through the hole at your target and angle it like you would if you were going to signal someone.

Then look at the reflection of your face in the back of the mirror. Somewhere on there you`ll see the spot of light that`s shining through the hole. You line that spot in the reflection up with the hole in the mirror and it`s aligned." Sure enough, the reflected sun from the mirror was shining on the target tree. "So you move the spot off the hole to stop the shine and back on to flash. Make sure you`re tipping it up when you do that or someone might get a flash that you didn`t intend."

"So I can flash light at someone, but how do I say anything?"

"Well, for that you need to know the code."

"Like the telegraph."

Jake smiled, "Yup, that`s it."

They had to polish the mirror again before they put it away because they had handled it. There were rouge and barrel patches in the cloth bag the mirror had come in. Deke wore his gloves so he wouldn`t put more finger prints on the steel.

"You know, Deke, I think your best bet is to stay with us. You could ride with the scouts. Nobody has to know you aren`t a member."

"Yeah, the way people come and go, and we could vouch for you," Big said.

"We`ll ride north at some point."

"Course you could get shot too," Big added, under his breath.

Jake frowned at Big and then continued, "Otherwise, I think you really ought to head back south. At least until the war`s over."

Deke was touched that Jake and Big hadn`t arrested him, and even took him seriously. He wasn`t worried about getting shot. He was mostly worried about losing Ned.

"I don`t want to lose Ned," he said. "The army will

take him.”

“No, not in the Rangers. We`re irregular. Most everybody has his own horse,” Big said.

“Can`t really join without one,” Jake added.

So just like that, Deke was going off to war.

CHAPTER 4

Kay thought she must be hurt, but she was too dazed to know for sure. Two big men came toward her, reaching down to grab her, with another coming up behind them.

"Now, lass, let`s see how you feel about Ities tomorrow," said one with a leer; but then he stumbled and seemed to lose his balance, tumbling to the floor. The other looked towards his friend and then dropped like an empty dress. There behind them, cradling a long wooden stick with a handle, stood the guard from the bank.

"Sorry about this, miss," the guard said. "We honestly didn`t expect there would be a riot."

Kay had a hard time breathing. Her corset was tight, and she was bent at an odd angle. The guard pulled her to her feet and steadied her while she caught her breath.

"Can you move? We have to leave," he said, giving

the crowd at the kitchen door a worried look.

She nodded yes, and they moved as quickly as they could toward the front of the shop. Whisked, really, since the guard was doing most of the work. Kay was quite wobbly and still dazed. The group at the kitchen door hadn`t noticed them yet and were still pushing on it. The door would give just a bit, but people were pushing on the other side too, and it got pushed closed again.

They made it out onto the street where men were knocking over and breaking everything – windows, carts – and dragging people they had caught down the street past them. But they parted for Kay and the guard, perhaps because of his uniform, or perhaps because of the club, but then perhaps because of the gun at his hip.

"They were going to rape me!" Kay said out of breath, almost in tears.

"Oh, no, miss. I doubt that," he said in a matter-of-fact voice. "From what I`ve read, they generally shave your hair and soil your dress."

"But why?" Shock had started to set in and she had begun to sob.

"They think the Italians are taking their jobs." He took a swipe with his club at a man who failed to move quickly enough.

"Are they?" she looked up at the guard.

"Yes, sometimes. And men who lose their jobs can be drafted, and their families may starve."

"But I don`t see the difference. Why hire foreigners?"

"Because they work hard for very little money." Kay thought about her aunt and her husband. "And the government looks the other way, because they need the manpower at the front," he added.

They made it back to the corner near the bank where there were wagons full of soldiers and police pulling up at the intersection. He let her sit down on a crate near the curb and knelt down next to her.

"I think you`ll be safe now. Can you get home?" he asked, with a worried glance back at the street.

"Yes, I think I can." Kay was trying her best not to cry, but she was shaking.

The guard shook his head. "I think you ought to come in and have some tea."

"No, no. Just give me a minute." She took deep breaths.

The guard looked around the street, caught the eye of his friend still guarding the bank door. They both nodded a greeting. "Take as long as you need, miss. We`ll both be here," he said.

Kay took a moment to look at herself. There were wine and tomato stains down the front of her skirt. It was probably ruined, she thought. Her back ached, but when didn`t it when she was wearing her corset. Thankfully, her bustle had cushioned most of the impact with the table. She pulled the remaining pins from her hair and let her copper curls fall around her shoulders, shaking them loose. Her arm and shoulder hurt, but her sleeves were too tight to pull up and look. At least nothing was broken. She tried to breathe evenly and slow her heart.

"Oh, I`ve lost my hat."

The guard had been staring at the soldiers, but he turned to her and chuckled. "Yes, you have, miss, but I don`t think you should go back for it."

"No," and she smiled. "It would be best to leave it."

"Can you make your way now?"

"I think I`ll sit for another minute," she said, but then changed her mind. "No, I think I can walk now." The guard helped her stand up. Behind them whistles blew, and the police and soldiers began to march down the street towards the riot.

"You really must go now," said the guard, giving the street behind them a worried look.

"Yes." She settled her dress and they began to walk down the street towards the bank. "How can I thank you?"

"Oh no, miss! Thank the bank manager, Mr. Reynolds, for letting me come and get you. It was my fault for sending you there," he said. "Really, it`s always been a nice place. This has never happened here before."

"It`s happened before?"

"Yes, but not here," he said, a little sadly. "New York, Boston of course. Chicago. But not here. Not till now."

There was the crackle of gunfire in the distance.

"Please, miss, go home," the guard said, at the bank steps.

"Yes. And thank you again." And she hurried up the street towards the trolley stop.

On the trolley, Kay noticed the woman next to her looking at the stains on her dress. She had tried to tuck them under when she sat down, but there was too much fabric and her arm hurt when she moved it. "Yes. I am a mess," she said and smiled at the woman.

The woman was older and seemed very sturdy. She looked at Kay with sympathy and said, "These things happen. Try alcohol. If it doesn`t work, you can always drink it." She gave Kay a strained smile. "You have a large bruise on the side of your face, dear."

"Oh," Kay exclaimed quietly. With her shoulder hurting she hadn`t noticed. She touched it gingerly. "I was caught in a riot."

"I thought I heard gunfire. It`s a good thing you made it out. Don`t worry, your hair hides most of it." Kay had lost her hat, but gratefully still clutched her purse and the papers.

"I just want to get home."

The woman sighed. "Don`t we all."

And so they chatted. They found they both hated needlepoint and the war. Kay thanked her and said goodbye when she reached her stop. It was afternoon, but the summer sun was still high in the sky, and the walk down her street was hot and humid.

When she got home her aunt peeked out the kitchen door to see who had come in. "Hello," she said. "What`s happened to your hair?"

"I was in a riot."

"Oh dear God. Let me look," and she hurried over and began her inspection, tutting over her dress and making noises of alarm, sympathy, and fright at her bruise.

"Please, help me out of this dress. I don`t think I can do it myself."

And so they retired to Kay`s bedroom.

"That`s a nasty bruise on your face. Anything else?"

"My arm."

Grace pulled off Kay's shoes, then unlaced her overskirt, her dress, her petticoat, her bustle, her steel crinoline, and then with a grateful sigh, her hated corset. Kay breathed deeply with relief. Then they went to work pulling her shoulder and arm out of her union suit. Her shoulder was wrenched and swelling, as was her forearm where the man had grabbed her.

"Oh sweet father on high, I`ll go for the doctor!"

"No, I don`t think he`ll do any good." Kay had a very low opinion of doctors. He`d probably try to bleed her with a dirty knife. "I just need to rest," and, to distract Grace, "and some food. Do we have any soup?"

"Oh no, but I can make some!" She hurried to the

kitchen.

Kay tried to work her shoulder. It was stiffening already, and she didn't want to be immobile. She forced herself up and went to her dresser to look at her face in her hand mirror. It was swelling too. She couldn't hide this under her clothes, she thought. When she finally got her garter, her long socks, her bloomers, and then finally her union suit off she found several more bruises, some turning rainbow colors. She pulled on her night bloomers, bodice, and dress, and thought about taking a bath. Her corset always made her itch terribly when she took it off, but her shoulder made it difficult to scratch. She thought that it would feel nice to wash off the heat of the day, but she doubted she could do a very good job of it with her arm hurting, and it was embarrassing to ask her aunt for help. But she put on her slippers and headed for the kitchen anyway.

Kay finally did try to bathe. Her aunt heated water, and Kay scrubbed and sponged herself out on the back porch where the water could run through the floorboards, especially her hair where that man had grabbed it. And when she finished she was cold and damp, which was a pleasant change from the humid summer heat. She had soup and bread for dinner, but thought about wine and spaghetti as she ate.

Then to bed, even though it was still twilight, but it was impossible to get comfortable. She thought about the day, then her father. She sorted through the papers, the things they had said, in her mind as she lay there, and then suddenly she realized, the letters just stopped. He might still be alive!

They rode along sweating under the sun. The

agents, with their hands tied, had a problem with the flies, which landed on them and sometimes bit. But there was little that could be done. They would blow at them when they could, but it was obvious misery. Deke had tied their bandanas over their nose and lower face, but the flies merely crawled under.

Suddenly, the one named Jay looked up, like he had an idea. "You know," he said, looking sideways at Jake. "If you let us go, ain`t nobody is going to have to know about the boy."

His partner`s eyes suddenly went wide and he looked like he was about to explode. "Shit!" he sputtered. "You idiot! You had to remind him!"

Jake drew his revolver, and before Deke realized what had happened, Jake had shot both men in the chest, then in their heads to make sure. Big pulled back on the reins of the spy`s horse`s as they tried to buck, frowning all the while at Jake.

Deke halted Ned and sputtered, "Why`d you do that?"

"It were a mercy," Big said, still frowning at Jake.

"They were just going to get questioned and hung anyway," Jake said, trying to smile. "I didn`t know how I was going to get you past headquarters anyway. We`d have had to go there to turn them in and somebody would surely find out you weren`t army."

What was left of the men`s bodies still sat upright, tied to their saddles, their blood running down, staining the leather and blankets. Jake and Big cut them loose and tipped their bodies onto the dirt. Then, after a little deliberation, they cut the saddle straps too and dumped them on top of the bodies. "Welcome to the war, boy," Big said, with a faltering smile.

"We going to bury them?" Deke asked.

"Not here," Big said. "Too close to the lines.

Anybody could come along while we were working."

Deke didn`t know what to think. Jake had just shot two people just because Deke wanted to see a city. It seemed a frivolous reason for people to die. But, on the other hand, they were going to die anyway, and it had been quick. And, as well, if Deke hadn`t been there it would have been Jake and Big getting shot. It was unnerving though, the speed at which Jake had made the decision. Deke was a bit confused.

They had spare horses now, and with a spare horse each they made good time. Deke had never had another horse than Ned, and he kind of kept his eye on Ned to see if he minded, but Ned seemed happy about the lighter load. Deke wasn`t sure he should get too close to this new horse. For one thing she was an army mare, which might be a problem for Ned who, having started off as an Indian horse, didn`t get gelded until he was older. And then too, Deke wasn`t sure he was going to get to keep her anyway.

They climbed wide grassy plains heading northeast towards the railhead at Tulsa. There were fewer streams but bigger trees and woods when they found them, and they almost got caught in a bog once. Despite Big`s worries, Deke never did see any sign of the army.

They were in Osage land. Big said that the Osage liked to move around a lot, but they did have some towns. The one they were approaching Jake called Tzitopa. Tzitopa mostly worked buffalo hide into saddles, boots, and equipment, which they sold to the army. The war was kind of a boon for these Indians.

Big whistled as they came in sight of the town. "Looks like they finished that machine works," he said. "They did that fast." The town was dominated by several smoke stacks which trailed black coal smoke. Mixed in with them were new brick buildings, some several stories tall. And spread around beneath them was a wide sprawl of houses and wide streets filled with wagons, dogs, and people.

"They sure have. You know, Deke, if you`re looking to buy a coat, this is the place to do it," Jake said, holding the lapels of his great coat. Deke was happier with his money than he was dissatisfied with his waterproof felt coat, so he just nodded. Leather coats looked nice and kept off the rain, but they were heavy and didn`t fold well.

As they rode into town they had to dodge wagons piled with salt, hides, lumber, and barrels, most driven by Indians. There were kids and dogs playing everywhere. Even though they were Indian, everyone dressed like they did in any town. Deke had seen Indian towns before, but never an Indian city.

"I don`t know about you two, but I`m going to find me a proper bath, shave, and a bed," Jake said. "Deke, you need to get that goose down off your face before we get to Topeka, or everyone will know you`re just a kid."

Deke had never shaved before and, although he had seen it, he was not sure how to go about it. When they pulled into a stable, Jake fished out the best of the agent`s shaving kits from the packs and handed it to him.

Big came back from talking to the proprietor and said, "We can leave our bags here. They have lockers we can rent and a watchman at night." Considering the extra gear they had, this was welcome news. Ned, tired and footsore, didn`t complain when he was led into his stall, but set to work on the hay in the trough.

"So what do we do now?" Deke asked.

"We find a hotel," Jake replied.

"There were three last time we came through," Big

added.

"How are you set for money, Deke?" Jake asked.

Deke shrugged his shoulders and said, "I`m alright."

"Well, let`s find a nice hotel. Tonight`s on the Union Army." Jake smiled and patted his coat pocket.

The proprietor of the hotel didn`t seem to mind that Jake`s money was Union. The Osage Nation, being neutral, dealt with whoever could pay. There were baths to be had next door. Deke hadn`t had a bath in a tub since he was a kid. Warm water was a rare experience for him, and these tubs were big! He could sit all the way in them. There was powder that when put in the water, scented it like flowers, and when splashed made large bubbles that stayed and didn`t pop. He soaked and watched the rainbow play of light on their surfaces. The men ordered food to be brought to them, in their tubs. The waiters just put boards down across the top and plunked the plates down on top. And there were clean towels. They wore their cleanest clothes, sending the rest away to be washed by somebody else! Deke just about howled at the moon at the thought of the extravagance of it all.

Finally, to top it all off, they went to the barbershop. Deke had never been to one before. His sun-bleached straight brown hair stretched down his back and was tied in a loose ponytail. He had always just cut the end off with his knife. The barber sat him in a padded iron chair and began to cut. Jake and Big sat and smiled, watching the barber work.

He said to them in thick, slow, accented English, "This one is free. Hair this long I can sell for wigs." The barber cut it close to his head, army style. Two old men came in and sat, huffing to each other in Osage, watching the boy`s hair come off.

Then the barber put soap on Deke's face from a cup with a round brush, and began polishing the razor on a leather strap. Deke was nervous. The razor glinted wickedly in the sunlight. "Sit still, don't move," said the barber, which made Deke all that much more nervous. He sat rigid rock still. The razor scraped over his upper lip and chin and across the underside of his jaw. As the soap was scraped off it went in a sink. Then the barber wiped off his face with a damp towel and brushed off his shoulders and neck. Deke's neck and ears felt cold. When he looked at himself in the barber's mirror, he saw an entirely new man. One whose ears stuck out.

Then it was Jake's turn. Deke watched carefully. He'd be doing this haircutting and shaving thing himself from now on. Big liked his bushy beard and just wanted a haircut, although he let the barber talk him into trimming his beard just a bit. When they got outside, Deke shook his head. The weight of his hair was gone, and he could feel the breeze on his neck and scalp. He couldn't help but laugh, which made Jake and Big laugh too. Big said, "Thank you, Abraham Lincoln, for this bounty!" And they laughed even harder.

Since leather was so cheap and available, they bought replacements for some of their tack and gear, including three proper pack saddles with panniers, which are big side bags, for the new horses. Deke got new boots even though his old ones weren't quite done in. Then they had a nice dinner. Jake and Big had cigars. Deke tried one and almost threw up. He was pale and woozy for quite some time, which made Jake and Big laugh and whack him on the back. When they rode out the next morning, they were clean and rested.

Where Tzitopa was an Osage city, Tulsa was Southern, but there were no border posts. Between Tzitopa and Tulsa stretched a proper road, and they were building a railway along its side. Deke noticed that the road was littered with black bits of coal, and he found out why when three wagons full of it passed them going back into town. They gained altitude as they rode, and the air grew a little cooler. When they got to the Arkansas River, there was a long wooden bridge on concrete bases, some parts being brand-new, and next to it, an iron trestle for the new railway. Looking at the city, Deke could see that it had been bombed. There were holes and craters all over, and fire had burned down whole blocks of buildings.

On the way through Tulsa, Jake and Big tried to coach Deke. "The head of the Rangers is Colonel Ford. You only need to say yes sir and no sir. You salute like this. You salute when we do, probably just when we walk in. You used to be a courier for General Johnson. He`s on the other side of town. Johnson drinks a lot. He can`t remember his own mother let alone you," on and on. Deke was more terrified than he`d ever been. He was very worried he`d make a mistake.

With the loss of whole blocks of buildings, people in town had to double up. Laundry hung across roofs, and there were extra store signs nailed up next to or across older signs. Deke wondered about Mr. Folkerson, if he had to share a store with someone now too.

Jake had a piece of paper that helped them through several checkpoints manned by soldiers in grey. On its outskirts northwest of town they met a sea, or at least it seemed that way to Deke, of men and tents. Smoke from cooking fires snaked up like some kind of topless forest. The rows of tents stretched on forever. Jake and Big knew where they were going though. Their path meandered down side roads until they climbed a low hill full of horses, men, and tents. They tied up their horses amongst many, leaving them there still loaded, and made their way towards a long tent. Men nodded as they walked by. Inside the tent it was hot and stuffy and full of an odd assortment of men.

"Ho, Big," said one as he dealt cards. "Jake, what happened to your nose?" another added. "Whose your new friend?" Men gathered around them. One slapped Jake on the back, which sent up a bit of dust. They were dressed in every kind of outfit Deke had ever seen. There were men in Indian leathers, long coats, short coats, tailored pants, moccasins, tall boots, short boots, shoes, and the strangest hats. Deke hadn`t known what to expect, uniforms perhaps, but this motley assortment left him confused. There was a card game around a table, some kind of game on a blanket, and a couple of men had been lying on cloth bags of supplies reading books.

Jake and Big nodded at friends as they pushed through, "Later, " Jake said. "We`ve got to report to the colonel."

They passed on into a second section of the tent. Big stuck his hand through the cloth flap and knocked on a tent pole.

"Enter," came a voice from inside.

The colonel`s office consisted of a cot, several trunks, a folding table, which he was using as a desk, and a single chair. Colonel Ford looked a lot like Jake, except he was wearing a grey officer`s uniform and his nose wasn`t broken. They saluted and Jake said, "Hayes and Wallace reporting back, sir!"

"Oh, shut up," Ford said, still writing on the piece of paper in front of him.

"Well, being as you`re in uniform I thought this was a special occasion."

"No, I have a meeting. You came back just in time. Who`s the kid?"

"This here is Deke Hayden. He`s a courier for

General Johnson. He wants a transfer."

Ford snorted. "Who wouldn`t, " he said. "You vouch for him?"

"Yes, sir."

"Big?"

"Yup."

"Good enough. I`ll get the paperwork and he can courier it right back over to Johnson."

"So, Jake, how are the Mescalero doing these days . . ."

Big tugged Deke`s arm, and they left through the flap.

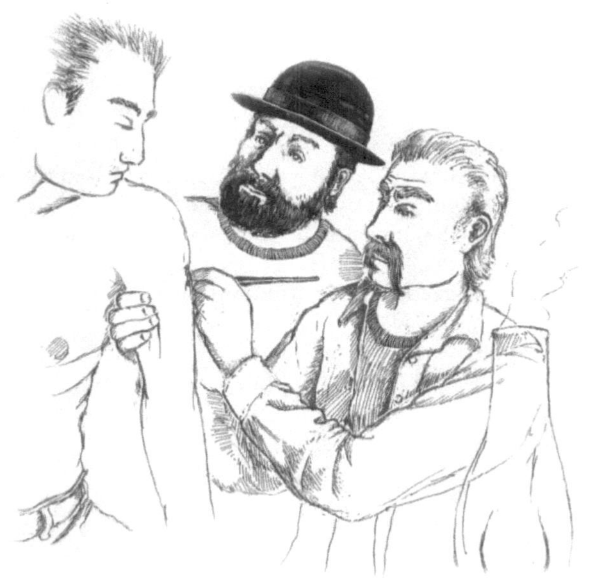

CHAPTER 5

"Boys, I would like to introduce you to Deke Hayden."

Deke hadn`t expected this as they left the colonel. These men were all old hard veterans, at least from Deke`s point of view. Their looks as they nodded in his direction just about sent him back through the tent flap.

"He`s a crack shot, practically feral, and honest to the core," Big said, with a smile.

That sent several eyebrows up.

"I`d like to see that," said a steel-eyed, leather

skinned, woodsman in an Indian jacket, Union soldier pants, and black boots that looked like they had walked a thousand miles.

Big snorted. "What do you say, Deke?" he said in Deke`s ear. "Let`s show `em."

Deke didn`t want to show anyone anything. He was thinking that Mexico might have been the right decision after all and was about ready to pack up and head south. But somehow he got pushed outside; so he walked over to Ned to get his rifle.

But he took pity on poor Ned, who had had a long day. "Give me a minute," he said, and he began unloading Ned and the mare. Ned`s fur was matted under his blanket and Deke tried to smooth it with his hand. Big handed him a brush and began unloading the other horses. Deke worked out the worst of it, and then checked the hooves. They were fit, but would need some work. Then he pulled his rifle from his saddle holster and turned to see that the men had come out and had been watching.

"Wait for me to finish," Big said.

Deke frowned at the men, put his rifle back, picked up the brush and set to work helping Big. Then their bags were just sitting there in the dirt. Deke looked around but could see no place to rack the saddles or anything.

"That tent over there," Big said, tipping his head towards a nearby tent.

Deke hoisted up a couple of saddles and took off towards the tent, then came back for bags, and then Big was there hauling too. Lastly, he picked up his own saddle, racked it, and then came back with his rifle and a box of cartridges.

One of the men said, "Can I see that rifle?" and held out his hand.

Deke silently handed it to him.

Several of the men glanced at the carved stock.

"That`s Navaho isn`t it?" the one holding it asked.

"Yavapai," Deke said.

"Bet you didn`t buy it either," the man replied, and handed it back.

He stared Deke in the eye, but Deke couldn`t figure out what it meant. Then they all turned and started downhill.

"Go on," Big said, still smiling.

So he followed. They had a target range, really more of a trash heap, set up at the bottom of the hill. A couple of the men picked up some hole-ridden cans and set them on top of sticks that someone had poked in the ground. Then they all stood back and looked at Deke.

Deke chambered a round and picked off the first can without thinking. Then he hit two more before he only clipped the fourth, cocking his rifle between shots. He drew his pistol quickly, clipping and then knocking the last can into the air on the second shot.

He could hear in-drawn breaths behind him.

"I wonder if he can do that from horseback," someone muttered.

Deke stood there absent-mindedly pushing more cartridges into his rifle`s magazine. The men looked surprised for some reason and Deke wasn`t sure if he should take it as an insult. "Should I shoot something else?" he asked Big.

"No, that`s good," Big said, with a chuckle.

Deke set the safeties and tucked the rifle under his arm pointing downward.

"If I`m staying here tonight then I need to clean up, otherwise I need to git so I can clear town before dark," he said to Big. The men were talking to each other, walking back up the hill. Some patted or whacked

Deke on the shoulder before starting up.

"I think you`re staying Deke," said a happy Big.

It took three days for Kay to work up the courage to tell her aunt her decision.

"I told you, I`m going west."

"You`re what?" for the third incredulous time.

"I`m going west to look for my father."

"A single woman like you? It isn`t safe."

Pointing to her bruise, "Oh, and it`s safe here?"

"You know what I mean. Unescorted."

"I`m not going to Boston."

"But you must."

"I`m going west to look for my father. He may still be alive."

"Not likely. Your mother said he was dead."

"No, he stopped writing."

"Then it`s as good as."

"No, it`s not."

And on and on. Really, it didn`t matter. Her aunt was not her legal guardian. She had no legal guardian any more. She was a free woman. But Kay wanted her aunt`s blessing. She needed her blessing because Grace was the only family she had left. To lose her would mean that she was truly alone. And so they argued.

They argued while Kay drew $800 from the bank. They argued more as she discussed her financial options out west with her lawyer and secretly drew up a will. Unknown to her aunt, she had $14000 transferred to her aunt`s bank in Boston. They argued when she checked train schedules. They argued as she divided her possessions into two trunks, her trunk to carry and her grandmother`s trunk to go with her aunt to Boston.

Grace finally stopped arguing when she found out that Kay had bought a small revolver for her handbag along with lessons in its care and use.

When she first told the shop owner she wanted a gun, he had looked at her askance, his eyebrow cocked. But then she pulled back her hair to show her bruise, and his look had turned to a frown. "We`ll have no part with murder, ma`am," he said.

She realized this had been a mistake, and so she said, "No, I`m going to travel west and I think I might need some protection."

He kept his frown and nodded, "Yes, ma`am, I suppose you might." But he clearly had his doubts, and so he took her into their indoor range along with a pistol. He showed her how to hold it, where the trigger was, and what it did. "Just point it down range. That`s right. Like this. Now squeeze the trigger –"

It went off with a bang and rocked her arm back so hard it was pointing upwards. The owner let out a little "eek" and gently pushed her arm back down from the ceiling so she was pointing down range again.

Kay thought the noise had been amazing. Her ears were ringing.

The owner looked at her enquiringly. "Do you still want it?"

Trying to catch her breath, she managed to say, "Oh yes."

When she got home that evening, she smelled of gun-powder.

Her aunt`s sullen silence after that touched Kay more than anything she had said before.

Jake took the transfer papers and signed General

Johnson`s name himself and had Deke take them back to the colonel, who didn`t even look at them. He tossed them in a pile he had in back of his desk. Jake said that the colonel somehow managed to lose that pile every time they moved.

Deke spent two weeks sitting around mending canvas, cleaning tack, fixing wagon wheels, and hauling supplies before doubt that he would ever get to go north began to creep into his mind. It`s not that he was unhappy. The more he got to know the Rangers, the more he liked them. They considered themselves to be, as they put it, "gentlemen soldiers," although others called them mercenaries. Some of them, like Big and Jake, were original Texas Rangers from before the war and had been with the scouts from the beginning. But many came from parts out west, just like Deke, and others had come from all over the world, Mexico, Canada, South America, and even Europe! Places Deke couldn`t even conceive of, they might as well have said the moon. And every one of them could shoot and ride.

And it was the sheer number of them. Deke had never been around so many people in his life. There were over 200 Rangers, although there never seemed to more than 60 around camp. And then around them on the sandy plain outside of town there were thousands of soldiers. Deke, when he was doing ranch work, had slept in bunk houses only when he had to. They were stuffy, dark, and noisy. He preferred to stay outdoors. But there was no place to go in the camp. The tents weren`t particularly stuffy, but noise travelled farther and there was more of it. From morning to night there were trumpets sounding everywhere. The troop had two of their own, and some of his first lessons were learning the company trumpet signals, then uniforms, then they moved on to flags. He had only seen a few flags in his life and never one waving above a galloping horse. He thought it was beautiful.

And people came and went too. Nobody stayed in one place for very long. The Rangers were the odd job men of the army, so for every Ranger in camp, there were two more out in the field, always leaving or arriving. But for those first two weeks Jake and Big were always there to give him advice.

Deke, being new and all, was under the command of the troop quartermaster, Sergeant Beauregard McDonnell, who put him to work all over the camp fixing and digging and hauling. The first thing he said to Deke was, "First off boy there will be no sarge or sir or Mr. McDonnell or whatever. Damn it, show respect for me when you speak to me and call me Beau or I`ll peel the hide from your bones!" Beau was a red–faced Irishman who always seemed to be at the point of exploding, was always playing cards by lantern light in the evenings.

Deke could read and write after a fashion, but he had never really learned his numbers, which Beau seemed to take personally. So every evening Beau would sit Deke down for half an hour and watch him struggle with addition and subtraction while Beau played cards. They filled the lid off of a crate with fine dirt and Deke wrote in it with a stick.

"That`s one dollar to you. Deke, you forgot to carry."

Deke grunted in frustration.

"Fold."

"No, no, Deke, it`s the tens you carry."

"I`m in."

"How about you, Zeb?"

"I`m thinking."

"Deke, how much is 9 and 4?"

"I`m in."

And on and on. It was pure frustration to Deke, who would master one thing about numbers but then immediately had to move on to another.

Beau had a Negro helper named William Cotton, although people around camp called him Black Bill. Sometimes though, when people were feeling mean, Deke heard them calling him Beau`s Buck. Both Beau and Bill claimed that Bill was a free man. Beau never said how he got there, and Bill never seemed to leave his side. Bill was a quiet man, which Deke suspected he had learned through hard years. Deke truly did hope that Bill was really free, but he was afraid to ask. Deke might find out something he didn`t want to know, and the spell that kept Bill safe would be broken.

Working around the camp helped him to get to know how things worked and the men who caused things to happen. He peeled potatoes and washed pots for the cooks who worked in two long kitchen wagons. He cleaned and oiled leather for the saddler, brushed and picked hooves for the ferrier, and pumped the bellows for the blacksmith. This was fair, too, as most veterans who didn`t have assignments were working there beside him as well. It was a good way to meet people and for people to get used to him.

As it turned out, Deke didn`t get to keep the mare, probably to the eternal regret of Ned. He saw her riding out a week after he arrived. Beau seeing him watch her ride out, frowned, said, "She yours?"

"Nope, a friend of Ned`s," which busted Beau up for some reason.

One night Jake and Big caught Deke when he was alone leaving the cook`s wagon and dragged him into a storage tent. "Deke, you`re going to have to see the doctor soon, and we`re going to have to do something about that arm of yours," Big said.

"I ain`t going to get no tattoo," and he started to pull away.

"No, no, boy, that`s the whole point," Jake said, and showed him a pen and a bottle of ink.

"What`s that for?"

"That is what we call - a temporary tattoo," Big replied.

Jake knew the right unit markings, and Deke sat there and let him draw on his arm. This was fortunate timing on their part, or perhaps Jake had inside information, because the next day the veterinarian, who was also the doctor, showed up at the farrier`s tent. He had just gotten back from an assignment the night before, and he was ready to catch up on his duties.

He seemed pleased when he inspected Ned. He checked his teeth, legs, hooves, and then his ears and eyes for mites and found Ned to be fit, which was reassuring to Deke considering the tools he had seen in the doctor`s tent. After inspecting Ned though, the next thing the doctor wanted to do was inspect Deke, which was not reassuring at all. He and an assistant practically dragged Deke to his tent and ordered him to take off his shirt, which Deke did slowly and with great reluctance. When he came at Deke with some kind of horn stuck in his ear, Deke almost bolted. But it turned out all he wanted to do was listen to his chest. He checked Deke`s teeth, hair, and ears, and then asked him to drop his drawers. Deke started laughing, partly out of sheer nervousness. The doctor stared back at him, which made Deke laugh some more.

"Do you mind telling me what`s so funny, son?"

"This is the same thing you do to the horses," Deke said.

The doctor looked to the side for a moment, then

laughed a bit too. "Yes, yes it is isn`t it? Now drop your drawers!"

Deke did not have crabs, lice, or odd lesions. His sight, hearing, breathing, and heart were clear and strong, and so the doctor pronounced him fit.

CHAPTER 6

Kay left her grandmother`s house in the early morning. There had been no meal. Just some cold bread and meat. Already buyers had come to look at the house, and Grace would stay until it sold. Kay would never see it again. The carriage driver, despite his peg leg and Kay's vigorous objections, took her trunk across the old plank and loaded it in the back of the carriage.

Kay and Grace hugged, and cried.

"Please be careful," her aunt said as she held tightly to Kay's hands.

"I will," Kay said.

"Please write."

"I will."

"Don`t go anywhere alone."

"I`ll always stay near people," Kay promised.

After more tears, Kay finally turned and walked to the carriage. The morning felt cool and bright, the hum of the city was immediate. She thought that she might have caught a whiff of fall in the air. She looked back at her aunt as she rode away and they both waved, and then there was only the road.

Her life seemed to be one long ending, with people dying and places drifting away. This was just one more ache.

Already the streets were full of people, horses, and wagons. They turned from the boulevard towards the city, where the men were still turning off the gas lights. She could smell the day`s bread just out of the city`s ovens.

At the train station she paid the carriage driver. The next Negro porter in line picked up her trunk to carry it to the platform and the waiting luggage cart. She tipped him and he tipped his hat, turning to get back in line. She stood near the cart, partly because she didn`t want to lose her trunk, but also because she felt that her luggage was probably more likely to get on the right train than she was.

The train station was a vast lace of iron and glass. So much enclosed space was breathtaking. Even the whistles of the trains seemed lost in it. The trains themselves were huge, higher than a house. The black iron engines barely seemed able contain their steam inside. It leaked out here and there, and occasionally jetted into the air when they blew the whistle. Men in dirty work uniforms climbed all over them.

On each platform there hung a clock, square in the middle, and she could see she was still early, and so she sat on a bench and waited. More people arrived. People came and sat on the bench with her. Eventually two men came over and began to push the cart away and she, and another woman both rushed over to the men.

"Excuse me!" Kay called.

"Oh yes, please!" the other woman said.

The men stopped.

"This is my trunk," Kay said.

"Yes, and I was wondering . . ." the woman added.

"Yes, ma`am, ma`ams?" one of the men said, looking back and forth.

"Am I in the right place for my train?" Kay asked.

"Yes," the woman said. "Me too."

"Well, let`s see your tickets."

So they both fished out their tickets.

"Yes, this is the right platform, and that`s your train." He pointed at the engine. "But you can`t board yet because we`re still loading goods," he added.

"Oh, but how do we know when to get on?" the woman asked.

"The conductor will tell you. They`ll be no mistaking it."

"We`ve got to go," the man's partner said.

"Yes, well, thank you," Kay replied.

"Yes, thank you," the woman said.

And the men sent the cart moving towards the train.

"No trouble at all," the man called over his shoulder.

Kay took a moment to look at the woman. She stood taller than Kay with pale straight blond hair and a long nose, which seemed to fit her thin frame. Like Kay, her dress was home-made. She seemed older too, but not by much. And then Kay noticed that she was being examined as well.

"So we`re going on the same train," the woman

said. She looked worried.

"Yes, it seems so."

"Oh, my name is Charity Carmichael," she seemed in a near panic.

"Kay Mapleton."

"I don`t mean to be forward, but are you travelling alone, because I am."

"Yes, I am," Kay replied.

"Could we sit together? I`ve never been on a train before."

Kay smiled. "I have, but never alone. It`s all very confusing."

Charity smiled too then. "I`m so worried I`ll make a mistake!"

And then they laughed.

"Where are you going?" Kay asked.

"Saint Louis to meet my husband. Where are you going?"

"Denver."

"All the way to Denver! I thought Saint Louis was far. So you`re going to have to stop in Saint Louis too." Saint Louis marked the end of the Baltimore and Ohio rail line. From there she would have to find another ticket west.

The Scouts, as they were called by the army, were ordered forward in the third week. They were heading to a place called Springfield. But in order to go, there was an amazing amount of wagon loading that had to happen first. Deke loaded bales of hay, bags of grain, filled kegs of water, carried bricks from the ovens and forge as they were pulled apart, lugged crates of this and that, and to finish it all off – an anvil. The tent had been packed, so he fell asleep that night under the open sky, not that he minded.

Then they were up again the next day and at it again. They had a cold breakfast of salt beef and bread because some parts of the column had pulled out that morning and among them were the cooks. The hill was starting to look empty, like it had mange. Some parts still had grass and some parts were worn down to the dirt. Deke noticed that a lot of the troops that had filled the valley were packing up and moving too. There was a big column of men moving down the road and through town, being joined by smaller columns as individual units moved out, but Deke couldn`t see exactly where they were going. From the sun, it looked like east.

When the last of the Rangers finally got moving, Deke rode alongside the wagon driven by Beau and Black Bill. Deke still lacked training and was not allowed to ride with the troop proper. He didn`t know how to hold column or formation. He barely knew what the bugle calls meant, so he had to ride back in the dust with the wagons.

The road was crowded with troops, all marching forward at the same speed, foot, horse, or wagon, which wasn`t to Ned`s liking at all. He was used to setting his own pace and tried to speed up. Pulling him back was tiring, especially when he would stop to eat grass out of pure spite. So after the midday stop Deke got permission to tie him to the back of the wagon. Deke rode from then on, high on top of one of the crates, which gave a good view of the road. After they were past the town they got up into low hills of oak and hickory trees, and grazed meadows mixed with ragged grey rock. Bill hummed songs to himself, although everyone was listening. The wagons threaded their way up a ravine, and Beau maddeningly kept asking Deke sums and differences.

That math was the only dark spot on what was a fine day; that was until it rained. It pelted down out of a rolling shelf of dark grey. Deke had to walk alongside Ned while he pulled his tent half off his saddle, which wasn't easy. Ned was not feeling charitable and kept moving to the side and Deke was too tired to fight. He pushed Ned back until he was walking crabwise and could go no further. Then Deke worked the tarp loose from the trapped horse. Wrapping himself up in the tarp, he climbed back up on his box.

Sometimes there were bridges, but more often there were just fords and several times water so deep that it washed over the bottom of the wagon floorboards, which sent Beau cursing. They never floated away though. It was at times like that that the soldiers on foot would string ropes across to keep men and gear from washing away, which meant that the wagons had to wait until the way was clear of men. Beau didn't mind. He'd watch the men as they waded through the water to gauge the river's depth and to pick the way least worn loose and deep by too many wagon wheels.

Whenever they stopped, Beau would send Bill and Deke out to collect whatever wood they could find for the night's fire. It got so it was an unsaid order. They would just get up and get to it. Bill never said a word that wasn't necessary, even when they were alone. He kept his eyes on the job in front of him, and so Deke did the same. Deke had been raised with Indians and he was used to quiet. The problem with wood hunting, though, was that everyone else was doing it too, and so sometimes they had to walk a ways from the road to find it.

The two of them were so quiet that they often surprised game. One time they came upon a lone buck. Bill stopped and stared. Deke for once didn't have his rifle and thought of trying with his pistol, but then thought better. He would probably only wound it, and they had no time for a long chase. So they both stood there and looked. It was then that Deke realized that he had never seen Bill with a gun.

Kay had bought a coach ticket at her aunt`s insistence even though she would be on the train for days. Her aunt didn`t want her to sit anywhere alone, and now happily she wasn`t. Charity was good company, although she seemed to be more enamored with needlepoint than Kay. She was clearly better wife material, unlike Kay, who never seemed to excel in any of the womanly crafts.

"My husband was wounded and so they discharged him. I`m going to help him get home."

"Do you know what kind of wound?"

"No," she said, clearly worried.

And that brought silence for a bit. Kay had seen so many men without limbs, with hooks or crutches. Charity was clearly fighting tears.

"We`ll get him home," Kay said with a smile.

"Yes, yes, we will," but her voice was distant.

Kay looked at the farms and woods as they passed by. Everything was so green. The rail fences, the barns, the animals seemed endless. Suddenly they passed a crossing where there were children waiting. They were waving at the train. Kay tried to wave, but it was too late. They were gone in an instant.

Charity, who, as it turned out was 18, had packed some food and for the first day she shared it with Kay. Charity ate sparingly, and Kay wondered if she had intended to make it last the whole trip. So when they woke in their seats in the morning and Kay felt she could stand to sit no longer, she said "Come, let`s go get breakfast!"

"Oh, but it`s too expensive."

"My treat. You`ve been feeding me, and it`s time I returned the favor." She had to practically drag Charity to the dining car where, after a short wait, the Negro waiter showed them to a table with white linen and a wide-bottomed clear glass vase with a pink flower in it.

They ate eggs, biscuits, sausage with gravy on top, and of course a gallon of tea. It went a long way towards making up for sitting in a seat instead of a bed all night long. The sunlight on the table and food was wonderful as the morning shadows passed over the table. Kay noticed that it was best to not pour too much tea in her cup because otherwise the rocking of the train would spill it. Her saucer was awash in tea, such that she had to pick up her cup with her napkin under it so it wouldn`t drip. With all the rocking, she could see too why the train`s crockery was so thick and heavy.

Then Kay decided that the corset must come off. She had three more nights on this train line. She found a Negro porter and asked him if there were any sleeper rooms available.

"Yes, ma`am, but they`re expensive."

"How much is expensive?"

"$3 a night!"

$3 dollars to be rid of her corset! She almost burst out laughing. "Is there one that sleeps two? And can I get to my trunk?"

"Well, ma`am, if you had it put in the luggage car, then it`s pretty much there for good. We can`t get in, at least not easily when the train is moving. The trains are pretty empty going this direction, so you can have a room. Of course, going back is another story."

"Then I would like one please."

The porter took her to the white conductor, who gave her two new tickets. The sleeper car had rooms with seats that could serve as two beds and two pull down beds above. There was a little closet where you could hang your things and a tiny sink.

"I`ll make the beds when you ask," the porter said.

"Thank you," Kay said, as he left.

Charity thanked the porter as well, and then thanked Kay, and then sat in the corner with tears in her eyes.

"Oh, please don`t be sad. My aunt wouldn`t have let me travel this way if I were alone. And besides, now you can help me out of this corset!"

All day long the train stopped and started at station after station, each looking much like the last. Some stops were longer because the train needed, as the conductor said, "water, coal, and sand." Kay could understand the water and coal, but why sand?

At these stops they were allowed out to walk around, which was nice, not that there was ever much to see. Kay had their trunks moved to their room. Train stations, she could tell, pretty much all looked alike and train tracks always seemed to face the back sides of farms. Except, of course, for the ones in the big cities like Pittsburgh where they had to change trains. Pittsburgh`s station yard was even more grand than Philadelphia`s. There was the vast brick, iron, and glass train yard, much the same as Philadelphia, but in addition they had a huge station as well, with full-sized restaurants actually inside the building itself. It was so big that there were birds flying around inside!

There was a great lobby filled with people waiting for trains, and on one wall was a signboard showing all the trains arriving and leaving. A man with a long pole constantly hooked and unhooked numbers and signs to keep it up to date. The floor of the great room was filled with rows of backed benches which were filled with mothers and children, soldiers wounded, soldiers ready for the front, and old men. Between the benches ambled a stout old man in a uniform who called out the train arrivals and departures in a holler that echoed over the tumbling chatter of the crowd.

They had entered the city by crossing over a long iron trestle which crossed a wide river. She saw river boats and steamers carrying cargo. The city itself was a grey sea of smokestacks and columns of black smoke. It made Kay`s nose itch and throat sore. Above the city was a hill where the airships docked. There were two great zeppelins there that day, along with a dozen smaller airships loading cargo. Kay wished she could travel all the way to Denver by airship. It would be so much easier, but airship travel was only for the rich and important.

Charity and Kay had three hours in Pittsburgh before their next train left. They were both so worried about their trunks that they watched the baggage car until they saw their luggage wheeled over to their platform, and then they double-checked that it was theirs and that they had the time right.

There was a train at their platform, but it wasn`t theirs. It was still too early. They walked back and forth through the tunnel between the tracks just to hear their footsteps echo and then watched trains arrive, until a trainload of wounded came in, at which point Charity turned away in tears. So they ended up in a restaurant drinking coffee! Kay had never had coffee before. She had it with cream from a tiny pitcher and sugar scooped with a tiny spoon from a little bowl. There was a post office in the station, so Kay posted her first letter to

Grace. It would arrive at Grace`s home in Baltimore before Grace got there herself.

The column pulled out of a ravine into low rolling hills. The road wound back and forth between them through shallow river valleys and ravines. Sometimes they would pass ranches with treeless pastures dotted with cattle. No one from these places ever came out to meet them. The column was long, so Deke figured that any onlookers must have gotten tired of waving by the time they arrived. When the collumn camped, Deke could see parts of it still winding back along the road. All the campfires looked like a string of stars.

Before they got to Springfield they ran across Tobi, sitting on a fence by the side of the road.

A lot of the same men who played cards, would sit with Deke and Beau during mealtimes, so Deke got to know some of them fairly well. One of them was Tobias Valois, who shaved his head, which seemed crazy to Deke, but Tobi claimed that with a hat it was cooler and easier to keep clean. Deke had not yet tried to use his new razor and did not think much of trying to use it on his head. Tobi had been a sailor, although some said he had been a coastal pirate, and was good at knife fighting. Deke admired his jokes, which he always seemed to be able to fish out in his French accent whenever the conversation lagged.

"Ho, Rangers, this way," Tobi yelled, waving his hat and then pointing down a logging road. "You are the last ones. Everyone is waiting for you."

Tobi climbed down, untied his horse, and rode up to Beau`s wagon. "Hello, Beau! Are you having fun yet, Deke?"

Deke draped himself back on the boxes and looked at the sky and said, "I like being carried from place to place!"

Beau called out, "How much is 23 minus 7?"

Deke looked back at the sky with a frown and said, "I liked being carried from place to place!"

Tobi laughed and said, "It`s down the road, Beau, you will see when you get there. I will ride ahead and tell them you are here."

The wagons turned off the main road onto the logging road while Beau called out again, "How much is 23 minus 7?"

"16," Deke moaned.

The new road was much less pleasant than the main road, being as it was poorly maintained and heavily rutted, so Deke returned to riding Ned. Clinging to his perch was too difficult as the wagon lurched this way and that. The road was narrow and there were trees and shade. And a breeze too, which kept away the flies.

The logging road was a short-cut to get them into camp northwest of town, bypassing the crush of troops coming in along the main road into the city. They ended up in a small town called Bois D`Arc. Really it was only a few buildings, but they had a store which Deke meant to look at if he ever had the time. There were more Rangers in camp there than townsfolk in town, and Deke figured the store was going to do brisk business. Tobi, when he saw him again, said they had a post office too, not that Deke had anyone to send letters to.

There was well water, plenty of firewood to themselves, probably even game in the woods, and a wagon track into town. But Beau`s wagons had most everything that made life bearable in the Army, and so everyone was glad to see them and there were plenty of hands to help unload. They were camped in a sloping field that had recently been plowed for second planting. This made the dirt damp and loose. The legs of their cots sank into the soil even when it had been stomped down. It was good soil for growing, but it stuck to stuff and got tracked in everywhere. It wasn`t much good for camping, and sadly, it wouldn`t be good for harvesting that fall either, at least after they were through with it.

CHAPTER 7

Kay put her corset in her trunk and left it there. She left her crinoline on the top bunk, and after the first day without it she thought that maybe it might accidently be left behind when they next changed trains. This being her own woman was heady! Instead she wore the day dress she wore at home. They sat in the coach car still, but it was so much nicer without the stiff crinoline. Now if only she could have a bath. The sink was no use with the train rocking about. After another day, Charity, with a naughty laugh, did the same with her corset. It was like being girls again. Kay felt like running down the aisles of the train, but of course there were limits.

They changed trains in Columbus and Indianapolis. The crinoline made it all the way. Really, she would have had to alter her dresses, because without it, the fabric would have draped more and been too long.

The further they got west, the more soldiers they saw. Kay and Charity sat in their seats while the train sat on the sidings and watched through the windows as troop trains, supply trains, and war trains went by. The war trains were the most interesting. There were iron cars with guns sticking out through little windows. There were train cars with long giant cannon built into them, and wide stubby cannon so big that Kay thought she might fit be able to fit her trunk down their barrels. She saw flat cars with wheeled iron boxes chained to the top that had guns sticking out and smoke stacks on their tops. Then there were trains of horse cars filled with horses, their faces visible through little windows, each with its own little stall, and flat cars with wagons, small cannon of different shapes, and curious mechanical guns. Trains went by packed with soldiers, sometimes passenger cars like hers or boxcars for the less lucky, often with soldiers clinging to the tops of the cars as well. And going the other way were the unending river of wounded being sent to hospitals back east.

Finally there could be no more delays possible, and the B&O line ended in Saint Louis. It felt strange leaving the train in a strange city with no idea of where to go. Up until then, Kay's journey had gone pretty much as she planned, with one thing leading to another. In Saint

Louis though, her plans ran out. It was like being at the end of the world. The platforms were full of soldiers, all of them in their way. Kay and Charity threaded their way between lounging soldiers and went to the ticket office because, they could think of no place else to go, and Kay needed a ticket for her next journey anyway. She was horrified to hear that there were no trains west. The lines were closed because it was too dangerous and some sections had been damaged.

"I don`t know why or how miss. Probably those damn Indians. Always trouble. Always upset about something." The clerk wore a strange hat with no top. Just a brim. Kay had never seen anything like it.

"Then we are going to need a hotel. Can you recommend one?" she replied.

"Ma`am, there are no hotels but ours. The city is full and the officers have all the rooms. And I`m not sure we can find space for you either. There`s a lot of people wanting to go places but with no way to get there." He looked frustrated and put upon.

Kay felt that this wouldn`t do, they needed this man, and so she tried to put on her best look of sympathy, "It must be difficult. You`re really the only one here anyone can talk to."

"Oh yes," he said, falling for it. "I see the same people four or five times a day. Sometimes they seem to feel it`s me personally. As if I control the trains. I can`t help the war or the Indians."

"Since we`re stuck here, do you have any idea where we could go? We can`t stay here."

"Well, you`re right there. Not with all the soldiers around, that`s for sure. You`ll have to check for yourself though. The rail line owns both the hotel and restaurant across the street and the granary and warehouses next to it besides," he said with pride. "Your baggage will be safe. Just go over and find out. Make sure you show them your tickets."

They thanked him profusely, and Kay thought it might be a good idea to think of something to bring him when she came back to ask again about tickets.

Fortified with purpose, they made their way through the station lobby, picking a path between sleeping and sitting soldiers. Some had rifles which gleamed wickedly, and their packs, helmets, and uniforms, which had interesting pockets and emblems attached. Kay was curious, but didn't want to stare. Some of them stared quite frankly back at them and did little to hide their intentions as the women passed.

The street outside was lit with hot dusty brown sunlight. Above it hung myriads of airships, all different sorts, some coming and some going. The city looked like a black forest of smoke-stacks with round balloon clouds floating over it, each tethered by thin strings. Kay had no idea why there would so many airships in Saint Louis. Perhaps, though, one might be heading west.

The street was a river of wagons and horses. There were others trying to cross, but it seemed a futile effort. No one gave any way to others. Finally a porter with a cart of luggage came out of the station and pushed into the traffic, which started an exodus. He would thrust the cart in front of horses causing them to balk, then took advantage of the moment, ignoring the driver's curses, to push further forward again. Once the way was open people flowed through. Kay and Charity made it across just behind the porter, climbing the ramp up from the street to the boardwalk behind him. Some stragglers, who had tried to dart across late to catch up, were stuck in the traffic out in the dung and dust. They waved their arms as they dodged about, but the traffic was too noisy to hear their yells.

The hotel was a large box of dusty unrecognizable color, three stories tall, with a simple square entrance and evenly spaced windows on each floor. It was called The Exchange Hotel. Kay and Charity wiped their feet before entering, as a sign by the door requested. Inside, the lobby was dark and cool, lined with hardwood and carpets. The desk had a vase with flowers. Kay felt she hadn`t seen color since they entered Saint Louis. The blossoms were a treat for the eye. The matron at the desk tisked over their tickets with a frown.

"We have a room. It is small," the hotel matron said. She had an odd accent. Kay felt she had heard it before.

"We`ll take it," Kay replied.

She looked at them with a doubtful glance and pulled a large book over. "Pay in advance."

Kay and Charity signed. Kay noticed that her handwriting wasn`t as good as Charity`s and sighed.

"I suppose you have luggage at the station," the matron scowled.

"Yes, we do," Charity said, with a worried look.

The matron sighed. "Give me your tickets and I`ll have it brought over," she said, with an annoyed glance at the street.

"Thank you," Kay said, and she really meant it. She didn`t want to try to haul her luggage across herself.

Even though Bois D`Arc was a ways from the battle, they could hear it in the distance. It was a distant rumble that came and went, like someone was blowing air in your ear.

Just when Deke had everything unloaded and settled and thought he could take a rest, Jake walked up and said, "We found something fun to do." Jake, Big, Tobi, and a new man named Clemett Schmitz were assigned a mission together, and they talked the colonel into letting Deke come along. Clem was new to Deke. He was short and thin and wore round brass spectacles. He spoke with an accent and said his parents came from Germany. He held his pants up with suspenders and had the nervous habit of running his ink-stained hand through his dark brown hair when he was thinking.

Before they packed to go, the colonel called them all to his tent. When he addressed them, the colonel admonished Deke, "Deke, I'm sending you along because Jake and Big asked, but I don't want you sticking your neck out for anybody, and to stick to what you`re told." He also told the four that they would have to answer to Beau if anything happened to him. Deke was touched. It had been a long time since anyone had worried about him, even though, in the case of Colonel, it was rather a stern worry. Then he told Deke his job was primarily that of courier. He had to carry drawings back and orders out. Deke was disappointed on hearing this, but held his tongue as he had been told.

Beau gave them three pack horses and told them to be careful with them. "They`re worth more than all of you together!" he said.

Their mission was simple and seemed to be in line with things Deke knew how to do. There were Union forces massing southwest of a place called Jefferson City. Deke had never heard of it, but it seemed that all they had to do was sneak in and count. It seemed simple. When he said so, the four men laughed.

"You`ll understand more when we get there," said Jake.

They were given rolls of paper in leather tubes, and wooden pencils. Jake let him try a pencil. Deke had never seen a pencil before and broke the point when he tried to write with it. With care and practice though, he eventually became quite adept at carving points in them with minimal loss of lead and writing smooth lines. His actual lettering, though, was appalling. The paper and pencils were for drawing maps and marking troop dispositions. There were little blocks of rubber too, which you could use to erase what you had written.

Although Jake and Big knew a few things on the subject, Clem was a real surveyor. The horses were weighed down with an assortment of wooden boxes containing the brass contraptions that surveyors used to do their surveying and a folding table for him to lay out his maps. There were books, too, that were full of nothing but lists of numbers. Deke wanted to look at the surveying equipment, but Clem said no, he'd see it all later when they settled down somewhere.

When they finally pulled out, Ned was practically prancing. He had been cooped up in camp for three days and wanted be anywhere else. That was until he saw the extra gear he had to carry. He tried to side step again as Deke went for the stirrup, but Deke had expected this and took an extra hop before lifting his leg up. When he made it to the saddle, Ned's ears were straight back. Deke leaned forward and laughed at him to show Ned that he knew what he was up to, and then stroked Ned's neck to show that it didn't bother him.

They rode down the little road into town while the morning dew was still shining and steaming on the yellow grass. Deke had a shoulder sack that was warm with fresh bread, and the smell of fires and cooking in camp was sweet. It was still cool and they had a slight breeze. Altogether it was the best kind of day for travelling.

On the way, Clem started teaching Deke Morse

code. "We'll be using it to signal each other," he said. "It helps though to have a sense of rhythm. Each letter is signified by a combination of long and short flashes. The most common letters have the simplest codes. You start a message with this . . ."

It took all morning to get to Springfield, and by that time Deke had a headache. The codes were very difficult to remember and if he lost track of where he was in the message, then it was practically impossible for him to get back on track. It didn`t help that Deke couldn`t spell a word right even it walked up and hit him in the head with a dictionary. The breeze kept away the flies, which was at least one blessing. They rode across a wide bumpy plain crossed by river ravines. There were patches of forest between meadows cut lush for grazing and fields ready for fall planting. This time Deke could see people, sometimes in the fields, and once they passed a man in an empty wagon. It took three hours to get to town. There was a slight hill crest just before town, and Deke got a good look at Springfield before they entered.

The town had only a few smoke stacks and seemed less ordered than many cities he had seen. There were fields mixed in with buildings. Many of the fields were filled with tents, and the roads were full of soldiers. The buildings were all wood, except for a few taller brick structures. Deke couldn`t see the center of it, but he heard a train whistle, so there had to be tracks somewhere. No one had bombed Springfield and Deke wondered why. Up above the city there were two teardrop-shaped airships with baskets under them. When Deke pointed them out, Clem said they were observation balloons. "Being high up lets you see things far away, especially on a nice day like this," he said. In the distance, on the other side of town above the trees, Deke could see at least a dozen large airships moored together, probably out in some field.

"We`re going to have to introduce you around General Terry`s staff," Jake said to Deke. "And get you some travel papers so you can move about without people giving you trouble."

"Yes, it would be sad if you got press-ganged in some alley," Tobi said with a smile. "Who would carry our reports?"

As they moved into town, Deke could see where rail fences around the fields had all but disappeared. Probably grabbed for firewood, he thought. There was little sign of disorder or drunkenness from the soldiers in the streets. When they came across their first saloon, he saw why. Its doors were closed with a rough sign nailed over it, "No liquor, don`t bother looking."

"Dry town," Big said. "Wonder what Terry did with it all?"

"Maybe he turned it into fire bombs and dropped it on the Union," Tobi replied.

"Could be," Big said to himself. "Be sad for the saloon owners though."

Deke saw a round object with a long white tail drop from one of the balloons. "What`s that?" he said, pointing.

The men squinted up at the balloons. "It`s a message," Clem said. "That`s how they send messages to the ground. The observer must have seen something important."

As they entered town, Deke could see that there were fires above the baskets, under the balloons. Clem said, "That`s what keeps them up. They`re full of hot air which rises. The bags keep a hold of it, which keeps the balloon and the basket in the air and the rope keeps it from going too high or drifting away." It seemed like some kind of miracle to Deke.

"Why don`t they burn up?"

"Well, sometimes they do. It`s very dangerous being an observer. If there`s too much wind then sometimes the balloons get blown off their ropes and go drifting, or the fires get knocked off their stands and set the basket on fire, or not enough heat gets up in the bag and the balloons come back to the ground. Sometimes too quickly. If there are enemy airships or troops nearby, they`ll shoot at the balloons, and there`s nothing the observer can do until he`s cranked back down."

"I saw an artillery shell go through one once," Jake said. "The bag collapsed and it dropped like a stone."

As Deke looked up at the balloon, he could imagine it happening. He began to wonder what he had gotten himself into.

With their trunks and the two narrow beds, there wasn`t much room left in their room. The matron had said the room was small and she was right. It had been meant as a small single room, but now it slept two. Kay, though, was glad to have it. She was in a strange city, but at least she had a place to come home to.

"I need a bath," Kay said. "I feel filthy." They had been travelling for four days and three nights on one train after another. Her hair itched and hung limp. She smelled. They had tried to bathe on the train, but it was impossible to keep water in a basin with the train lurching about.

"We certainly do," Charity added, with a smile.

They climbed down the four flights of stairs to the lobby and approached the front desk.

"Is there some way we can bathe here?"

"And wash clothes," Charity added.

"This is an old hotel. You have your basin in your room. We have no place to hang clothes either. There are laundries in town, some nearby, and bath houses." She seemed put out by the question, as if the idea of a hotel with baths were new. "But they aren`t decent places for young ladies."

"We need a proper bath. Where then can we go?"

"You should go home."

"I`m trying to go there," Kay said wistfully, ignoring the implied insult. "But it seems to be getting further and further away."

"And I`m not going back without my husband," Charity said fiercely.

The matron stopped and frowned. She looked down and sighed. "Mine died in the war with the French."

"We went to war with the French?" Kay asked, confused.

"Gott, gibt mir Kraft!" The matron said, under her breath and then shook her head.

"No, the war between Germany and France." She saw neither Kay or Charity had any clue as to what she was trying to say. "Eighteen years ago?" It was clearly futile. "But then why should well-bred young women care about the news or history?" and she smiled a little. "Perhaps before you leave Saint Louis, you will have more appreciation for its value."

"So you want to find your husband," she continued. "That will be difficult, but I know some places where you can start. As for the baths. I can draw you a map. You will need it. You must be careful in the streets here. It is dangerous."

"We saw the traffic."

"It is not only the traffic. The city is full of soldiers loose in the streets."

"We saw them too."

"You will have seen too many before you leave."

She took a sheet of letter paper from a drawer and dipped her pen in the ink and drew them a map. It was two blocks to the laundry, on the next street over. Easy. But the baths were more difficult. They would have to cross streets, and even though it was only three corners away from the laundry, their route took them past five.

"It is the safest route," she replied, when asked. "You can eat along the way too. It will be cheaper than here. In the old days, we would have sent your laundry over for you. But help is very short. It`s only me and the cleaning women now, and I can`t leave."

"We understand," Charity said.

"I will lend you a sheet to carry your things in. Do not stay out after dark. It is good it is still light in the evenings."

They changed into their cleanest clothes, which turned out to be the dresses they started in, minus the corsets of course! Then piled everything on the sheet and pulled the corners together into a bag. Then Charity, being as she was the biggest, pulled it over her shoulder and they headed downstairs.

The desk matron bid them good luck, and then they were back on the boardwalk and the noise.

The laundry was easy. They made two lefts and never left the block.

The woman behind the counter was an American Indian, the first Kay had ever seen! She had long straight black hair tied back in a ponytail with a beautiful clip made from beads and colored thread. Her skin was brown and wrinkled, but not like the color of a Negro. It was more like a tan. Other than that, she looked just like any other woman. She saw them staring and gave a slight smile that wrinkled the corners of her eyes, like she knew a joke but wasn't about to share it.

She looked at the sheet and said, "Ah, you are from the hotel. Let's see what you brought me." They opened the sheet and the woman sorted things into piles. "You've been travelling. I can finish these day dresses tomorrow, but the better things will take an extra day. We are up to our eyebrows in uniforms," she said. "There is some sort of party, and all of these officer boys have suddenly realized that they haven't washed in weeks."

Before she was finished, a soldier came in with a canvas bag and dropped it on the counter. "Captain Hall needs these by tomorrow night," he said with authority.

"Ha! A captain! I have generals in line. Check back tomorrow. I don't know if we can get it done by then. The day after for sure, but tomorrow . . . I don't know."

The soldier looked both worried and annoyed. He huffed and thrust the bag across the counter. "Take them."

When he had left, the old Indian laughed. "I will charge him double."

Kay liked this woman. "My name is Kay and this is Charity," she said.

"It's good to meet you, Kay and Charity."

"We're going to the baths here," and she showed the woman the map.

"Oh, quite a journey for two young women with the town like this. That is not the best place to go though. That woman at the hotel doesn't know everything." She took out the grease pencil she used to mark tags and added new lines to the map. "Go here," she pointed. "Tell them Wah-Shinka at the laundry sent you."

They thanked her and went into the street again. The traffic wasn't so bad on this street, and they needed to cross it, but after some debate they decided to stick to the instructions. At the corner they stared at the corner they needed to be on, another river of traffic blocking their way.

Suddenly a Union soldier barged by them, followed by two others, straight into the traffic. They looked distraught and ill. They had come out of a store with the numbers "606" painted on the front. Kay and Charity knew a good thing when they saw it and jumped to follow. The soldiers didn`t seem to care, one had tears running down his face, but they broke the traffic, and Kay and Charity made it across. After that, they only had a minor side street to cross.

At last they came to a door. It was only thing they could see where the woman had pointed to on the map, and so they knocked. A young Indian woman answered.

"We were told to say that Wah-Shinka sent us," Kay said. The woman didn`t say a word, but nodded her head and let them in. Inside it was cool and dim. There were three Indian women sitting in a small simply furnished room. Against one wall was a pile of cushions. There were two chairs with small tables beside them, a bookshelf with a varied assortment of books, and in the center a beautiful carpet. Light streamed down from windows set high in the walls. Beyond, through the next doorway, they could see a courtyard and could hear water, like a fountain, and the voices of women. On one of the side tables was a half finished cup of tea!

The woman who had let them in snorted. "She is always finding lost children."

One of the women was sitting on some of the cushions knitting! She had a beautiful round face. When she saw Kay looking, she smiled and held out her work. It was a little sweater.

"It`s for my daughter."

"Oh, let me see!" Charity bubbled.

Kay rolled her eyes. She was terrible at knitting.

CHAPTER 8

The general had taken over the best hotel in town, with the lobby as his command center. Deke`s eyes took a few moments to adjust to the dim lamp light after the bright sun of the street. He could see the general himself talking to other officers off to the side of the lobby. Jake led him over to a young man in a smart uniform. Jake actually saluted, so Deke did to.

"Colonel McDonald," Jake said.

"Jake," McDonald greeted him with a smile.

"We`re going out to scout that troop concentration."

The man`s smile got bigger. "That`s good news. I`m glad they sent you."

"This here`s Deke," he said, dragging Deke forward. "He`s our courier and he needs papers."

Colonel McDonald smiled a tight smile at Deke and held out his hand. After a second of confusion, Deke held out his and they shook. "A pleasure," he said. Deke wondered if it really was.

"Time is short. We can have those cut immediately." He turned and yelled, "Baker!" A short, older, bald man popped up, as if from thin air as best as Deke could tell. "This man needs courier papers immediately."

"Sir!" the man barked, and then he motioned for Deke to follow. They went into the office behind the hotel front desk and from there into rooms in the back that had been converted into work rooms. Deke thought that maybe someone used to live there because there were dark rectangles in the faded wall paper where pictures had hung. Baker led Deke to a man sitting at a desk. The desk was stacked with books and loose paper. Baker, as stiff as before said, "This man needs courier papers."

The elderly, bespectacled man behind the desk looked up with a bored look. "Does he? Well, we can do that." He carefully pulled a book from under a stack of paper and paged through it until he found the end. "Name?"

"Deke Hayden." He had to spell it out for him.

"Unit?"

"Rangers," Deke replied.

"Rangers?" the man frowned.

"The Scouts," Baker said.

"Oh, the Scouts. Yes."

"Duration?"

This stumped everyone for a minute.

Finally Baker said, "Give it three weeks. We can cut him new ones if he needs it."

"Three weeks," the clerk said, and he scribbled it in his book.

"Commanding officer?"

"Jake Hayes," Baker replied.

"Jake?" The man harrumphed and reached behind to a bookshelf and pulled down a book. "That isn`t right," he said, as he thumbed through the pages. "Ah, here he is." He put the book back and turned back to the desk.

"Jeremiah Hayes," he wrote.

"Jeremiah?" Deke almost laughed.

"Something wrong with that?" asked the man.

"No, sir."

"Area of operations?"

"That would be Saint Louis," Baker said.

The man pulled three slips of paper from a drawer and sheet of black paper from another. "Fresh sheet, just for you," he said. He eyed Deke and asked, "You can sign your name can`t you?"

"Yes, sir."

The man cut the black paper in two and sandwiched it between the three forms and began filling it out with a glass pen, which he dipped in ink. Then he had Deke sign. "Press hard. We`ve got two copies." When he peeled away the black pieces of paper, there were two extra copies of the travel paper.

As they waited for the ink to dry, the man said, "You will keep this with you at all times. You may be required to sign it again to make sure you are you. You will notice that it expires in three weeks. If you need an extension you must come back here." Deke nodded through this and yes sir`ed at the end.

"Good man. You are dismissed!" and the man waved him towards the door.

In the lobby, Colonel McDonald and Jake were leaning over a table with a map. The colonel was pointing at things on the map so Deke waited. After a bit, Jake noticed Deke and said, "Ready?"

Deke nodded.

"Well, OK then. Let`s go," Jake said, rubbing his hands together.

They rode out to the north. Beside the road there

were fresh poles with telegraph wires strung between them, pointing the way forward. No sooner were they on the road than Clem started in again with Morse code.

"6 Cannon."

"Da di di di di, da di da di, da di, da da da, da di."

"You left out an N and the start, and end."

"Can we stop using those? It takes too long."

"No."

So Deke spelled it out yet again.

North of town were open fields dotted with airships held down with cables tied to loose webs of rope draped over their gas envelopes. Above drifted two great zeppelins, their aluminum and wood under carriages gleaming silver in the afternoon sun. They were moored to the earth with thick cables fixed to huge iron winches. And on the horizon there were eight more coming in towards the field in a long ragged line.

The airships had their own camps with tents, wagons, and piles of crates and boxes. It clearly took far more men to keep them in the air than it did to fly them. The smoke of campfires drifted with the breeze, as did those airships that were only tethered to the ground. Deke wished the wind direction would shift just so he could see them all swing around, or stay and sit for a bit to watch that line of airships land. Instead he had to tell Clem the count of the airships he saw by type, in Morse code.

Past the airships they rode through low hills, stream–filled valleys, and the occasional buffalo herd. It was getting on towards dinner when Deke noticed he could smell coal smoke. They'd been passing canvas covered wagons. Deke had figured they were empty wagons heading to the front, but when he asked Jake about them, Jake said. "Mostly they're full of lead. The hills around here are loaded with it."

When they were stopped in a tree-filled gorge with a stream, Deke stooped down to fill his water bag but Big stopped him. "Don`t. We`re too close to the lead mills. It might be poison." Deke had seen ponds poisoned by alkali, but something so green and alive being poison seemed wrong.

They spent the night camped near a town called Wyota. There was an area north of the town set aside for troops, and they shared it with the rest of the soldier boys who were heading north. They had music that night from those who could make it. Jake and Big smoked as they listened. Tobi was off gambling, and Clem lay on a blanket, staring at the stars. Deke watched the soldiers from a distance at the edge of the firelight. He had never gotten close to their camps before for fear of being pressed and had never actually seen how they lived. They didn`t seem so different.

The next morning the soldiers were slow getting out and so they were on the road again alone. As they rode, occasionally Clem would stop and pull out a compass and his watch, scribbling in a little book he kept in another pocket. When Deke asked, he said, "I need to keep track of where we are. There are damn few landmarks around here."

They made good time and were on the Osage River itself by midday. The river was wide, and from on top of their horses they had a clear view of the far bank. "That over there is the Union," Jake said. "Or at least it is until somebody can figure out how to get across."

"You could build boats," Deke said.

"That`s the generally the way it`s done," Clem replied. "But an army needs a lot of boats to cross something like this. Big ones."

"They`re hard to hide," Jake added. "Both sides patrol the river with airships and scouts so nobody is crossing in force without the other side knowing it. At least not here. The problem is that they`re already across through Saint Louis and there`s a rail line between Saint Louis and Springfield. Both sides use that line to supply their armies. One side rips it up as they retreat. The other side builds it back as they advance. Both sides have built spur lines into other parts of the front."

"The reason we`re here Deke is that it looks like the Union is going to try to force a crossing somewhere south of Jefferson City in order to flank our line. We`re here to update and correct the existing maps of the area in preparation for the battle and to note troop positions, both ours and those across the river."

"Where possible," Big said, giving Jake a serious look.

"If we can," Jake said, with a small smile.

Kay and Charity had found a women`s club run by the local Osage Indians!

"We needed a place for our ceremonies and there was no place private in the city. So we rented a store front and then everything grew from that. Now we own the building and use this part for our club," Myka said. She was the woman who had let them in. They were all soaking in the warm pool. "For some ceremonies we have to bathe." The pool was like a large wooden cistern, about three feet deep. The hot water came from a boiler in the back. They all took turns shoveling in a little coal.

You had to bathe before entering, and the women had built a bathing nook where warm water sprayed down from a fixture like the end of a watering can. It made it so easy to wash your hair! The women didn`t seem to care much about clothes, which was lucky since

Kay and Charity didn`t have any bathing clothes. It was like skinny–dipping with Kay's brothers when they were little. She watched the women at first, but except for the brownness of their skin and the odd accent, they were just like any other women.

"And if we have to soak in water, then it might as well be hot!" said another woman, Kimani, and they all laughed. She was born Shoshone but was Osage by marriage.

"We`re so grateful you let us in," Kay said.

"Oh, don`t worry. All women can join. We have to stick together, although not many white women want to sit with us. Maybe you will meet some later."

"Yes. We used to have quite a crowd in the evenings, but it`s no longer safe. We have to close now long before dark."

"It`s no longer safe even during the day!" another said, and they all sighed. There was a general nodding of heads in agreement followed by quiet while everyone sat and soaked.

There was, though, something nagging at the back of Charity`s mind. "What does 606 mean?" she asked. All of the women burst out laughing. Kay and Charity looked at each other and shared their confusion.

Myka looked at a friend and said something in Osage, then lightly clapped her hands together once.

"Clap," the friend said. At which point they all broke out laughing again.

"The soldiers get diseases from whores by having sex with them. 606 is a new cure for one of them. There is a man." Myka spat that last word out, "who claims to be a doctor. He runs the store down the street. He sells cures to the soldiers."

"His medicine is fake," an old woman said, her mouth barely above the water. She dunked the back of her head down into the water to warm her hair.

"You would certainly know, Grandma," Myka said, and then to Kay, "She knows all the old medicines and tricks. She`s writing a book." Kay thought she might like to see that book.

While they were dressing, many of the women were surprised at the amount of things Kay and Charity had to put on.

"This is crazy," the old woman said, looking at Kay`s crinoline.

"Yes, it is," Kay agreed. "Unfortunately I need it to make most of my dresses fit. What I need is a dress maker."

"Myka can help you there," the old woman said.

"Grandma," Myka said, frowning.

"Well, you could. You know you are a good seamstress."

"Oh, could you, Myka?" Charity asked. "We don`t have time. We have to look for my husband. We can pay you."

"No, no money," Myka said.

"Is he in the army?" Kimani asked.

"Not any more. He was wounded."

"Finding him, then, will be difficult."

"He told me the hospital in his letter."

"That will help, but it will still be difficult. Everything at the hospitals is in confusion. We have members who work at them."

"Which hospital?" another woman asked.

"Jefferson Barracks."

"That will be especially difficult. It`s very large. I will ask if there is some place with records and someone who can help you."

When they left, Kay made a small donation to the club and made a promise to come back at mid-day, the day after next. That was cleaning day and the club would all have a big lunch together. They would come back tomorrow as well, when they had their clothes back from being cleaned, to drop off some of their dresses so they could be altered by Myka. Charity had borrowed a book from the club`s small library, <u>The Woman in White</u>, which Kay thought she might read as well if Charity liked it.

The time had grown late, so they decided to eat at the hotel. Crossing the street though, was a problem. The soldiers from the clinic broke the traffic from the other side. The women couldn`t follow in their wake. They decided to try up the street where it had seemed easier before, and it still was. They made it across, although an unhappy dodge had put Kay`s shoe in a fresh pile of manure. Kay resolved then and there to do something about their wardrobe. They were not dressed for this kind of city.

When she was finally going to sleep that night, after the noise of the street outside had quieted, Kay noticed an odd sound. It came and went, very low and elusive. It sounded almost like someone blowing in her ear.

They woke late the next day. Kay had slept clean in clean sheets in a bed that didn`t bounce and rock. She didn`t have to get up at 3AM to change trains. She had no schedule to keep that day at all. She fell back to sleep several times, finally giving in to her bladder and staggering down the hall to the water closet. Charity was already awake but deep in her book. She said, "good morning" as Kay stumbled by.

Back in bed, Kay found it difficult to move, but she couldn`t sleep. If only I had looked for a book too, she thought. Staring at the late morning sunshine and listening to the sound of the street, she decided that she didn`t care that she wasn`t properly dressed. Her night dress was practically as good as her day dress. Propriety be damned. She got up, went down the four flights of stairs and walked up to the front desk and asked the matron if she knew where she might get a newspaper. The matron handed her hers with a small smile.

Kay climbed back up the four flights of steps to their room, flopped back down on her now cold bed, pulled the covers back over as she laid down, and began to read. If only she had a cup of tea, she thought. It would be perfect.

The newspaper however, turned out to be filled with nothing but awful news. Saint Louis was looking to hire more police. They were looking for wounded veterans who could walk a beat. Kay wasn`t sure what "walking a beat" was. It sounded violent. There was a story about the Sullivan offensive going well with miles of territory being taken. She had no idea where Sullivan was. Miles, though, didn`t seem like much. There was a "Women`s Auxiliary Drive for Rags for Bandages," which had grim implications. Then there was, "Escaped Slaves Starving to Death by the Hundreds in Oakville Camp," which sounded even grimmer. The ads were no better: "Protect Your Home and Family from Rebel Vandals, Buy Swenson Guns." "Stock Up For Hard Times, McCracklin Canned Goods," and "Plows for the One-Handed, Schwartz Plows." It was all awful.

Kay looked over at Charity, who was still reading her book. "Want to get breakfast?"

Charity turned a page and without looking up said, "Sure."

They dressed in their city dresses and thumped down the stairs. Kay gave the paper back to the matron. "It`s all so awful," she whispered, frowning.

"It is isn`t it? Sometimes though, you can learn something useful. For instance, this Sullivan offensive.

That`s just outside of town, not 30 miles away. They need bandages, so there were a lot of casualties. Refugees are starving, so they`re shorting their supplies to feed the army. The trick is to read between the lines."

"Read between the lines," Kay repeated. What an odd phrase, she thought. "30 miles. That`s close," she said, frowning.

"Too close." The paper made more sense to her now. They asked the matron if they could borrow another sheet to carry their dresses to be mended and she handed one over, but not without making a mark in a book first.

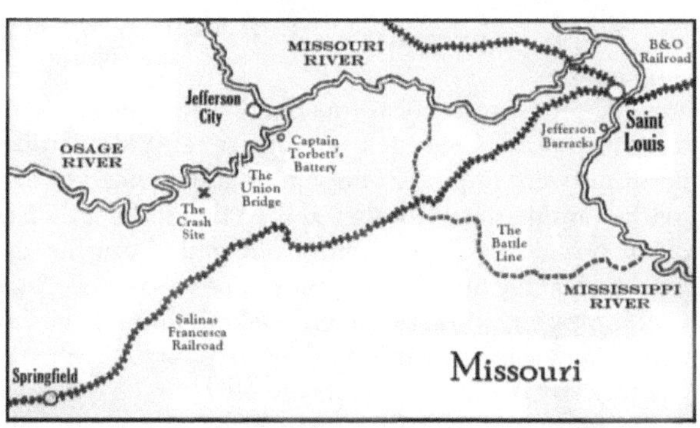

CHAPTER 9

The Rangers followed the river, travelling along farm trails, logging roads, old keelboat tracks, and anything else they could find that bordered it. The river meandered back and forth, and twice Clem led them across country on shortcuts rather than follow its twists and turns. All the while Clem kept checking his watch and compass. On towards evening they began to meet sentries, and more and more often they were challenged to identify themselves. Late that afternoon they came across artillery emplacements being dug by teams of Negro slaves.

"Yes, sir," said the white sergeant in charge of the slave`s guards. He pulled off his helmet and wiped his brow, like he had actually been doing work. "There is fun a comin` across that river and with a little luck, we will be gone somewhere else when the party starts." They all paused and looked at the river. "Sometimes," he said to himself, "I can hear their bugles."

"Be a bad place for us for them to cross," Jake said. "No good roads in here."

"Yessa. I guess that`s why we`re a diggin`!" the sergeant said.

There were more teams digging trenches closer to the river, and Clem felt that these and the artillery positions were important enough that they needed to be marked on the map. So they pulled down the little table off of one of the Army mares and pulled out the map from its leather tube. "I`m pretty sure we`re here," said Clem, tapping with his pencil. Deke couldn`t see how Clem knew which river loop they were on. When asked, Clem said, "Well, I`m not absolutely sure. I`m guessing based on directions and distances we`ve travelled, and of course eyeballing the shape of the river loop. Of course the map itself might be wrong. Rivers shift too. But I don`t think we`re too far off."

From then on Clem not only stopped to check his compass and watch, but sat atop his horse with his binoculars at every high point they came to, scanning the countryside, especially the far shore. He often found things to note on the map. Whenever they stopped to rest, Clem would let Deke look around with the binoculars too, but only if he told Clem what he saw in Morse code.

As they followed the river, the sound of the front grew louder and more distinct. Deke could make out specific thumps sometimes, and at night there was a glow on the horizon to the east.

The day came when Deke saw the first obvious Union position he`d ever seen. It was an artillery battery on the other side of the river on a low bluff down across the water. Deke could see the earthworks across the river but nothing else until Clem pulled out a telescope and perched it on a tripod. It was shiny brass and Clem let Deke look through it. He could see tiny figures in blue lounging on the earthworks parapet and the muzzles of four cannon.

"There`s probably more we can`t see," Clem said. "They`re there to keep our boats from crossing."

Deke felt like he was seeing some sort of mythical beast as he looked at the Union soldier boys. He`d heard so much about them, and now there they were. Up until then, he almost hadn`t believed they really existed.

"I`m not going to be precisely sure about their location until we find some landmark I can use to orient myself. We`ll probably have to start from Jefferson City itself and work our way back," Clem continued.

When they came to Jefferson City the next day, Deke noticed that the country had opened up, with more cleared land, less woods. This gave the Union less cover to hide in, and they could see dug-in troops plainly guarding the approaches to the city. There were Southern troops dug in here too, guarding their bank. The Rangers rested on a hill in a vineyard eating grapes as they looked at enemy soldiers through the telescope. Deke could see vineyards down there too and suspected that many of the Union soldiers were probably eating grapes as well.

There were two bridges across the Osage River from Jefferson City, both demolished. Far to the west they could see the dark Osage water mixing with the brown water of the Missouri River.

Down in the hollow below them there was a mortar battery. There were three mortars, each about eight feet long and about two feet wide tapering towards the muzzle. They were mounted on circular tracks that allowed them to rotate, and around the track was an iron ring that marked the angle they were pointing. The shells came up past Deke`s waist and had to be lifted with special carts that winched them up to the right height to load in the breech.

That day they were treated to the sight of them firing. The battery captain sent a runner up to them as they ate grapes and watched the Union troops across shore. "Captain says you'll either have to come down to the pit or move further away. We're going to fire."

Apparently the Union was making an effort to rebuild one of the bridges across the Missouri River on the far side of town and time had come to destroy it yet again. No one was sure why the Union was doing this. It might have been just to force the battery to fire. Each time they fired, there was a chance someone would spot them and changing the battery's position without anyone noticing was difficult.

These were the biggest cannon Jake had ever seen and he was all for watching. After a little discussion they decided to go down.

"Where can we hide the horses?"

The runner thought for a second. "Put them behind the observation trench. It always seems to be a blessed spot." Deke noticed, when they got there, that there did seem to be a lack of shell holes.

Captain Thaddeus Torbett was working at a table in the back of the mortar pit when they came down the stairs. He ignored their greetings, concentrating on his work instead. He had a big canvas bag which sat on a scale. He was measuring black powder into it with a little scoop. There were three other bags sitting on the table as well. He explained what he was doing as if he were lecturing class. A class full of deaf people. Captain Torbett, like most artillerymen, had grown a little hard of hearing.

"Today, we are going to destroy a bridge and maybe some annoying artillerymen too. We have the bridge already targeted, so that's really just a matter of formula. We've hit it so many times that we know precisely the amount of powder to use based on the temperature of the barrel," he said in a loud voice. He was measuring out powder now with a little scoop, watching the scale, humming affirmations to himself. Then, like a surgeon who had just finished an operation he stepped back and said, "Sew it up, Private."

The crew had already opened the breeches of their guns and had shells in their hoists, so the captain moved over to another smaller table. "Next is the fusing. We`re going to want an air burst first, just over the bridge," and then with a just a tinge of mean glee, "to clear off the workers." On another table he had a small cylindrical device, like a spring, and a treaded tube. "We know from experience that to get the correct height on the airburst we are going to need a 4.7 second flight which just happens to equal a two inch fuse." The Captain measured and cut a 2 inch piece off what appeared to be a stick of lead. He walked over and showed it around like a child with a favorite toy. "The core is compressed gun power. We are using a dual-action fuse today for this shot, just in case we overshoot and actually hit the bridge. Can`t waste a shot, you know," and then he chuckled to himself.

Deke and his compatriots all glanced at each other. This man was not only deaf but just a bit touched.

"We can skip the swabbing since this is the first shot of the day," he said, smiling. He fitted the pieces of the fuse together and walked over to the shell. "And now we insert the fuse." He screwed it into the point of the shell.

"For our counter-battery suppression rounds we are going to try something new." He stopped and thought for a moment. "What do you think Pettigrew, for an air-burst right over their heads? Try 7.2 seconds?"

The corporal looked like he was counting to himself on his fingers. "Sounds right, sir!"

"Hmmm . . ," said the captain."We`ll give it 7.5! That`s three." He cut off two more pieces of lead and fitted them in the fuse housings. Then he walked over to the other two shells sitting in their cradles and screwed in their fuses as well. He pulled out another detonator from the box and screwed it into a fourth shell sitting on the ground. "This one`s plain impact," he said with disappointment.

Stepping back, he lifted his arms to the sky like a conductor leading an orchestra, and yelled, "Load shells!"

The crews rolled their shells over to their breeches and slid them in, pushing them in with large wooden rods with soft leather tips.

"Load powder!" yelled the captain. Crewmen walked over to the table and picked up bags of power. The Captain shouted, "Wrong bag, Klein!" and the soldier jumped. Klein quickly picked up the correct bag with both hands and lugged it to his gun where it was gently shoved in the breech. Then the breeches were closed and locked. Another soldier went over to the table and put the leftover powder bag in a metal box under the table.

The corporal stood at attention and yelled, "Breeches set!"

"Advance the shells!" yelled the captain. Polls were inserted in the muzzles of each gun to push the shells back against their bags.

"We are going to fire this first shell at a low angle to spread the shrapnel across the bridge lengthwise," he said with pride. "Gun number one, elevation 32 degrees!" he yelled. Two men manned a crank and aimed the gun up towards the sky. "Azimuth 8 degrees!" and another crank was manned, the gun turned towards the town.

The corporal stood at attention again and yelled, "Gun set!"

"These next two are counter-battery fire and we need a high angle to rain shrapnel down in their trenches. Guns two and three! Elevation 58 degrees!" The cranks cranked and the muzzles of the guns rose. "Azimuth 352 degrees!" And the guns swung around.

And the corporal again yelled, "Guns set!"

Then the captain turned to them. "This is how it will all work. There will be two volleys, first one shell and then three. You may stay out for the first shot, but we may have incoming rounds during the second. They`ve been trying to find our position just as we`ve been trying to find theirs. They will try to use our smoke to find us." He looked off into the distance. "We know generally where they are, and I`m hoping that they`ll come out of their holes when they hear the first round," he said, smiling an evil smile. "That`s when I hope to hit them with shrapnel! If you stay out for the first round then it must be out of the pit. Cover your ears. Don`t wait until you hear me yell fire. Lay flat on the ground." There was perhaps just the slightest bit of glee again in his voice. "For the second volley we all must go in the bunker."

They all decided to stay out. He waited until they were climbing the stairs and then yelled, "Gun one, set cap!"

They were lying down at the back of the lip of the pit when they heard the captain yell, "Prepare!" and most of the men in the gun crews came up out of the pit.

Deke thought that he might have heard the command "Fire!" but he was too busy bouncing six inches off the ground to be sure. The entire Earth shook. Dust came loose even from the trees above them. He tried to keep his eyes open, and he thought he saw the shell arc skyward then lost it. 4.7 seconds later there was a large explosion on the other side of town, like a clap of far–away thunder.

"Return!" the captain yelled over the ringing in Deke's ears.

They all ran back down into the pit. "Gun one, swab!"

The crew lowered the barrel and pushed a big wet sponge down and through with a pole.

"Gun one, load shell!" While they were loading, the captain said in his over loud voice, "Now that we have woken them up, we will take care of the bridge itself! Gun one, load powder!" This was the bag in the box.

"Breeches set!" yelled the corporal.

"All of you, into the bunker!" yelled the captain.

They ran down the steps, through the door of the bunker into darkness.

"All guns, set caps!"

They heard a whining whistle and then an impact.

"Prepare!" And the gun crews crowded down the steps into the bunker with them. They could see the captain outside through the door and three crewmen standing as far from the guns as they could, holding strings. More impacts shook the earth.

"All guns fire!"

The crewmen yanked the strings and rolled back away from the guns. The world lifted six inches and dropped back down again. Deke could feel it through his skull. And then they all just sat for a bit in the dusty darkness and listened to the incoming rounds. After a few minutes it all stopped. The corporal lit a lamp with a match and hung it on a post. There was a general sense of relief.

"Can we go out?" asked Big.

"Not for a few minutes. They'll fire extra shells to try to catch us," said the corporal.

Sure enough, there were three more impacts. Deke could hear the ricochets of shrapnel in the pit.

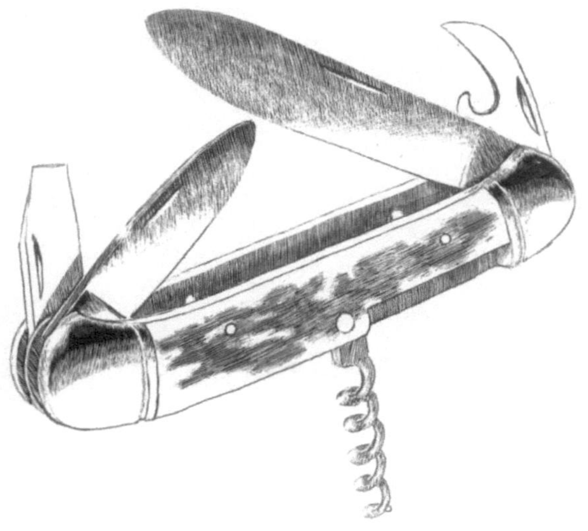

CHAPTER 10

Kay and Charity picked up their laundry and went to the women`s club, where Myka looked at their dresses and decided what could be done. Myka wasn`t a professional seamstress, so she found it difficult to estimate the time necessary to make the alterations, but she would bring what she had to the club the next day. Kay found a book, something called <u>Wives and Daughters</u>. And that was it. Really, it was a rare, delightfully uneventful day.

The next day they went to the club early and helped sweep and scrub. The tub was drained, cleaned, and refilled. The coal box for the boiler was shoveled out. Plants were watered and trimmed, shelves dusted and restacked, and from the kitchen in back, good smells began to drift about.

There wasn't a single dish that Kay had ever tasted before. There was corn, but not like she had ever seen it. It was roasted with spices. There was fry bread, assorted beans, and chicken flavored with herbs she didn't recognize. They had berries and cream for dessert! It had all been spicier than she was used to, but she enjoyed it. They ate together at a long table and then worked together to clean up.

Myka had finished a dress for Kay, and it fit, so now she had two she could wear. And after lunch they were introduced to Anpo, who washed clothes at the Jefferson Barracks hospital laundry.

"I can take you there tomorrow if that is a good day for you." She had a small quiet voice, but her eyes seemed to smile.

"Please," Charity said.

"It's not a nice place. Really. Do not wear clothes that you care about." She seemed to look at them with concern.

"Is it far?" Kay asked.

"Yes. I'm hoping to go by boat. My brother fishes and usually takes me there and back in his boat, but this won't be the usual day and he may not want to. I will know tonight."

"We can pay him," Kay said.

"With him, that may help." She stopped for a second in thought and then looked at them again. "Please be sure you want to do this."

"I have to know," Charity said.

And Anpo looked down and nodded.

They had good fortune to find a guide. Saint Louis was one of the gateway cities to the west and in the best of times was large and busy, but it had swelled with the arrival of the Army. And the Army, always hungry for transport, took everything it could. So finding some form of transport to the hospital was fortunate. Boats and stretchers were about the only two ways left to get there.

They met Anpo the next morning.

"My brother, he will do it for three dollars." Kay didn`t know if this was a lot or not. The carriage to the train station had cost her thirty five cents, but this was all day and a long way.

"Carry us there and back?" Key asked.

"Yes."

"Then we`d best go."

Anpo led them through dusty, noisy streets, down boardwalks, past stores, noisy saloons, police stations, stables, smiths, and into an open air market.

"Best to buy food here," she said.

Kay hadn`t thought about food. They bought cheese, bread, and grapes. They were expensive. Food was in short supply.

Kay and Charity were completely unprepared for preparing or eating food. Neither of them had brought a bag to carry the food, a knife to cut it with, or even a cup to drink out of. Anpo, though, had come prepared with a bag, knife, and cup that they could share. This was almost more than Kay could stand. "Anpo, I`m going to need a knife and a bag of some sort of my own. Not for today, but for . . . I feel so useless!" it almost came out in a sob of frustration. "I`m so tired of not having useful clothes or useful shoes! I`m so tired of not being . . . useful!"

Anpo and Charity stared at her. "We`re too near the river. There are no clothes or shoe stores here, but we can buy a knife," Anpo said.

Kay tried to calm down. She suspected she was more tired than she knew. "That would help."

"Then we need to go this way," and Anpo turned them right at the next corner. They were near the docks by the river and it was mostly warehouses, but there were shops tucked in here and there. Most were maritime equipment or fishing gear, but half a block in from the corner was a tobacconist. Charity sneezed when they entered and then sneezed again, pulling out a handkerchief from her purse.

"I`m so sorry," she said.

The proprietor put down his paper and smiled. "What can I do for you ladies?"

"She would like a pocket knife," Anpo said.

He stood and moved towards a display case. "Ah yes, we do have a selection. Something for a lady." They crowded over to see.

The proprietor picked up a small, thin pearl-handled knife and put it on top of the glass. "This might work," he said.

Kay peered at it. "It`s so small. I can`t see that it would be of much use."

"It`s for cutting thread and yarn, perhaps fabric."

"No, but how about that one?" she asked. She pointed to large, thick knife.

"A canoe? That`s for fishermen and cowhands. Something more ladylike would be more appropriate," and he started to reach for another knife.

"No, I want to see that one," she insisted.

He paused, blew air out his nose, and then reached over for her choice. "It has six blades, two knife blades, a cork puller, a can opener, a screwdriver, and an awl. The knife blades lock."

"Nice," Anpo said.

"Bone handle. Carbon steel blades. Made in Solingen, Germany."

It felt substantial in Kay`s hand. "How do I open

it?"

"There`s a notch on the edge of each blade," he pointed as he spoke. "Watch your fingernails."

She pried the largest blade out, opening it until she felt a click. "It`s lovely." The blade gleamed in the light from the street.

He looked at her doubtfully. "Have you ever owned a knife before?"

"No."

He sighed again. "There are a few things you need to learn."

He showed her how to safely open and close it. How to clean, oil, and sharpen it. The best way to cut rope and leather. How to peel an apple. How to pass it to somebody else when the blade is open. And how to drill holes with the awl. Half way though Charity said, "Oh, now I want one too!" But she balked when she saw what they cost.

"We can share, " Kay said.

Kay bought the knife, a tin can of oil with a long spout and a little screw cap, and a sharpening stone. She also talked the owner out of a soft rag for oiling it. The owner wrapped the lot up in brown paper and tied it with jute string. She put it in her already heavy handbag and felt it get heavier.

The morning was well underway when they arrived at the docks. They walked along between stacks of crates, bales, and sledges, past stone covered docks, some with steamers waiting. They went past gangs of Negro workers loading freight, passengers leaving and boarding, and flocks of crows feeding on the leavings of the river`s fishermen. The river was over a mile wide and they could see the far shore in the distance across the brown water churning like milk in her tea. Past the docks was a beach of baked mud and again Kay hated her shoes. The heels sank in. She tried to keep her weight on her toes. Along the shore were smaller boats pulled up on the clay bank, fishermen smoking, telling stories, and passing the time. Some stared as the women passed.

Anpo led them past boat after boat until she saw one sitting canted on the beach with a figure reclining in its bottom. It was a man and he was snoring. Anpo gave him a nudge and he moaned. She gave him a harder nudge and, sucking air, he rolled over and fell in the clay.

"Ow!" he said between snorts. "Anpo, is that you?" He looked around blinking at the light.

"This is my brother Shou Gah Lee. Some say the elder dropped one of the stones on his head when he was named," Anpo said.

"Anpo, I`m so tired of that story." He was rubbing his eyes.

"He can barely speak his own language."

"What should we call you?" Charity asked.

"Shou will do."

"It`s good to meet you, Shou," Kay said.

"The same," he said. "It`s late."

"We had some delay," Anpo said.

"Then we had better get going." Shou wore short baggy pants, a loose baggy shirt, and topless shoes that were somewhat like slippers. On his head he had a wide--brimmed hat that was woven out of straw. Kay felt like there hadn`t been a day gone by that she didn`t see something new these days. He looked the women over. "Anpo, they`re not dressed for this."

"I know. It`s all they have."

"What should we do?" Charity said.

"Take off your shoes and stockings. You are going to have to wade into the water a ways. I can`t push the boat in if it has too much weight in it. You`ll just have to lift up your dresses above the water."

Kay was so glad they had worn their day dresses. The women sat on the edge of the boat and took off their shoes and socks, which involved some tugging on their garters beneath their skirts. When they stood up, the mud squished between their toes. It felt cold and strange. Kay hadn't squished barefoot in mud since she was a child.

With the women off, Shou heaved his boat towards the water. After a bit it was deep enough to float free of the bottom, but the water was past his knees. "OK. Anpo, show them how to get in."

Anpo waded out, her legs making wakes in the brown water. When she reached the side of the boat, she faced her back to it, pushed down with the heels of her hands, slipped her bottom over the edge and fell backwards into the bottom of the boat. The keel grounded as she got in, but lifted free as she moved down to the end.

Kay and Charity looked at each other. Charity said, "You go first."

Kay thought of arguing, but then out of the blue she reached down and hiked up her skirts and marched in. The water was cold and the bottom slippery and sticky at the same time. When she got to the boat, the edge seemed to wobble precariously. She was faced with a dilemma. Hold on to her skirt or the boat. Finally, she just sort of leaned sideways and rolled in. Her dress got wet, both from the river and the bottom wash in the boat, but she was in. It rocked as she moved back.

"Keep low as you move," Shou said. "Next!"

Charity made a whining noise, but she hiked up her skirts and slowly waded in. The boat wanted to drift to the side, but Shou was pushing it back. This made it more difficult for Charity. Kay moved forward to help, which grounded the boat and steadied it. With Kay`s help Charity made a much more graceful entrance. With the women at the stern, Shou slid the boat off the shore and jumped in.

The boat was fourteen feet long and tapered to a point at each end. It had a locker in the stern in which they had placed their belongings. "Someone needs to move to the bow," he said. Both Charity and Kay started to move. "Wait. Just one! Anpo, you stay back and steer."

With the load distributed, Shou sat himself amidships, set the oars, and rowed the boat into the current. Kay was afraid to move once she was seated next to Anpo. It seemed every move made the boat wobble. But Anpo wasn`t afraid and sat holding the tiller with the breeze blowing her long straight black hair. Out in the water Shou turned around in his seat facing the stern and began to slowly row down river.

The trip took three hours. They ate their lunch in the boat, which gave Kay a chance to use her knife. Shou gave it proper scrutiny and admiration, much to the amusement of the women. She cleaned it with river water and rubbed it with oil before putting it away.

The hospital was up on a bluff above the river. There was a dock, and Shou tied up to it. Kay was so grateful she didn`t have to wade ashore.

Shou pulled out a fishing pole and said, "I might as well make the time count. Let`s see what`s hiding around here," and set to fishing.

There were wooden steps up the bluff, which felt good after so much sitting. At the top was a train station. There was no one at the ticket counter, no baggage handlers, no carriages waiting to take away travelers. On the landing were stacks and stacks of stretchers, too quickly washed and still bloodstained.

They crossed the tracks and started up the road towards the top of the hill. They could see a row of buildings and several columns of wood smoke at the top. The grass around them had been grazed down, but by what they couldn't see. The wind was out of the south, and from the hill they could see down river. There were no boats, but the countryside was green and the fields were plowed.

Near the top they were passed by a line of ragged Rebel soldiers in pairs carrying stretchers stacked with yet more empty stretchers guarded by two tired Union soldiers. They were all thin and their eyes were sunken and dark. Their stares were blank and distracted.

Anpo stopped. "I want to warn you," she said. "This will difficult. This isn't a nice place."

"I have to know," Charity said.

"I know. I would want to too," Anpo replied, and she started up the road again.

As they rounded the first building, Kay was first struck by a smell, then a vision, and then, when she could comprehend it, a sound. They were lying in loose rows that went on and on, a low moan drifting over them like a breeze. Wrecked and ragged, blue, black, grey, red, brown, and there was a green tree that was moving in the wind. The buildings were red brick and there was smoke in the sky, and crows. She was lying on her back looking at the sky and someone was talking. It was Charity. She was crying.

"Kay? Please wake up."

She could smell that smell. "I'm awake." She coughed.

They helped her sit up. Charity hugged her.

"I need to get up," Kay said weakly.

They tried to help her to her feet, but she sank back down to her knees. Her head hurt and the smell made it hard to breathe.

She tried again and made it this time. It was still there, all of it. She could see them, broken and dying. There were screams in the distance over the low general moan. She could see blood staining the steps of the first building and the dirt, the red stained dirt that went on forever. Moving here and there were men and women, carrying water, picking up stretchers and bringing others.

She started moving towards it before she knew she was doing it. Then she stopped. "Where do we go, Anpo?" She noticed Anpo had been holding her arm.

"We need to find Nurse Dibble. She`s in charge. She has the books."

They could see figures moving back and forth so they started down the rows. Men called to them. Sometimes for water, sometimes just help, but often the women couldn`t understand what they were saying.

Charity wanted to stop. Any of these men could be her husband, but Anpo held her back. "You can`t help them. You won`t find him that way." And so they kept going. "The laundry is this way too. We can ask there."

Threading their way between, Kay saw blackened skin, bones, faces cut away. Men lay in puddles of their own blood and urine. She saw grey mixed with the blue. Most had no boots or helmets. Sometimes even their belts had been taken from them. Once they had crossed the wide yard and approached the second row of buildings she almost fainted again, falling to her knees as her vision blurred. She could hear Charity throwing up.

She tried to look up, but her eyes kept sliding off the stacks of bloody, gangrenous limbs outside the surgery. A Rebel in a bloody smock swept a wave of bloody water out the front door with a push broom. He called inside, "Sergeant La Croix, there`s ladies out here bein` sick."

A man in blue appeared in the doorway. "Damn it. How`d they get here?" He walked down the steps motioning for the Rebel to follow. "Put that broom down Geach and help me."

He walked sternly over and said, "You aren`t allowed in here. This is a military area."

Charity looked up at him and said, half sobbing, "I`ve come for my husband."

"You can`t. It isn`t allowed." He looked at Anpo and said, "I know you."

"I work in the laundry. We need to find Nurse Dibble."

Geach helped Kay to her feet. She breathed for a second and then put on her bravest face, at least the best she could, faced the sergeant and said, "We aim to find him."

"Your wife would come for you," Anpo said.

The sergeant started to speak, but stopped. Started again, but stopped at a loss for words.

"I know where she is," Geach said. "Can I take `em?"

The sergeant shut his mouth which had been hanging open then said, "Sure." Then he turned and walked back to the surgery shaking his head.

"Come on," Geach said, and he started an aching trudge towards a door two buildings away. Kay thought his thin bones might snap any second. "There was a courier that came in. She`s talkin` to him or writin somethin for him to take back for sure."

The building they approached didn`t have blood stains on its steps. When they got to the door, Geach motioned them to go on up. "Go on. I`m not allowed in there." Then he turned and walked back.

In the entryway there was a guard who scowled at them. "You`re here for . . ." and he let it trail off.

"I`ve come for my husband," Charity said.

"We would like to see Nurse Dibble," Anpo said.

The soldier leaned back in his chair, groaned and rubbed his tired eyes. "Anpo, damn it, you know what`s going on here. We have six times the casualties we can handle. You can`t just bring people here!" Then he leaned forward and looked at them. Charity still had tears running down her face. They all three must have looked grim.

He blew out through his cheeks and then slapped his hand on the desk as he stood up. "I`ll ask." He left through a doorway, and they could hear voices. When he came back, he didn`t say a word but just motioned them towards the door, looking back towards his desk.

Anpo led them in.

Her office was small but it had a window that let in light. Her desk was facing away from it. There was a soldier sitting in a chair, probably the courier. He was just a boy. His face was pale as he looked up at the women as they entered.

"What do you want Anpo?"

"These women need to look up a patient."

"Oh, yes, of course." And she paused. "I`m sorry, but I have nothing to offer you. We`re even out of tea."

"That`s not a problem ma`am," Kay said.

"Did he write?"

"Yes he did," Charity said.

"Do you remember the date?"

"It was June 3rd."

Nurse Dibble got up from her desk, went to a shelf, and pulled down three books. "Then it will be in here." When she brought them to her desk, Kay could see the start of tears in her eyes. "These aren`t in any order other than the patient`s final disposition. You`ll have to start at the beginning and go down the lists until you see him."

Then looking away from the women she walked to the door, motioning for the courier to follow. They heard her say something to the soldier in front, and then they were alone with the books.

They each took a book and started at the top of the first page. The books were full of lists, final dispositions, either discharge date or reason for death. Too many died of gangrene, loss of blood, or fever.

Anpo finished her book first. It had started before the date of the letter and she got to skip the first half. Kay was working her way down what must have been her 30th page when she saw it. William Carmichael, fever, June 8th, 1892. He was dead. Kay didn`t know what to do. She just folded up in her chair sobbing. This was too much. There were never any happy endings. She heard Charity crying too. Then Anpo.

CHAPTER 11

Deke wanted desperately to check on Ned, but they were up in the observation trench instead. "Damn it all! Godsell, there were twice as many shells incoming than there were supposed to be. Our counter battery fire did nothing!" Captain Torbett said.

"Sir," the private said. "Sir, there`re two new batteries, at least, judging by the smoke." Deke edged over the lip of the trench.

Outside he could still hear Torbett. "Tar-nation, show me where!" Walking down the hill to the depression where they`d left the horses, Deke found Ned, which brought a smile. They were all still there! Deke thought that maybe the spot really was truly blessed. He was busy trying to make amends to Ned for leaving him out during a shelling when he was joined by Clem, who was out of breath from trotting down the hill.

"They want my telescope up in the trench." He pulled the box off the pack saddle and trotted back up.

Deke dug around in his bags and found Ned`s brush. He worked Ned`s back and then had moved on to his pale mane when Clem showed up again. He looked at Deke and shook his head. "You and that horse." He grabbed the map tube and his pencil box and ran back up the hill. Then Deke dug out his hoof pick and cleaned and checked Ned`s hooves. They all needed tending and he was working on his third horse when Big came down the hill. "Deke, that can wait. Come on back up."

Up in the trench, Clem was making a copy of the parts of the map he had drawn on. He had the map rolled out on top of a shell crate and had a thin piece of paper on top of it. He was tracing the markings in ink. Over on the other side of the trench Jake was writing furiously on a piece of paper. He stopped for a moment and said to Deke, "We`re going to send you back with what we`ve found so far and to get supplies. Go down and pick two pack horses to take with you."

Now it was Deke`s turn to run down the hill. He set to work on the pack horses. Then Big came down again and worked on moving the contents of the panniers into just one so Deke could go back empty. Deke led Ned and the two pack horses up the hill. Jake met them near the top. He had a packet of papers sealed with wax.

"Take this back to McDonald," Jake said. "I want you to follow the river back the way we came. Report anything new you see to McDonald. We`ll be somewhere along the river when you come back, but I don`t know where." Then he handed him a piece of paper with a list on it. "These are supplies we need. McDonald will tell you who to talk to about getting them. Don`t stop for anybody except when you have to pass a challenge. Don`t give that packet to anybody but McDonald. Deke, this is important. This is not the time to take off. This is serious. Camp alone away from others, not at all if you can. That means no fires at night. No hunting. Stick to salt beef and hardtack. If you think that you may be captured, not that I expect this to happen, but if it does, then try to burn or hide the packet. A lot of people are counting on you. That`s the standard courier lecture. Now you come back soon and in one piece."

"Have fun Deke," Big said with a smile, and he slapped Deke on the shoulder.

Deke mounted Ned, tipped his hat with his forefinger and rode away.

He rode back along the river as he had been told. The first night it rained and he had to camp. He was glad the panniers were empty because there wasn`t enough room under his tent half for them. The next morning he inspected the soggy leather. They were still new and he`d have to oil them when they`d dried a bit or they would turn hard.

When he came to the first set of trenches they had encountered, he noticed that the Negroes were gone. The trenches were being dug by soldiers this time. This struck him as strange and in line with his orders, so he asked an officer.

"We think they came across two nights ago, killed the guards, and made off with our blacks," the officer said. "We showed up to occupy the earthworks and found them half done and full of bodies. We found boat marks along the shore too."

Deke couldn`t see any boats on the far shore, but it was pretty far away. He wished he had Clem`s telescope.

"I was just talkin` to them three nights ago too. That sergeant said he could hear them on the far bank," Deke said.

"I can believe that."

"I`ll tell them at headquarters when I get there.

They`ll decide what to do."

And Deke rode on.

As he neared Springfield, he noticed that the zeppelins were gone, and half the smaller airships too. Their crew camps were there, but the ships themselves were nowhere to be seen.

The town too seemed deserted; the rows of tents were gone from the empty fields. Headquarters though, was still there in the hotel and McDonald was still his same cold self.

"So what did you bring me?"

Deke handed over the packet. The colonel pulled on a pair of spectacles, pried off the seal, and started reading. Deke didn`t know what to do, so he just stood there. Two pages of Jake`s scrawl took time to read, so it took a while for McDonald to make it all out.

Then he yelled, "Baker!" And Baker appeared. "Go wake the general. He`ll want to see this."

Deke had given up as completely forgotten when McDonald finally turned back to him. "Anything else?"

"There`s the slaves," he said. He told him about the Union raid. "Oh, and this," he said, pulling out the list. "We need supplies."

"We don`t have much. The Union`s been bombing our rail lines. There`s delays all along our supply lines. We`ll see what we can do."

When Baker came back, McDonald had a quiet word with him, then handed him the list. Baker nodded and then turned to Deke and said, "I`m to find what supplies we can for you from the general depot." Baker talked as he skimmed the list. "It`s quite a wish list. The paper will be difficult, but considering your mission it`s understandable. Anything canned or preserved left with the troops. We have foraging parties out just to feed the command post. Ha! Coffee, we have coffee," and on through the list he went.

Deke left with half the list unfilled, with most of the missing being food. They said not to hunt but Deke was tempted, just to have something to bring back. Before he left, McDonald gave him another packet sealed with wax to take back.

The first inkling Deke had that something might have gone wrong at the front was when he passed through Wyota. There were wagons of wounded a field hospital. Deke couldn`t help but stare at the rows of mangled bodies lying in the dirt. The ground around the surgery was stained red. There were men moaning and occasionally screaming. Ned shied away as they approached, and Deke couldn`t disagree, so they edged around the town.

The closer he got to the river, the more war he heard. He could hear explosions and even rattling gunfire. The air was full of smoke which gave the sunlight a brown tint. Straight ahead, right next to his path, was a column of it. Something had set the gully next to the road on fire, which got Deke kind of curious. What could set green brush on fire? Riding directly down to look seemed like a bad idea to Deke, so he found a tree–lined feeder stream that led into a gully. He followed it for a bit until he got to the point where things were burning. The fire was sucking a brisk breeze down the gully, blowing at their back. Deke had to hold his hat on. Green brush doesn`t want to burn, but sometimes nature insists, and there was fire in the trees in that gully. The path down the stream was clear though and he and Ned picked their way down it slowly.

Up ahead there was a hole through the woods letting in sunlight. A mound of wreckage sat draped over bent and splintered trees and brush. It burned eerily with a mixture of clear shimmer and orange flames, like some kind of invisible fire. The wreckage had been an airship, probably shot down as it had flown over the river. Deke didn`t know who was in it or who it belonged to, but he didn`t see anybody alive, so he edged Ned backwards the way had come before some piece of ordnance decided to go off.

Back on the road, Deke couldn`t decide which direction to go except perhaps towards the shooting. If he couldn`t follow the river, then he could follow the front line. But finding the Rebel line was difficult. He didn`t see it until he was practically past it. By the side of the road he saw Rebel grey lying about in the trees. Most of them were lying on their backs, many with wounds. Those on picket were looking the wrong direction and didn`t see Deke until he was right on top of them. Deke almost got himself shot. As it was, he had to put his hands up until they had looked over his pass.

"Boy," the sergeant said. "There isn`t anything but blue from here to the river. I don`t know about your Scouts. Haven`t seen 'em. But you should either turn around or get down off that horse before somebody shoots you."

"Which way does the line go from here?"

"Our flank is that away," and he pointed south east. "But after that, your guess is as good as mine."

Deke nodded and said, "Much obliged," and rode back along the road the way he came.

Deke didn`t know which way the Rangers might be, but it wasn`t far to the river travelling west so it seemed more likely they`d be the other way, east. He rode down the road until he found a trail going east. It led down to a stream in another gully, but there was nobody there. Thinking he would reconnect with the Rebel line he turned north and rode splashing through the water.

He`d been riding for longer than it seemed to him he should have need to, so he took the next path east out of the gully. It wound around a bit and ended up on a road full of wagons heading south. The drivers were all dressed in regular civilian clothes; Deke didn`t stop to think about this, but turned north. He was heading down the road, looking for the line when he ran into Union cavalry. Actually, to be precise, they ran into him.

Deke heard horses off in the gully to his left, and then up from the brush came two dozen Union soldiers on horseback. They were on him before he could react, so he sat there because sometimes it`s best to just say nothing. The officer leading them pulled up his reins and brought their column to a halt. He eyed Deke, and rode over.

"Now who are you?" he growled and spat.

Deke frowned at him as if he was an annoyance. "Courier," he said.

"Courier? Let`s see your papers."

So Deke pulled out his pass and handed it over.

The officer eyed it suspiciously then looked at him and said, "So why are you out here?"

Deke half pulled the packet out of his shirt pocket so the officer could see the wax seal.

The officer growled like this had been a bad day and handed Deke his pass back and said, "Well OK then, get on with it." He then turned to his men and rode on down the road.

Deke just sat there dumbfounded.

His body had been buried in the grave pits south of the hospital. The Union no longer had the manpower to spare for single graves. Even using prisoners took food. The graves were dug by steam shovel instead and covered the same way. Over each grave pit, a single grey slab had been placed listing 250 names. Charity and Anpo walked down the rows until they found the stone with his name. The enormity of it left them all feeling helpless.

They saw, in the distance, two other women who had managed to find a way to the hospital in the distance, searching the stones for their kin, stooping at each to read names. One stood and covered her face in silent pain. She had folded in on herself, the world now separate and hated. Searching the stones was the last desperate act, for as long as the search continued, there was still hope.

Where the trip down the river had taken three hours, the trip back took five. Shou caught two catfish while he was waiting, and they were both well over two feet long, but nobody felt like congratulating him. It was a silent trip home. It was closing in on dark when they made it back to town, and there were clouds building in the sky.

Anpo talked her brother into escorting the women back to the hotel. He had wrapped his fish in canvas and carried them with him half under his arm. By the time they made it to the hotel it was dark and raining. Kay and Charity started to cry again as they thanked Anpo and Shou, which started Anpo crying and left Shou standing there looking uncomfortable.

Kay held Charity as they walked across the lobby. Her sobbing was loud in the quiet room. The matron came up to the desk from the back, but turned back when she saw them. Her eyes looked troubled. They had to rest half way up the steps to their room, Kay sitting there with her arm around Charity. At their room, Charity stumbled through the door into the dark room and fell on the bed. Kay picked up a candle from the bedstand, lit it from the wall sconce in the hall, and set it back in the room on the table. In the candlelight she could see Charity staring at the ceiling.

"We should eat," she said.

Charity was silent.

Kay looked down at her dress. It was filthy. She began to pull it off, but then stopped. Instead she began to unlace Charity`s shoes, pulling each off to thump on the floor, pushing her feet onto the bed. "I`ll be back," she said, and pulled herself to her feet. She could hear the rain pelting against the window.

In the hallway, by the dim gaslight, Kay made her way down through the lobby and onto the wet dark boardwalk. Next door was the restaurant. Its door was locked, but there was light inside and people. She knocked. She could feel the damp seeping through her shoulders.

"We are closed!" said a male voice inside.

"Please, we need food. I have money."

A mustached face looked through the window. His eyebrows shot up and then the face disappeared. There was a moment and then the lock turned, the door opened a bit, and a woman`s face appeared in the space between. "Can I help you?" She was perhaps 40 with very dark hair and a gravelly voice.

"We need food. Please, I have money."

The woman eyed her dress frowning. "Yes. Yes, of course." She opened the door.

Kay was just reaching the point of her hair dripping and she stepped in quickly. "I`m sorry, but I'm afraid that I`m going to leave a puddle on your floor."

"That`s not a problem, we haven`t mopped yet." She had a cigarette and she took a long drag and blew it up towards the ceiling. "We don`t have much food left. It`s getting hard to get with all the trains and river boats stopped."

"I hadn`t heard that."

"It`s those damn Rebels and their balloons."

"What do you have?" Kay`s voice sounded small and tired, even to herself.

"We still have bread and fish stew."

"That will be fine."

"You don`t want to know the cost?"

"It`s been a difficult day."

"I can tell. You`ve been crying. Your dress tells so many stories."

"My friend`s husband died," and the tears started, which made her angry at being so foolish. "She needs food."

"So do you, I think," she said gesturing with her cigarette. "Maurice!" she called, and the man with the mustache popped out of the kitchen. "We need two bowls of stew and two loaves. Wrap them on a tray." She turned back to Kay. "I`ve seen you before. You`re staying at the hotel."

Kay nodded.

"You can return the dishes tomorrow." She eyed Kay again and then asked, "If you don`t mind my asking, where did you go?"

"Jefferson Barracks."

"Hmmm . . . I shall make a point of never visiting there," she said with a slight smile and took another drag on her cigarette.

Kay nodded and drew a breath to laugh, but it came out a half sob.

She carried the tray back up to the room. Charity was just where she had left her. She pulled the towels back from the bowls of stew and the smell filled the room. Kay could see the steam in the candlelight.

"I brought you some food."

Charity`s head turned slowly. She looked at Kay and said, "He was all I had."

Kay said nothing for a bit. "I think I know. I`ve lost just about everybody I ever knew." She looked at the stew. She was hungry now, but she wanted Charity to eat. "Please, Charity. Please eat. I know how you feel. It will help."

Charity took a breath, rolled slowly over and put her feet on the floor. "I`ll try," she said.

She didn`t each much but she ate some, and she had some bread in the morning. Kay helped her out of her clothes. She bundled them up in one of the extra sheets and carried them the next morning down to the laundry.

Wah-Shinka tutted over the blood stains and her story. "The urine and mud will come out, but I think the blood will leave a mark."

"Yes," Kay said. "I suppose it does."

Then she went back to the hotel and literally dragged Charity out of bed. Charity relented when she realized that Kay was ready to drag her down the stairs in her night dress. They made their way down to the club.

"Is Anpo here?" Kay asked.

"No," Myka said. "She had to work."

"Oh," she said. "How can she? Go back there?"

"She wants to help," she said, and then looking at Charity sitting on the bench across the room, "So do you."

They scrubbed and soaked until the smells of Jefferson Barracks were gone. Myka had a dress for Charity, which was a blessing. Charity had nothing to wear that morning but her night dress. It was odd how they had ceased to care.

"We are going to need better shoes," Kay said

displaying her ruined high heels. "And I think we need a dress maker. I love you Myka but one dress a night is not quick enough. To ask you to do all our dresses, especially so quickly, is too much."

"Yes, I thought of that too. I will ask around."

Both their handbags were looking rather sad as well, Kay thought. What they needed was something they didn`t always have to hold in their hands. It was strange, but all this gave her an odd feeling she couldn`t explain. She felt like a bug losing its shell.

Everyone at the club, it seemed, had somehow heard about Charity`s husband, and apparently every woman in the entire state of Missouri at one point or another that day had decided to show up at the club to give Charity a hug or to hold her hand. Some even brought food, which was set out on the table. Kay considered that to be an unreasonable kindness considering the current shortage.

Kay planted Charity in bed back at the hotel that evening and decided to find out more about the trains. There were no luggage carts to help people across the street that day, but it was evening and that seemed to make the traffic lighter. She made her crossing in quick jumps and steps. Drivers yelled at her for crossing their path, but she ignored them and concentrated on getting across.

There were soldiers lying on the sidewalk in front of the station. Some of their eyes followed her, as she went in, with uncomfortable intensity. Inside there were more. Every seat was taken, every wall, every corner. They wore ragged uniforms and sat with their rifles, packs, and helmets. The station smelled of unwashed bodies and tobacco. The soldiers watched her as she crossed the lobby.

The ticket counter was closed. Behind the bars was

a slate board with "No trains due to Rebel bombing," written in chalk.

As she was walking back to the door a soldier called out, "Hey, little missy, why don`t you stay with us for awhile?" and there was a general chuckle. Someone made a grab at the hem of her dress, but she pulled loose and backed towards the door. Her hand instinctively slipped into her purse where she could grip her pistol. But there were no more grabs made and she backed out onto the boardwalk.

Back in the hotel, she plunked down on a chair in the lobby. There were two old women knitting and a man with a newspaper. He turned its pages back and forth furiously and finally plunked it down on the side table, muttering to himself, "This is all just rubbish!" He strode out of the lobby back to his room.

Kay got up, walked over and picked up the paper.

"Jefferson City Offensive Off to a Roaring Start!" There was a photograph of Union soldiers standing over three huge cannon sitting crooked and bent in the plowed earth. "Miles of countryside taken." She had heard that before. "Call Out to Nurses," and there was a drawing of a well-dressed woman tending a handsome officer with a bandaged head. Good luck with that, she thought. "Disaster in Boston!" A molasses tank had exploded, killing hundreds, possibly the work of Rebel spies. It had made a flood down the streets all the way to the harbor. "Women`s Auxiliary is Ready!" There was a picture of twenty women in black dresses standing in line holding rifles. Kay wondered if they were wearing their corsets. She smiled and thought, I have the most wonderful attitude today. Mixed into the newspaper banner, along with a boat and train, was an airship. I've tried the boat and the train, she thought. I`ll have to try that next.

When Deke looked it over, he realized that there was no place on his pass that said CSA or Confederate States of America. Nowhere on his gear did it say CSA. He didn`t even have a tattoo. He felt that maybe Jake and Big had meant it to be like that. And he still had a week and a half on his pass to find out what happened to his friends. So he rode on just as if nothing had happened, over the roads he was ordered to ride on, following the river. He was challenged twice and accepted without suspicion.

There were huge holes dug out of the earth here and there, and once or twice an hour he would hear the whine of something big rocketing over his head and the thump in the far distance where it hit. All the time he rode, he passed soldiers and full wagons going in and empty wagons going out.

When he asked about the holes, a soldier replied "It's Big Mary. It's a railroad cannon."

Deke didn't know what a railroad cannon was, but he could sure see what it could do.

"It's named after Abe's wife!" The soldier said, and then let out a cackle of glee.

At the first trenches, down by the river where the Union had first crossed, there was now a bridge made out of boats with planks stretched between them, and a road being built by Negroes, already being heavily used. These were probably the same Negroes that were snatched from there in the first place. Deke supposed that they were free now, but it didn`t look like it made much difference. Past the bridge they were digging grave pits. Deke looked over the mounds of stacked stripped bodies, but he knew none of them.

At Captain Torbett`s battery, there was huge hole dug out by some enormous blast. The guns were knocked all askew and bent. Up on the hill, the observation trench had been filled in on purpose. Deke suspected that Captain Torbett was in there along with his crew. Down in the hollow the blessed spot was still blessed and untouched. He could see dung on the ground, all of it old. Some of it was probably Ned`s. He circled the area, but there were horse tracks going every direction and every piece of equipment and gear that could be taken was gone. Deke was stumped. He could hear the front, booming and popping in the distance. He decided it would be best to go back to Springfield.

Taking the route he knew best, parallel to the river, he rode Ned along one of the trails they had taken, leading the mares behind. The trail was now worn down until it was practically a road itself. That`s when he heard a popping, fluttering sound behind him which kept getting louder. He turned in his saddle, and there coming down straight at him was the huge circle of an airship. Except for the popping of one half–working motor, the thing was silent and was practically ready to land on top of him.

"Sheeee-yit," he yelled, grabbed onto the pack horses`s reins and spurred poor Ned. "Git!" he yelled. Ned didn`t like spurs, but he knew the sound of an emergency when he heard it and took off, almost yanking the mares`s reigns out of Deke`s hand. They ran, but Deke could hear the thing behind him. He suspected it was a lot faster than they were, so he looked around fast for an out. Up ahead he saw a meadow on his left. The ground might be soft or uneven under all that grass, but Deke was in no position to be picky. He pulled Ned over to the left. Looking back he could see that the airship passed just behind the mares, only four or five feet off the ground.

When it hit the ground, it dragged itself across the earth, making a furrow right down the trail they had been riding on, plowing up the grass and knocking over brush, trailing orange–edged, shimmering, clear flame as its gas bags vented and burned inside the envelope. Then the undercarriage dug in and stopped, and the envelope flopped forward over the gondola still half full of gas. "Damn, they`re going to burn up!" Deke said. He dropped the mare`s reins, turned Ned and galloped back towards the balloon.

CHAPTER 12

Over the next two days, Kay and Charity, with the help of friends, found: dressmakers to alter their clothes, sensible boots, shoulder bags, and hats that kept out the sun and rain. They tied their hair back in pony tails. Charity declared they looked more like Indian women every day. Not only were the clothes more comfortable, being able to run made crossing streets much easier and safer.

Then Kimani came to them with news. "We've found you a ride west," she said. "There's an airship captain who owes some of us a favor. He's leaving tomorrow. He wanted a $1000, but we know things about him that he doesn't want others to know and we managed to talk him down to $100."

"Where's he going? Can he take Charity?" asked Kay.

At this Charity frowned. "I don't know if I should go," she said. "You've done so much and I've done what I set out to do."

"You said you didn't have anywhere to go," Kay replied, with a smile.

"Yes," she sighed.

"Then you might as well come with me, unless you want to stay here."

Charity didn't know where she wanted to go or even where she could go. She frowned.

"It's dangerous here. You should at least go back north," Kay said. "Where's he going?" Kay asked Kimani.

"Kansas City," Kimani answered.

"I bet there are trains out of there. That's north of the lines," Kay said.

"Not by much," Kimani said.

"Still, it's north and most of all, west," Kay replied.

They had left their crinolines, corsets, and other northern womanly gear with the dressmakers. It made Kay feel lighter just to see it all gone. When they packed, they found that their belongings barely filled half their trunks, so they decided make to do with just one. They asked the matron at the desk if she knew who might want it and she said that she might.

"Maybe it is time for me to travel again too," she said.

Kay hired a carriage to carry them to the aerodrome the next morning. It was easy because there was so little work, even for the few carriages, with both the trains and boats not running. She stepped out the front door and looked for one passing in the street near the station.

The hotel matron looked them over as they checked out.

"You look much better," she said. "A lot more ready than when you came in. I was worried about you both the other night when you came in late."

"Yes, that was a bad day," Kay said.

"I suppose you found your husband," she said, looking at Charity.

Charity looked down and in a small voice said, "Yes."

"Just like mine. It will be a long time before it gets easier. You did not have children?"

"No. I miscarried once."

"That is common with the first." She stared at the street. "Well, now you can travel," she said, closing the register book. "I travelled all the way to America. I think maybe it`s time to go. This is not a nice place. How are you leaving?"

"Airship," Kay said.

"Yes, it would have to be that. There are partisans on the river."

"Partisans?"

"Yes. They set a mine on a warship. You didn`t hear?"

"No."

"You should read the newspaper."

"Read between the lines."

The matron smiled, "Yes."

Before Kay left, she posted another long letter to

her Aunt telling her about their adventures so far and that their next stop was Kansas City.

The carriage took them across the city to the north, to a wide field grazed low by sheep. It was there that the airships were moored. Some were close to the ground, some wrecked and burned, and some had tents set up around them, but only one had a man waving at them.

"That the one, ma`am?" the driver asked.

"I think so," Kay replied.

The waving man`s head was shaved bald and he had a big handlebar mustache. He wore a brown felt jacket, a stained shirt, work pants tucked in high–topped black leather boots. He leaned on a pole with a hook on the top as he stood there watching the carriage approach.

As they came closer he called, "Are you Miss Mapelton?"

"Yes I am," Kay replied.

"And this would be?" He asked, scowling at Charity.

"Charity Carmichael," Charity said uncertainly.

"Miss Carmichael," he said, turning to her with a sudden ingratiating smile and a slight bow. "Captain Thaddeus Fenton at your service." Kay didn`t like something about that smile. Like the man himself, it seemed disingenuous. "Miss Carmichael is here to see you off?"

"No, she`s coming with us."

"I was given the impression that there was only one," he said with a slight frown. There was something flinty and hard behind it.

"Strange. There were always two of us."

"Then that will be two fares? Up front?"

"We were told $100." Kay only had $238 left and that wouldn`t leave much if they couldn`t find a working telegraph and a bank.

"But that was for one."

"I don`t see your cargo nets full." Kay eyed the airship. "Perhaps $125?"

"Miss, the extra weight costs us kerosene and gas." Fenton slowly shook his head no.

Kay squinted at the man, "Then $140?"

Fenton squinted back. "We could make the trip for $175."

"$150."

"$170 or it`s off," he said, crossing his arms.

Kay sighed. "$170," and she paid the man.

The captain chuckled to himself at some inner joke and then yelled over his shoulder, "Digby!" A thin scruffy crewman in an old tweed suit came out of the cabin door on deck.

"Yes, Captain?" he piped.

"Get the women`s luggage."

"Aye aye, " he replied.

The airship was like a flat–bottomed boat with a wide deck ending in a small cabin. On each side of the cabin were the engines, and Kay could see that they were meant to be raised and lowered. They were held up by a steel cable that angled up towards the center of the ship to a short vertical post at the top of the cabin. Below the post there were two winches. Draped under the airship`s envelope, hanging above the decks, were nets, some with boxes in them.

When Digby saw their one trunk he said, "What, that`s all?"

"Yes," Charity said.

He frowned in confusion for a second, then shrugged and lifted it onto his back. "They`re travelling light," he said as he walked by the captain.

"Good, that will make up a bit for the extra passenger."

Digby pushed the trunk up on deck and then followed up the ladder. The captain waited at the bottom. "Ladies?" he said.

They didn`t need his help, but he seemed inclined to give it, Digby helping them up on deck. Once they were up, the captain climbed up and pulled up the ladder. Digby untied a rope and lowered one of the cargo nets. The captain used his pole hook to pull it down further so Digby could push their trunk up. They stowed the ladder in a net on the other side.

In the center of the small flat lower deck there was a copper tank flanked by two wood boxes, one with a shovel clamped on to it. All of it bolted to the deck. The tank had two pipes going down through the deck and one going up into the gas bag. The Captain jumped up and down on the deck a couple of times then stood quiet. "We`re heavy," he said with a frown.

Digby unclamped the shovel, opened one of the wood boxes, and said, "What, half a pound?"

The Captain thought for a second and then said, "Yes." He opened a lid on the tank and Digby tipped in a small amount of grey powder. They closed the lid and pulled the red ball handle of the lever next to it. There was a kachunk sound inside the tank, followed by sizzling, and Kay could see the pressure gauges attached to the tank begin to rise.

"Does that make the gas to fill the bag?" Charity asked, clearly intrigued.

"It`s not a bag, it`s the envelope!" Fenton said, roughly.

"Oh."

Digby trotted into the cabin and came back with an assortment of goggles. He handed the captain a leather skull cap with goggles that buckled under his chin. He handed both women goggles. "You might need these," he said. "Cold wind makes you tear up." He added, with a half smile, "can`t have that can we? You might want to give me your hats too. They get blown away unless you can tie them down."

Then both men climbed up to the crowded upper deck, past the tiller wheel to the two winches. "Right, together, an even 90," the captain said, and they began to lower the engines. They lowered them down until they were even with the lower deck, but with the props still just above the ground.

They then each unhooked rubber hoses from the railing, leaning out onto the engines, and pushed the hoses onto nozzles sticking out of the engines. "Set?" the captain asked.

"Set," Digby said.

They both braced their heels against the edge of the deck in brackets set there for that purpose. Reaching out over the motors, they grabbed handles set in their side. "Ready?" huffed the captain, clearly not liking being bent over.

"Ready," Digby replied.

They both pulled on the handles, which came out on chains as they leaned back. This turned over the motors. On the second pull both motors gave a loud pop. On the third they sputtered to life. The wind from the props whipped by them. The men pulled loose the tubes and turned off the valves. The ship began to pull against its mooring lines.

Digby climbed down to the lower deck. "We`ll let them warm up for a bit," he said to the women. "You two need to hold on to something. You can stay in the cabin, but it`s a mess in there, or you can stay out here and hold on to the rail. I suggest putting your backs to the cabin wall cause we`ll be tipping upward and moving forward. Don`t hold on to the gas generator. At the moment it`s kind of hot and besides, it`s full of acid and you might get it on you."

The captain came down and tapped Digby on the shoulder. "Let`s go," he said. They went to the railings on each side and unlashed the ropes that looped through the landing rings on the ground and pulled the ropes loose. Kay could feel a lurch in her stomach as the ship came loose from the ground. She held on harder to the rail in fear and anticipation.

The captain left Digby to hank the ropes and climbed up to the tiller wheel. He pulled back on the throttles next to the wheel, and the engines woke up. Kay and Charity were pushed back against the cabin wall as the nose of the airship leapt upward. The sound of the engines was deafening.

They climbed and climbed until they were close to the clouds and their ears popped. When the captain felt satisfied with their altitude, he throttled down the motors and Kay and Charity could again hear each other. Kay was near a railing. She peeked around the side of the cabin and could see Saint Louis behind them, the ground yawning far below. Behind the props, Kay could see the big rudder vanes shift from side to side as the captain steered.

There was nothing between them and empty air but the steel tubing of the railing, leaving them both a little afraid to stand up. The wind was fierce. The ship swung slowly around until they were running parallel to the Missouri River, all the time climbing. Kay could see the sun glint off its surface as she tried to clear her ears. In the distance to the south and west were columns of smoke from fires. It was the front line. There were men fighting and dying there, and here they were drifting high above in clean sunshine.

"Oh, cows!" Charity said, pointing.

They were so small from above. Then a hawk came up for a minute to look them over.

Kay finally worked up the courage to stand up. She saw Digby come down to check the gas generator, so she staggered over to him, the wind whipping about her, and asked, "should we be so close to the Missouri River? Aren`t there Rebels there?"

"No miss, they`ve been pushed back." He frowned at her. "It`s best to follow it for navigation," he added. Then he turned abruptly and climbed back up to the upper deck.

This seemed to Kay to be unwise, but she went back and sat down next to Charity who was having the time of her life. "This is incredible!" she said. "Oh, birds!" She pointed at their white shapes. There were tiny houses and roads.

After an hour and a half, they came to a fork in the river. The airship took the left fork. "This isn`t right," Kay mumbled to herself. When she was sure of their direction, she stood up and faced the Captain on the upper deck and yelled, "Where are we going?"

He pretended not to hear.

"Where are we going?" she yelled again.

He frowned and huffed. "Take the wheel," he said to Digby and came down the ladder.

"We have to make a stop," he said.

"Where?"

"Springfield."

"That`s Rebel territory!"

"I have to make money. We have no cargo this trip. You two barely cover cost," he said, coming down the ladder.

"You said Kansas City!"

He smirked. "Well, Springfield is out of Saint Louis and it`s west. We have things besides cargo we can sell there. Springfield is a lovely place to sit out the war. There`s lots of jobs good looking young white women can do there. We may even have some lined up for you," he said, looking the women up and down.

"You God-damned . . ." Kay was cut off as he flat-handed her hard across the side of her face and she fell back against the cabin. Charity stared wide eyed at him.

Kay`s hand ended up in her bag almost without her thinking. He stood there laughing. She would not be hit like that again! She drew her pistol. At least she had only intended to draw it, but somehow it went off. The bullet passed his side. It crossed the deck and pinged through the side of the gas generator, drilling a neat round hole. "You crazy bitch!" he yelled and stormed forward to slap the gun out of her hand.

She fired again. This time it went through his stomach and he fell backwards through the spray of acid that was jetting out the side of the gas generator.

"Captain!" Digby yelled. He had been pulling something down from the cargo nets when he heard the shots.

Fenton was writhing on the deck, clutching his gut, blinded by acid. Digby rattled down the ladder and went for Kay, who turned and shot him too, hitting him in the hip. He was spun around, knocked off his feet. Kay grabbed Charity`s arm. She had just shot the crew! There was nobody up there steering. She pulled Charity towards the ladder. Charity was staring at Fenton who was still curled up screaming. Kay pulled her around Digby, who was lying unconscious on the deck in a rapidly growing pool of blood.

"Get up there," Kay said to Charity, but Charity was in shock. "Go!" She put the pistol back in her bag and used both of her hands to push Charity up the ladder.

At the top they could see that Digby had been pulling down long rolls of red cloth on paper tubes. They were Rebel flags still furled. "Hellfire and damnation!" Kay cried. "The Rebels won`t know we`re not Union!" She let go of Charity, rushed to the wheel and began to undo the rope loops that held it steady and on course. Something whizzed by their heads.

"Oh dear Lord God have mercy on us," Charity cried.

"Those God damned bastards," Kay yelled, as she swung the tiller over to the right, the wind whipping her hair around her. This was not a moment for propriety.

There were more shells whizzing up from below, and up above Kay could hear a whooshing of escaping gas over Fenton`s screams and the crackling clatter of the engines. The ship turned with agonizing slowness. Finally there was a loud clang from the engine on their left and something ricocheted upwards through the gas bag, tearing another hole in the envelope. The left motor cut out with a tumbling sputter, its silence almost louder than when it was running. The airship went back into a slow turn to the left – back towards Rebel lines.

They were past the river and Kay could see that the ground was closer. It was just a matter of time before they hit, and there was nothing she could think to do except to look for something to hold on to.

Grabbing Charity, Kay pulled her down on the deck between the railing and the wheel housing and then squeezed in beside her. The second motor began to fail, sputtering and catching. She could hear torn canvas flapping in the wind. Then they were scraping across the ground until the prow of the undercarriage dug in, throwing them painfully back against the railing.

CHAPTER 13

Deke pushed his way under the sagging envelope and climbed up on the ship`s deck. There was blood all over and up above he could hear cursing. He saw two women tangled up against the railing, one trying to stand up.

"The ship`s on fire!" he yelled.

"I know!" said the shorter one, who was now standing. She started trying to rouse the other. "Come on Charity!"

"You shot him," Charity said, in a failing voice.

"It wasn`t like I meant to! They practically insisted on it!" Kay said, with a tinge of panic. Then she yelled to Deke, "She`s about to faint and I could use some help!" She pulled the taller woman up until she was sitting upright, but she was plainly having trouble.

Deke climbed the ladder, pushing the envelope

cloth up to make way.

"Come on!" Kay said.

Deke grabbed Charity's hand and together they pulled her to her feet then laid her over the edge of the stairs. He held her shoulders as he climbed down while Kay held Charity`s feet, but he slipped and fell and Charity fell on top of him.

Kay scrambled down and rolled Charity off and pulled Deke to his feet.

Deke thanked her and then asked, "Why`d you crash?"

"I`ll tell you outside. We need to go. We`re going to burn up!"

Together they carried Charity out from under the airship envelope out into the sunshine. Kay could see the ripple of heat in the air above the airship envelope as gas met air and caught fire.

Then Kay turned and ran back towards the burning airship.

"What are you doing!" Deke yelled, following.

"I need my money back," she said. "It`s just about all we have and we`ve got a long way to go."

Deke ran after her, grabbed her by the shoulder and spun her around. He could see determination in her eyes lit by the fiery shine of the airship. "I`ll go look. Just stay here," he said carefully in the voice he used with Ned on his bad days.

Kay thought for a second and then nodded. "It`s in the captain`s right pocket. He`s on the lower deck somewhere."

Deke nodded, ran to the airship, and then climbed carefully back under the sagging airship envelope, pushing his way up on deck. There was lots of blood but no captain. He was about to go check the cabin when it occurred to him that when they hit everything must have slid forward. As he started sliding forward himself, he noticed that the deck was sticky. The varnish on the wood peeled up and stuck to his boots like something had dissolved it.

He had no time to think about that though because, about halfway past a big copper drum with a hole in it, he saw a pair of boots. When he lifted away the canvas, there was a man with a brimless leather hat on that buckled under his chin, and goggles too. The hat was fur lined, which was about the damnedest thing he'd ever seen someone wear. He was about to pull it off to look at it when he remembered his situation and that there were flames right above his head. Besides, the side of the man's face was badly burned. He had died curled up, gut shot by the smell, and Deke had to pull hard to roll him over. There in his pocket, right where she said, was a wad of money. He pulled it out and stuffed it in his pocket and then worked his way back out.

"Did you get it?" the short one said. She had been down on the ground throwing up and looked pale, but she still had that look in her eyes.

Deke squatted down next to her, nodded his head, and handed the money to her.

"Thanks," she said. "It may save us." Especially since we might be in trouble with the law, she thought.

Charity was lying flat on her back on the ground, peaceful as the dead.

"So what happened," Deke asked again.

"We got shot down. That Digby couldn't get the Rebel flags out in time, because I shot him!" This didn't make much sense to Deke. She looked like she had a case of the after–fight shakes, so he decided she needed a minute or two to calm down.

They didn't have much time before they were going to be found by somebody, so he left her to look after Charity and went to get the horses back. He expected Ned not to wander off, but these Army mares were hardly to be trusted. Wander they had, but no further than the edges of the field. When he returned leading the horses, Charity was awake with Kay squatting next to her.

"We better get out of here," Deke said. "Someone will be by soon, I expect. That is, unless you two want to be found."

Kay shook her head. "Not by soldiers."

"That`s just about all there is around here," Deke replied, a little out of breath from chasing horses.

Deke handed Kay his water skin so she could wash her mouth out. He wondered why they wanted to avoid the Army. He`d never seen any sign that it cared much about civilians, especially when there was a battle. Most times the Army seemed to be of the opinion that civilians should just get out of the way, preferably on their own. But this woman seemed to have her own opinions about soldiers and she probably had her reasons.

"So you shot the crew?" he asked Kay. She didn`t look like a desperado to Deke.

Kay just nodded. She was still kind of pale, and didn`t look ready to talk yet.

"Well then, let`s see if we can get this here Charity up on one of these pack saddles." He eyed Charity doubtfully. She was sitting up now. "They aren`t really meant for riding," he added.

"I can try," Charity said.

"Good enough!" Deke replied with a smile.

Deke had Kay hold the reins while he cupped his hands, got Charity to use the correct foot, and boosted her up on top of the saddle. She went over belly first. Unlike riding saddles, there are about as many types of pack saddles are there are horses and mules to use them and these luckily were not the kind that had pieces of wood sticking up, like you see the Army use sometimes. These were built by Indians and were designed to be versatile. So although Charity didn`t exactly have a seat, she did have a flat spot to perch on, which she did after a lot of rearranging of her dress.

"It`s not so bad," Charity said.

"We`ll see how you feel after an hour," Deke replied.

Kay had been watching Charity and had done some planning ahead. Her ascent, although still ungraceful, went quicker.

"By the way, my name`s Deke."

"Kay," she said, and gave him a weak smile.

"Charity." Charity was looking at the distance to the ground with apprehension.

To Deke they looked more like two kids lost in the woods than murderers. They had no gear and nothing to even carry it in, except a couple of shoulder bags. Deke could see that they needed more help than they probably thought. He climbed up on Ned, took the reins of their horses and led them away from the burning wreck down the river towards Springfield.

"Where were you two headed anyway?"

"Kansas City," Kay replied.

"You were going in the wrong direction."

"We sure were. The captain decided to take us to Springfield instead. Wanted to find us jobs entertaining, even though we didn`t want them."

"Damn inconsiderate," Deke said.

"He was some kind of smuggler," Charity said.

"Or maybe a spy," Kay added.

Crossing lines meant he probably could be hung as a spy too, Deke thought. But this left him stuck on the horns of a dilemma. His friends were missing, he was behind enemy lines, and now he had two ladies who had to be set down somewhere.

"I was headed to Kansas City myself but kind of got delayed," he said, which was entirely true.

"Well Deke, that kind of delay saved us from a burning balloon, so for some kinds of delay we are truly thankful," Kay said. "So, are you going to show us the direction to Kansas City?"

He was silent for a moment. He couldn`t take them through the lines.

"I can do that, at least," he replied. Ned snorted, but Deke couldn`t tell if it was in approval or not.

They were going to need gear or better still a hotel for these women if they were going to sleep warm and dry. The day was still young, but he doubted they were going to find anything with the battle going on around them. They needed to cover distance, but he had to make several stops to adjust things, and it was getting on towards noon when they neared the bridge he had seen earlier. The now free Negro workers were putting the finishing touches on it.

It had been widened enough for both wagons and people and had ropes strung beside it in the water for people to hang on to when they fell off and across the sides to keep them from falling off in the first place. Wagons were coming across in a line, and next to them marched a line of soldiers. At least they were until a man sitting on a crate next to the shore, with his watch out, blew a blast on a bugle. Wagons with wounded and the walking wounded had been lining up on the ex-Rebel side of the shore, wanting to go back across to the Union side, and it was their turn. When the last of the full wagons coming in made it off the bridge, the wagons of wounded and men hobbling beside in blood red, bandage white, and tattered blue started crossing back.

"So that's how we're getting back across the river?" Kay asked.

"It`s about the only way, although I expect there`re more bridges being built down river."

He saw Kay nod slightly, but he couldn't tell how she felt about it, a thin ribbon of wood and boats stretched across that wide expanse of thick brown water.

"We better get in line," Kay said.

"Those poor men," Charity said to herself.

Kay knew she was thinking of her husband.

Deke, Kay, and Charity were standing on the shore, still on horseback, getting ready to try to cross with the wagons, when they heard a low whistling scream that rose until it was a clap of thunder. Out in the river, about a hundred yards upstream, there was a huge column of water that rose and blossomed out like a thistle flower, and the whole river seemed to jump upward, hazing over in a nervous mist. The horses shied back, heck even Ned shied, and Deke couldn`t blame him, especially when a big wave crested over the shoreline and slapped into men, wagons, and finally their horses.

Charity couldn`t hang on when her horse fell. It got right back up knee deep in water, but she was still down in it. The water was trying to get back in the river and wanted to take Charity with it. Deke leapt down and held on to her. Together they dug in their heels until the flow eased up. They were drenched, but Deke was pleased that he had managed to keep his hat. Charity poured out the water from her bag and fished out her drenched needlepoint with a sigh.

Deke finally got Charity back up on her horse, and both women thanked him profusely. Charity passed her bag to Kay, who began pulling things out to dry on every possible spot she could find on her saddle and horse. Charity looked in the panniers beneath her and declared that there was a sack of something in there that was turning to mush.

"There`s no time clean it out now," Deke said.

Deke had seen this before, but only at a distance, and the shells had been coming from the Union side. It was another Big Mary, only this one though belonged to the Rebels, and they were definitely after the bridge. He turned and looked back at the bridge as the water settled and was amazed to see that it was still there. "I guess being built of boats has its advantages," he said, to himself.

Kay looked at him questioningly, but Deke nodded towards the bridge. "If that cannon is like the Union one, we have about half an hour before it fires again. We better get across quick."

Clem, Big, and Jake were up in an observation trench about a mile away from the bridge, mostly by virtue of Clem, his telescope, and math skills. The retreat had left the Rebels a bit disorganized. The railway gun and engineers had arrived, but the spotters hadn`t. Judging by their first shot, a near miss, Clem was quite good at observing and artillery spotting. Clem left the telescope and sat down at his table with his books to compute the correction for the next shot.

The bridge was about a mile away from their position, with telegraph wires stretching back another four miles to the railroad spur where the cannon itself sat. They had approximately 22 minutes until the gun would need their aiming corrections.

"This barrel droop chart is fascinating," Clem said. "I wonder how they figured it out?" He was enjoying the practical application of math.

"Probably trial and error," Big said.

"Yeah," Clem replied, absentmindedly. "I guess so."

Poor Tobi was now the courier, since Deke was missing. He was off riding towards Springfield with his own packet of maps and notes.

Jake took Clem`s spot at the telescope. He could see the bridge between two hills and the river spread out behind their tops. The soldiers were running around like ants, pushing wagons back on the road and fishing men out of the river. The next shot, there would be no helping the men in the water or on the bridge.

Then from behind the edge of the rightmost hill he saw some figures on horseback making their way towards the bridge. What caught his eye was the color. They were clearly not soldiers, two of them women in dresses. He slid the focusing tube back and forth a bit to try to catch the best focus. He could swear he knew the cow hand in front, leading the two women. And those women weren`t riding on saddles, they were sitting on panniers of familiar design.

"Big, look at this." He turned the scope over to Big.

"What am I looking for?"

"Three riders, two of them women."

Big tinkered with the scope for a bit and then let out a big whistle. "So that`s where he got off to. The women look sweet."

Jake grabbed the scope back, "I missed that." After some tinkering he smiled, "Deke, you never cease to amaze. There couldn`t be more than two eligible women in a hundred miles and you found them both."

"Where`re they goin`?" Big asked.

"Looks like they plan to cross the bridge."

"That`s not good."

"Well maybe this shot is going to have to be

delayed until they do," he said. And then he said to himself, "Say hello to Philadelphia for me, Deke."

A captain was gathering able men, organizing details and empty wagons. They began moving up the shoreline picking up and loading stranded fish, many still kicking. Deke guessed that someone was having fish tonight for dinner.

They made their way forward to the bridge, through the crowds of wagons and wounded soldiers. There was a sergeant checking papers at its head. Deke turned back in his saddle and said, "I need you two to think of the names for your husbands. You two are officer`s wives, captains I think."

"We aren`t going to get shot are we?" Charity asked.

"No, not you. But I might," Deke said.

"Sweet Mother of Jesus, what a day," Charity replied.

"Hallelujah," Kay added, with a smile.

At the top of the bridge they were pulled aside by the bridge guards. Deke showed them his damp pass and introduced the women as officers` wives. The women sat and stared into the distance with a look of wan boredom. The sergeant barely looked, snorted, and waved them through. They rode straight across in the line of wagons carrying wounded, the horse`s hooves clomping hollowly on the boards. It took a long time to cross and Deke worried more and more as the minutes ticked by, but no shells fell from the sky.

On the far side there were wagons picking up fish too. The road through the woods was crowded with wagons and men, waiting to cross the bridge.

"That was easy," Kay said, after they had made it to dry land.

"Yeah, " Deke replied, looking confused. "Kind of strange."

Kay stared at Deke.

Deke looked back at Kay. "We took too long to cross. The gun should have fired."

That got a little yelp out of Charity.

"What are you, Deke?" Kay asked.

"I`m an Army courier," he said, and then he smiled, "Just not this Army." That brought a smile from Kay which Deke thought looked nice.

As best as he could figure, the road they were on was going to Jefferson City and then Saint Louis, which wasn`t where the women wanted to go. So, just out of sight of the bridge he turned them left, off the road, and took off through the woods heading west.

"Why`re we going through the woods?" Kay was frowning.

"That road goes to Saint Louis and it's nothing but army columns all the way there. All the inns will be full of officers and all the food and wood will be gone. I'm hoping that if we head north, we`ll run into a road heading west with no soldiers."

As they rode he told them how he had come to be behind enemy lines. This got an even bigger smile out of Kay. That brought the sun out a bit for Deke. That was until the next shell came in. It screamed down and ended in thunder. The bridge was gone, wagons, men, and all. The wave from the explosion pushed into the woods and almost reached them, but pulled back with a sizzling hiss. There would be no going back for Deke.

"Guess I`m going to Kansas City after all," he said. "I`m sure not going back that way."

When they stopped, Deke had to help them down

off their perches. They ate lunch, and Deke was surprised that the women didn`t complain about their saddles, or really the lack of them. They couldn`t be comfortable.

Kay asked, "Did you desert?"

Deke laughed. "No. I never joined in the first place." He pulled up his sleeve and showed them his shoulder. "See, no tattoo."

"Do soldiers go out and get them?"

"No. They tattoo you so you can`t desert."

"That`s awful," Charity said.

"Sure is."

He told them about Big and Jake and the Rangers and how they had smuggled him in. When they got back up on their horses, Charity spread her dress around her, draping it over the horse`s back to get the maximum amount of sunlight and air. Deke, though, expected they would both still be damp tonight. Humidity makes drying clothes difficult sometimes.

It was afternoon and the woods were beautiful, but there was still no sign of a town, which left Deke a little worried.

Since he had told them about himself, it was only fair they told him a little of their stories. They told him about their lack of family, Charity`s search for her husband, and Kay`s search for her father. It seemed they were all three orphans.

Deke was really starting to worry when finally, at dusk, they came to a town called Vincentville. It didn`t have an inn, but it did have a barn, and a general store with a post office, but the best piece of luck was that it had a saddle tree shop! For a few coins the women got to sleep that night in the barn, in the hay pile, in the loft. The owner would have nothing to do with an unmarried man sleeping in the same room as two unmarried women. Deke had to sleep in back of his house. "You better be there in the morning too, " the man said, as he went inside for the night.

The women bought blankets, clothes, and sundries at the general store. While they washed in the trough as best they could, Deke stayed out of the way, while making sure everyone else in town did too. For a little more money, the general store owner`s wife fed them a hot dinner.

Neither Charity nor Kay had ever slept outside at night and, despite Deke`s instructions, they were a little unsure as to what to do. The store owner had left them a lamp, but they had to keep it away from the hay, which meant that one of them had to blow it out and then make her way back to their blanket in the pitch dark. There were animals all around, including bats in the rafters. Sleeping in hay is nice as long as it`s fresh and you have a blanket to keep it from poking, and they had a comfortable night, once they managed to get to sleep.

When Kay woke, she had sunk down into the hay pile and started the day with a sneeze and a view completely blocked by hay. She had no idea what time it was, just that it was light. Pushing back the hay from her face she could see the early morning sun in the rafters and cobwebs shining through the holes in the roof.

There, sitting on the edge of the loft in front of the hay pile, with his back to her, was Deke. He looked thin and his clothes well worn. He was rubbing oil on the horse`s harnesses.

Without turning he said, "Morning."

Kay stretched and then realized just how sore she was. "I`m going to hurt so much today."

"Better saddles will help," he replied.

"We can get those?"

"Yup. There`s a shop here that makes them. It`s

pure heaven-sent luck."

"I wonder if that store owner has tea."

"A fire would be nice. A pot for hot water might even be better. I have coffee, but no way to make it."

"Sugar and milk?"

"No," he said. And then he added, "Sugar and milk?"

"For the coffee."

"It`s good in coffee?" He seemed to think about that for a bit.

Then he said, "We need to think about what we`ll need for the next few days. There`s no stage service here."

A few days on the road with a strange man. He seemed nice, and for some reason she felt like she could trust him, but they didn`t know him and he was just a little bit odd.

They ate breakfast with the general store owner`s family again. Deke traded in the nearly new panniers for two good used saddles and saddle bags. Kay paid for the difference. She told them later that her wad of money was a fair bit more than she had given Captain Fenton.

The store owner didn`t want to sell regular saddles to women, said it was unseemly, and he only had one side saddle. It was new and expensive, and it was clear he didn`t think women should be riding at all, even with a side saddle. Kay listened to Deke and the old man argue until finally she let out a growl that climbed from the very center of her exhaustion, nerves, and lack of lunch. She slammed her hands down flat on the counter and yelled, "Do you want our money or not?" He gave in, but it was clear that there weren`t going to be any "deals, discounts, or bargains."

After a bit of inventorying and thought, they bought supplies: coats, utensils, tent halves, and pants and hats for the women. The women busted out with laughter when they tried on the men`s pants in a clean stall in the barn. The clothes were baggy and stiff, but a vast improvement over dresses and garters when it came to riding horses. They left Vincentville a far richer town than when they entered. And before they left, Kay dropped a long letter in the mail to her aunt. She left nothing out.

Out of town and to the northwest they rode, away from Jefferson City, the battle, and the Army. It was two more days across rough country trails before they found a proper road and made it to Warrensburg. On the way, to pass the time, Deke told them the story about the bombing of Abilene and then about the good time he, Jake, and Big had in Tzitopa thanks to the three spies and their money. It seemed he couldn`t stop telling them the Indian names for things and stories about them.

Late in the afternoon on their first day out of Vincentville, Kay and Charity saw Deke slip out of his saddle, pulling his rifle with him in one smooth motion. He walked towards a pond quiet as the wind, with a fixed intent, and then slipped into the brush like a snake. There were two shots. The women didn`t know what to think, but Ned seemed unconcerned and just stood there nibbling brush. They waited a bit more and then Deke popped back out of the brush with two big ducks. He held them up with a smile and said, "Dinner."

It was June and it stayed light late. Deke built an early fire because the ducks would take awhile to cook, pitched tent halves, and fixed beds, while the women dressed the birds. Deke was appropriately impressed with Kay`s knife. They stuffed the ducks with wild basil, sliced apples, and potatoes, and roasted them. There was a stream so they washed clothes and hung them up while the ducks cooked. It was a nice evening, but Kay intended to try to keep awake, at least for awhile after they went to bed. She had her pistol beside her under her blanket just in case Deke turned mean. As she was doing this, she realized that he had to know she had one, but he never asked her about it.

But she was asleep as soon as she lay down. The next morning, she realized she was sore in whole new ways. Stretching brought the best and worst feelings she had ever felt. There was a beetle walking across the ground in front of her at eye level. She watched it walk by on its six legs. It had no idea she was there.

Charity moaned. "I can`t move."

"It`s amazing. Whole new ways of hurting," Kay replied. But she managed to sit up. Then she waited until Deke`s back was turned, and slipped her pistol back in to her bag.

Deke had rebuilt the fire and had it down to coals already. He had been up for a while.

"Coffee?"

"Yes, please, but first I have to take care of some business."

"Back of those bushes isn`t bad," he said nodding towards the brush.

It turned out he had dug a hole there for that purpose at the base of a tree they could lean on. How long had he been up?

There were eggs, bread, and the last of the duck for breakfast. They had hung their food up away from the bears and raccoons, and even though there were little foot prints on the saddlebags, the raccoons had been stumped by the buckles. Black coffee was a shock at first, but it went down well with the eggs, and it was warm.

Riding that day was not particularly pleasant. They were chafed and sore, but the woods were beautiful, it was summer warm, and the shade of the trees sweet.

Deke pointed out bee hives, beaver dams, deer, and a beautiful red and white snake. Then he showed them how to work a signal mirror. There were no people, though, no roads and no towns. They swapped stories about their lives as they took measure of each other. And this time Deke shot, over the course of the late afternoon, three rabbits.

The next day they found Warrensburg, where they slept in a barn again, this time with no difficulty from its owners, and cooked meals from the blacksmith`s wife.

The next day the riding hurt a little less. When they finally reached Kansas City the day after next, Kay and Charity could ride on their own without fear. They had also decided they could trust Deke.

They came out of the woods and found they were in the Kansas City Aerodrome. It was a big grazed field on top of a hill on the far side of town from the river. There were only a few airships there, all small ones. Kay wondered if any of them were heading to Denver. But then the thought of another airship ride made her shudder.

The city itself stretched across a wide flat wash that ended in the Missouri River. There was a lack of smoke- -most of the homes didn`t appear to have steam yet. Kay wondered if they lacked gas-light as well. The harbor had river boats moored at the docks, but none were moving or even showing smoke. To Kay the city looked like it had more streets than houses. Clearly its people had great plans for the future, once the war ended.

Suddenly Charity started tugging on Kay`s shoulder and pointing "Look!" she said.

Kay tried to see what she was pointing at, and then she saw it, a small bit of movement and smoke. It was a train heading west!

The hotels were all down near the waterfront, and

they found one with baths! Before they approached the desk though, Deke sat down and pulled off his boot. Kay was puzzled until he pulled out a flattened packet of bills. "No, no," she said. "I want to buy the horses from you. We`re going to need them. I can pay as part of it."

"They aren`t exactly my horses," he replied.

"Rebel horses in Union territory are as good as yours. Besides, some of this money came from that Rebel captain." She frowned and then said, "I really need to find a bank though." And then she smiled again. "Or maybe some proper Rebel spies this time! Then we can thank Jefferson Davis instead of Abraham Lincoln!" Deke laughed at that, and begrudgingly let her pay. When they finally settled it that evening, Kay insisted that Deke take $180 for the two horses, which was a deal for both of them considering the cost of horses during wartime and the fact that Deke had gotten them for free.

That night, after they had bathed, they put on clean city clothes and had a real dinner. It was the first time Deke had had time to realize just how beautiful these women were, especially Kay. She had a way of seeing things clearly and plainly, and her smile was something amazing to see.

That night, as Charity and Kay were falling asleep in their room, Kay heard Charity say, "I think he likes you."

"Me? Nonsense," she scoffed. "You`re clearly prettier and far better wife material."

"Perhaps, but he likes you."

That just about scared Kay more than the airship captain.

CHAPTER 14

The next morning, with the advice of the man at the front desk, Kay set out for the nearest bank. It was two streets away. They wanted to charge her 6 percent and to wait 24 hours before she could receive her money! This seemed outrageous to her, so she walked further down the street to the next and there they only wanted 3 percent. They explained the wait as well. They had to wait for telegraphic confirmation from her bank in Philadelphia that she had funds to cover the draft. This seemed reasonable, so she wrote them a check for 500 dollars.

When he got up, Deke went to visit the horses. The stablemen had done their work well and they all seemed to be in good shape. He had bought a bag of early season apples from a market stand and the horses happily crunched one down each. On the way back to the hotel he stopped to look in the window of a watchmaker. There, sitting on a piece of cloth, was a shiny brass compass, $12. It was oil filled and had a dial marked in degrees and about five other types of lines he didn`t understand, each exquisitely engraved. Deke already knew he didn`t have that much in his boot, so he headed back towards the hotel.

As he was going up the steps, crunching on an apple, he ran face to face into Kay.

"Oh," she stepped back. "Good morning."

"Good morning to you too," Deke said. "Would you like an apple?" He fished one of the nice ones out and offered it to her. For some reason her cheeks were red.

"Yes. An apple would be nice," and she smiled just a little bit and took the apple.

She was about to leave and he didn`t want her to go, so he said, "Wait till you see what I`m buying."

She stopped and smiled just a little bit more. "What?"

"A brass compass." Deke crossed his arms, stared off into the distance, and struck a heroic pose. "I won`t ever get lost again."

"Somehow, I can`t think of you as ever getting

lost." And she smiled just a bit more, which was sunshine to Deke.

"Well, you`ll see when you get a good look at the plains. Even Indians can get lost out there when they get off trail."

"Then it`s a good thing we can take the train."

"Yes, yes it is."

Then they both turned and marched towards their destinations, each kicking them self for acting like an idiot.

Deke was in a double quandary. He wasn`t sure which way he was going, east to the cities or west with the women. They surely needed help, but he was shy and unsure. He went back to the watchmaker and bought the compass, and in front of the shop he tipped it out of its felt bag into his palm. It glinted gold in the sun and its needle turned lazily in its case. He turned the case until he had lined the needle up with the "N". At least he knew which way west and east were, he thought. Which way should I go?

He was near the train station and so decided to check the train schedules. The boards on the boardwalk thumped under his boots as he walked. There were women and children walking along the street. It was nice, he thought, not to be in a city full of war and soldiers.

In the train station he stopped to listen to the telegraphs in the telegraph office. There were men sitting at desks writing down messages. They were faster than he was, which Deke admired, but he could still pick up bits of this and that. "River traffic halted", "BDR 515.", "Weather SJ MI fair 8W", "Rebel attack Hays", "Caution all routes Denver", Deke didn`t like that one, "Weather Top KS fair 12W", "Rebel attack Camdenton", and on and on. It didn`t stop. One message ended and another started.

Deke thought that Camdenton was near that new bridge across the Osage River that they had crossed not four days ago. It was a shame, he thought, that all the work those poor slaves had done had gotten blown up.

"So what are you up to?" said a voice behind him.

Deke turned to see a man in uniform standing with his hand on the handle of his gun in his holster. "Listening to the news," Deke replied.

"You understand Morse?"

"Yup, although this is faster than I`d like it to be."

"Hey Magill!" he yelled over his shoulder. "Come over here."

"In a minute," Magill replied.

The man turned and called, "No now!" and then turned back with his pistol leveled at Deke. "I think we may have a spy."

They took Deke down to the police station where they found his travel paper and the wax sealed note. Its Rebel origin was clear from its contents and Deke was locked in a cell without his guns or his new compass.

Deke didn't show up for lunch, which vexed Kay.

"He`s probably off getting drunk somewhere," Charity said. "Don`t worry."

Kay checked at the front desk. "No ma`am, he hasn`t checked out. Oh, did you hear? There`s going to be hanging tomorrow!" the clerk said.

"A hanging?"

"Oh yes! They caught a Rebel spy!" he seemed genuinely excited.

"When?"

"In the afternoon apparently. I do wish they wouldn`t be so quick about it. Hangings are so good for business. But the military . . ." and he threw up his hands in exasperation.

Kay felt her stomach tighten. "Where`s the jail?" she asked.

The jail was downtown, three streets away. When she got there, what she saw was a solid block of brick in a bare dirt lot, with a heavy tile roof. There was a crowd over by its side, so Kay walked around to see. The crowd was looking at a small barred window in the side of the jail wall. Under the window sat a bored looking man sitting in a chair with a shotgun across his lap. The crowd was held back from the window by a split rail fence.

Kay heard someone say, "Oh, I saw him!"

"He just looks like some kid."

"He`s a spy. Gotta kill em. They`ll be bombing us next if you don`t."

She pushed through the crowd until she could see the window. A face passed by it. She was sure it was Deke. He was pacing his cell.

She ran back to the hotel and found Charity in their room doing her needlepoint.

"Deke`s been arrested. They`re going to hang him."

Charity`s eyes widened, "You`re kidding."

"They think he`s a spy!" Kay was frantic.

"Well, maybe he is."

"He`s not a spy. He must have done something stupid and they found those papers of his."

"Then let`s go down and tell them to let him go," Charity said.

"And why would they listen us? What are we going to say? We just met this man when he saved us from a burning blimp? They might even arrest us too."

"Then what should we do?"

"I don`t know. Let me think," and Kay sat down

on the bed with her head in her hands. "We don`t have much time." She flopped back on the bed and stared at the ceiling and after a couple of minutes she said, "The real trick will be how we get him out of town. There`s by horse, by river, or by train. If they were just chasing him then I bet on him to get away, but if it`s the three of us then I think we`d lose. The river is slow and there`re no boats on it. We might even get shot crossing in front of somebody`s or other`s troops. That leaves the train."

"You`re not thinking . . ."

"I`m just thinking!" she said, rubbing her eyes with the palms of her hands. "It would be best if we could fix it so he could escape on his own, but there`s so little time. There`s a guard outside so we can`t pass anything in. I wonder how they get their dinner?" Kay was silent for a bit and then she said, "I`m going out."

"Don`t do something stupid too."

"I won`t. I just need to understand this thing better."

Kay practically ran to the bank and told them that Charity was going to pick up her money. They said it would be ready in the morning. She gave them Charity`s name and a description. Then she went to the train station and bought a ticket in a private cabin on the noon train to Denver, along with three spots in the horse car, and shipping for two crates to Topeka. She knew they couldn`t leave Ned so she went to the stable and paid them to deliver the horses and tack to the train tomorrow. Lastly she went to the warehouse district and bought two packing crates, a hammer, a box of nails, and two screw top jars. She had them label the crates "Bibles" and the names "Rev. Hammer" and "Topeka", and had them carried to and stacked on a cart in the corner of the train platform for the Denver train. She had all her props in place.

When she checked the schedule, she found there were no trains arriving from between 2:00 and 6:00 AM. She would have to do it then.

Then she went back to the hotel and had dinner with Charity. She was so nervous she could hardly eat. It all depended on Charity now.

When they were back in their room she said to Charity, "I`m going to break Deke out of jail."

"I knew it!" she said. "You are out of your mind!"

"I can`t let them kill him without trying to help."

"Then there will two hangings. Maybe three!" she said, eyes wide.

"No. I have a plan. It`s practically no risk to you. I`m going to do everything that`s dangerous. But I need you to do a few things."

Charity flopped backwards onto her bed and this time it was she who stared at the ceiling. She said in a strained voice, "So tell me the plan and let`s see if you`ve thought of the perfect crime."

"To begin with, you have to pick up my money from the bank. If I don`t make it, you`ll need it to continue on," Kay said.

"Not crazy yet," and at they had a nervous laugh.

"You`re going to have to get on the train tomorrow, but change your mind and get off at Topeka."

"Still not crazy yet."

"Lastly, you`re going to have to nail us in crates, actually probably only Deke."

"Crazy. I don`t know how to hammer nails."

"I have some nails and a hammer. We have some daylight. We can learn, and Deke can show you some there."

"If he knows how."

"He`s a frontiersman. He has to know how to hammer nails."

"I haven`t agreed to this yet, but I`m willing to see if I can hammer nails."

They went down in the alley and bent nails, one after another until they could get one in reasonably straight. They started out with little taps to get the nail set, then holding the hammer in two hands, they hit the nail harder and harder until it went it.

"We`re too slow," Kay said.

"Maybe Deke will have a better idea."

"Worse comes to worse, we can just take the horses and ride out of town."

They needed to get Deke`s things from this room, but it was locked. So they went back to their room and looked at the latch on their door. Kay decided they could open it if they had something flat to push into the latch, but they didn`t. They went through all their things. There wasn`t anything flat and stiff.

"Oh, if I still had my corset, a piece of boning would do it," Kay lamented.

However, a search of their room turned up the steel banding under their mattresses. By stretching the spring, they could get one off. Kay slipped it up her sleeve and they went out. Charity watched the steps while Kay worked on the door. It turned out to be disturbingly easy.

They packed Deke`s things in his bags and took them to their room.

There was nothing left to do but to wait.

Kay expected to have to spend pretty much all day inside the crate so she drank little with dinner and peed her heart out before she left.

"Please be careful," Charity said. She started crying from worry. Kay looked a little pale herself.

"I`ll do my best. Remember. Wait a half hour then go to the station."

Kay had changed into her pants, left her bag with

Charity, and slipped her pistol in her pants pocket. She felt light headed and the world seemed unreal and bright.

She walked downstairs and into the night. Out on the street she could hear every sound in the city. There were dogs barking, wind, and water over the stones in the shallows of the river. The streets were empty and dark with no gas light and only the occasional dim shine from this window or that. The jail was dark too when she got there, approaching from the back. The guard was there by the window still, asleep in his chair. She had made all sorts of plans about how to overcome the guard, but he was just sitting there snoring. She was going to hold him silent at gunpoint, tell him how she had killed two men and wasn`t in the mood to make it three, make him drop his drawers and lay on the ground so he couldn`t make any sudden moves. In the end though, she walked up to him and whacked him in the head with a brick.

Deke had heard her and his face appeared at the window. "Kay?" he whispered.

Kay said nothing, but pulled the guard`s gun belt off and passed it to Deke. Then she found that the fool guard had the keys to the front door. As she walked around to the front, she heard Deke making noise inside. She hoped he had some plan because all she could think of was unlocking the door and walking in, pistol drawn.

She was fumbling through the keys when Deke opened the door for her. He opened it about six inches, his face lit by the candlelight inside, and said to her, "Stay there. I`ll be out in a few minutes." And that was it. He came out and locked the door. They sat the guard back on his seat, gave him all the keys, and checked that he was breathing.

When they were finally away from the jail, Kay

said, "We go to the train station next."

"Why?"

"We`re leaving by train."

"Why?"

"Because they`ll catch us on horseback."

Deke thought about this as they walked. "They won`t catch me," the emphasis on the "me."

"No, but they`ll know we`re with you."

"Yes, but they don`t know you broke me out."

"What will we say?"

"Tell them the truth. I rescued you from a burning balloon and that`s all you know."

Kay felt almost disappointed. She had made so many plans.

They met Charity at the station, which was pitch dark and locked up. Kay hadn`t thought about them locking up the station at night. The crates were inside on the landing. Charity hugged him when she saw him. She had all the things Kay had bought and Deke looked them over and laughed. But then he looked at Kay. "I need to get my stuff and go."

"It`s in our room."

"You broke into my room?" He looked like he was going to laugh again.

Kay nodded.

Then he was quiet. He seemed to be deciding something. Then finally put his hand on her arm and leaned over and kissed her carefully in the darkness of the train platform.

She stood there stunned.

"I`ve got to go," he said.

Kay pulled her room key out of her pocket and gave it to him. "Go."

"Wait for me in Denver," he said and then he turned and ran.

Kay had tears in her eyes, and when she looked over at Charity, there glinting in the dim light from the street, she saw Charity did too.

CHAPTER 15

Deke, his saddlebags over his shoulder, was staring into the black darkness inside the stables. "There`s surely somebody in there keeping watch," he thought. But there was no way that he was going to be able to get in to find out without being seen. So he decided to do it straight. He sat down, pulled off his boot, and took out his money.

"Hello?" he called. "I need my horse. Hello?"

He heard a snort from the back, then "What?"

"I need my horse. Sorry about it being so late, but it`s an emergency."

"We`re closed. I can`t take money, the boss isn`t here, so you have to come back in the morning."

"I`ve got to go now, my brother came and said the house caught fire and my Mom`s burned bad. He`s getting my cousin and we have to go."

"I can`t."

"I`ll pay you double. We need to go now. I was planning on staying that long anyway."

There was a drawn out grumble, "Double huh?"

"Three horses, my cousin`s and mine."

A match was struck and he could see a grizzled old face with a bushy mustache as he pulled the glass off a lamp to light it. The man stood, picked up the lamp and walked forward. Deke noticed that his hand was on his gun.

"Mine`s the palomino," and Deke walked over to Ned. Ned nuzzled him looking for apples.

"Well OK, he`s yours at least. That`ll be $6."

"$6!" said Deke genuinely astonished. "Mister, it should be $3."

"Yes, but you say this is an emergency and it`s I don`t know what time in the morning."

"$6."

The man snorted and crossed his arms.

"$5," Deke said.

The man licked his lips and smirked, "OK, $5."

Deke counted out the money and saddled the horses with absolutely no help from the old man. Before he rode out, he looked at the man and shook his head. "$5, damn." He meant it. His wallet much lighter, Deke rode towards the center of town before he headed out just in case the old man was watching.

Between the Union and the Rebels, there were no bridges left standing across the Missouri river so he couldn`t go north. He didn`t want to ride all the way to Denver which meant he was going to have to meet a train eventually. It was in some ways unfortunate that it was the middle of the night, because he could really use a look at the route maps in the station.

One thing he did know was that he had to leave town by the road or they`d see his trail right off, and he had to do it fast. So he set out for the edge of town at a trot through dark empty streets. When he made the main road, he forced himself to slow to a walk. It was hard but he knew that if they had any kind of tracker with them, he would see the tracks and know it was someone in a hurry.

Having been raised out in the wilds of the Plains kind of taught Deke more than a little bit about tracking, not that he'd admit to it. And having been raised around others with similar skills left him with notion that these skills were somewhat more common out in the wide world than they actually were. So in as much as being on the run went, he tended to over compensate.

Deke watched for a stream to follow to get off the road. He passed the first one and then a second just because he knew they would waste time checking them without his help. He could see the false dawn by that time and knew time was short, so he took the third and headed south towards the open prairie. He let Ned speed up to a trot, even though it would get his shoes wet, and began to eat up ground. When he found low hard earth, he left the stream and used his shiny new compass, which he had retrieved from the vest pocket of that sheriff, to keep his sense of direction as he sped across the open grassland.

It was almost dawn and he still wasn`t cold, which didn`t bode well for the day. Finding another stream, he rode in to cover his tracks again, riding back towards town. He then turned south covering his tracks with a drag, for about 30 feet, until he was deep in the grass. Ned by himself could walk backwards, though he didn't like it, but those army mares couldn't, so he rode south at a gallop for 15 minutes, then galloped back to confuse the direction of the prints. Then he left the trail a third of the way down. He carried on like this all day long.

That night he left the horses and climbed a hill. He couldn`t see any campfires, but then they probably wouldn`t do something helpful like camping on top of a hill anyway.

It was nice that he had saddles for all three horses. This made changing mounts easy so the next day he decided to go for distance. If they had a posse, even if they had just the sheriff and a tracker, they probably didn`t have two spare horses each. He set off at a trot going southwest and just kept it up from dawn to dark. He passed buffalo herds, prairie dog towns, and antelope. He was watched over by eagles and hawks, drifting in the heat above.

That night he looked again for fires and saw none. The next day he went for distance again, this time straight west. He took streams when he could and tried to obscure his exits. When he camped that night it kind of started worrying him that he hadn`t seen anyone following.

That night, there was a rainstorm. He figured he was way ahead of any followers and any tracks between himself and them were gone. Of course, for the rest of the day his tracks were going to be as obvious as fleas on a dog, there for anyone to pick out, what with mud and all. He found a stream and stuck to it for as far as he could go.

They never did catch Deke. The Kansas City Herald three days after he left printed the headline: "Posses Return, Rebel Vanishes!" It was a disappointment to the town. There was blessed little entertainment back then. People had worked themselves up for the inevitable fair that came with a hanging. Women had baked, pulled their best dresses out, and men had missed the games, like the town pool for how many times the prisoner kicked before he died.

The deputy at the jail window that night had a

cracked skull, concussion, and brain swelling, and there was some doubt whether he would live, but he woke up after a week and was walking around town in three. Kay and Charity having been questioned at length, were let go. The stable apologized to them, solemnly informing them that the Rebel had stolen their horses, refunding their money for stabling and shipping. Charity and Kay were remarkably forgiving about it. And two empty crates labeled "Bibles" were delivered to Topeka where they sat unclaimed.

Kay and Charity left town by train. But not before Kay posted another letter to her aunt telling her about their latest adventures and current location.

On the train they plunked themselves down in their seats in their plain trail-worn dresses and tossed their hats in the seat across from them. The Negro porter brought in their saddle bags containing their few meager possessions, wished them a good trip, and left.

Kay lifted her feet and looked down at her boots and started laughing.

"Yes?" enquired Charity.

"I was thinking about that first day at the train station."

Charity laughed too. "I wonder where my corset is today?" she said. And that brought more laughter.

"It`s dancing with my garters!" which brought even more hilarity. They really were tired.

Then they sat quiet for a bit. "This sure has been a long trip," Kay said.

"Amen. At least they can`t make us change trains on this line. It`s straight a track to Denver."

But they did. They sat in Salina, waiting for a new engine because theirs had broken down. Then they had to change trains in Hayes because the train had to be broken apart and reformed at the rail yard there, although they got the same sleeper car back and might as well have been left there asleep. But it was after Hayes that the last straw dropped for Kay.

They were trying to sleep when Kay thought she heard the conductor bellow in the hall, "Look out folks, we`re a gonna be a stoppin!" It was luck that led them to sleep on the side facing the engine. When they began applying the train`s breaks, Kay and Charity were pushed back against the wall instead of falling on the floor like all their things that were sitting on the seat across from them. As the train was squealing to its slow halt, they could hear gunshots and in the hallway someone wailing "It`s a hold up!"

In unison they both groaned the wail of the rising dead. Kay, who was on the bottom bunk, reached down over the edge of her bed and looked for her pistol. She finally had to sit up to reach it, muttering in frustration and annoyance.

In the hallway they could hear doors slamming open, screams and bellows. She stood up and started stomping towards the door muttering, "I have just about had enou . . ." When she was interrupted by their cabin door slamming open. There stood a dusty disheveled man with wide brimmed hat, a great coat, and a drawn gun pointing up at the ceiling.

"Everybody, this is a . . ." he said, but was cut off when Kay slapped the gun from his hand with a vicious swipe from the shoulder, sending the chambered round through the ceiling. Then straight armed him back into the wall and down to the corridor floor.

"I know it`s a God damned hold up!" She screamed, and then leveled her pistol at him and yelled, "Go hold somebody else up or I`ll shoot you someplace that hurts!" Then she slammed the door.

The bandit just sat there on the floor saying, "God

damn, God damn."

They were left alone after that.

The good thing about a hold up was that they had to fix the tracks, which meant that Kay and Charity had six hours without bumping, rocking, stopping, starting, or being woken to change trains.

Charity kept the bandit`s pistol, although it was a little large to be drawn easily from her bag. Kay made a mental note that they really needed to get something more appropriate for her in Denver.

They had breakfast in the dining car, which was free! Apparently many people on the train no longer had any pocket cash and the train company was truly sorry about it.

Once they got started again, the flat rolling grassland just went rolling by hour after hour. Two women sitting alone always seemed to attract more women, and Charity`s needlepoint created a point around which conversation could start. Poor Kay was surrounded by needle pointers, knitters, and crocheters, every one of them far better at it than she. But they learned a lot about Denver that way.

"Henry and I have waited all year for this. Denver is going to be so much fun," said a plump woman dressed in grey.

"Oh, I lost count," said a thin school teacher, with glasses and a frown for her knitting.

"We heard there was an opera," Charity said.

"There`s so much more. There are dance shows, restarants, and shopping. The shopping! They get things shipped in from San Francisco now, things from China."

"That sounds nice," said the school teacher, as she began to undo her row.

"The trick is to keep a reign in on the gambling. I have to watch Henry all the time."

"Where is he now?" Kay asked.

The woman in grey chuckled. "He thinks I don`t know it, but he`s in the next car passing a bottle."

They came to a large city, Namaqua, the capital of the Arapaho Nation. Its station was new and its rail yard extensive. Not much could be seen of the city itself because of the flatness of the land. What they could see were smoke stacks and their trails of smoke. There were a lot of these. The Arapaho had invested heavily in manufacturing. The station buildings themselves were beside the platforms and they got to them by way of long covered bridges that crossed over the platforms, and around which smoke billowed as trains passed under. They had an hour and a half wait so they decided to explore a little.

The station had a cafe and just to experiment, they bought two cups of something called chocotl. It was thick, warm, and very spicy.

"This definitely isn`t coffee," Kay said.

"I think it may have chocolate in it," Charity added.

"How can you tell? It`s so spicy. I can feel it in my fingers."

"That`s funny," Charity said, smirking.

"No, really."

There was an Arapaho visitors bureau displaying examples industrial products and Arapaho culture. Apparently the Arapaho produced and refined oil, made products produced from buffalo hide, grain, and wine, which they got to taste. There was beautiful artwork, painting, pottery, baskets, and weaving, all of which were terribly expensive.

The next day, after they pulled out of the town of Namaqua, the train turned northwest. They could see the mountains growing in the distance from their seats in the coach. They looked like a wall across the horizon, blue and capped in snow. Kay and Charity had never seen their like before, stretching in each direction until their snow capped tops disappeared below the horizon. Charity thought they looked cold, but to Kay they looked like they held secrets, but cold too she agreed.

Denver itself crept up on them the flatness of the land hiding it until they were almost upon it. It had broad strait streets lined with red brick buildings, many with their own smoke stacks showing modern steam plumbing. With so much brickwork, Kay suspected that one of those smoke stacks out there must be a brick factory. Closer to station were saloons and dance halls. It looked kind of rough to be a center for shopping. More like some kind of carnival.

As they climbed down the steps of the train to the platform, Kay saw several rough men spread out on the platform eying the crowds as they left. One of them pulled the cigarette slowly from his mouth as he locked eyes on them. He called, "You two here looking for work?"

Another with slicked down black hair yelled at the first, "Back off, they're in my area!"

The first flicked away his half burnt butt and yelled back, "Yours starts at the broken brick."

"The blond then. Hey honey, you lookin for a job? We've got a sweet location."

"If you like fleas," muttered the first.

The second stared at the first with a hurt look.

The women just stood there for a moment, then Kay followed by Charity slowly shook their heads "No."

Then both men started to approach them reaching in their pockets, until they saw the women step back and their hands in unison reaching in their bags. The men stopped, staring at the women's bags. The first started laughing followed reluctantly by the second, whose eyes kept shifting back and forth between the first man and the women.

"No harm meant ladies," said the first, and he drew out a card. Both men came forward with cards extended at arm`s length. Kay and Charity reached out and took the offered cards.

Kay`s card read "The Windibank Hotel, for the discriminating gentleman," and then an address.

"No offense intended, you look like you might be looking for work. With your looks, you could make a bundle here," the man said.

Charity gave a nervous laugh and Kay said, quickly followed by Charity, "Thanks. No, thank you."

The men each gave a slight nod and edged back towards their posts they had been leaning on, scanning the remaining crowd as they went. Suddenly, the first perked up and started following a man in a nice suit. "Pardon sir . . ." he called.

The station hummed with the noise of crowds. The women had their saddle bags over their shoulders when they had stepped down from the train onto the covered wood platform, so there was no luggage to look for. As they walked past the other platforms and then to the front lobby, they were called to and hooted at by hucksters and shills lining the station hall. Everyone was handing out flyers and cards for venues of entertainment.

They had no lack of taxis out in front, both steam and horse, but the confusion was too much for them and they didn`t know what to do, which to choose, so they retreated down the street. At the corner they practically bumped into a deputy which seemed strangely lucky to Kay. She wondered what he was going to try to sell them.

"Can I help you ladies?"

"We`re looking for a hotel, a real hotel, where we can sleep," Kay said.

He eyed them with a professional interest.

"Personal or pleasure?" he asked.

"Personal."

"I thought so," he said with a bored sigh. "It`s best to get out of the downtown area. All the taxis take commissions from specific hotels, but you seem sturdy. I suggest you walk up the street five or six blocks and start looking for yourselves. The further away the better."

Despite her misgivings, this sounded like good advice to Kay and a walk after so long on the train would feel good. So they thanked him and set out down the street. Kay noticed that some people walked down the street a ways before getting into carriages or meeting friends with horses. They looked more like normal people coming home. So it seemed likely that even the locals avoided the station when they could.

They passed discount train ticket offices, saloons, assayers, investment offices, gambling halls, cat houses, mining supply stores, dance halls, flop houses, pawn shops, food vendors, Indian trade stores, fine clothiers, dubious bath houses, China imports, restaurants, and one steam car dealer. The China import shop stopped them for a bit with geometric designs, inlays, and clay pots so big that Kay could see no use for them except maybe to store a body. The Chinese, she thought, must lead very strange lives.

About three blocks along, the street opened up and there, set back from it on one side, across a big garden with its own driveway was an opera house made of red brick and white wood, and across the street a park. Workmen were pulling down a grandstand in the park and sweeping up. Considering all the red, white, and blue, there must have been an election. The opera house had beautiful scrollwork and carvings, obviously all lit with gas light lanterns at night.

"What it must look like lit up at night," Charity said.

"I think we all should go when Deke gets here."

"Do you think he`ll make it?"

"They won`t catch him," she said, with certainty.

"How is he going to find us in all of this?"

That stopped Kay. "I don`t know, but we better think of something."

They picked a hotel that wasn`t too fancy or run down, and it was on a side street with less traffic. They walked into its busy lobby and asked at the desk. The man, and he was a man whole and fit, which was something Kay hadn`t seen behind the desk at a business in a long time, told them that the hotel was full.

"We`re always busy in the summer with people fleeing the circus downtown. We don`t even need to advertise. People just walk in, like you, trying to get away from downtown."

"Where can we go then?"

"Try the next street down. This is the first place people see, so try the second."

Outside, Charity stopped Kay. "Look," and she pointed at the side wall of a wood building. It was speckled with leaflets, mostly from the election. "We can make one of those and pin them up all over."

"Why?"

"To find Deke, silly."

"Oh. Oh!" she smiled. "You are a genius!" and she hugged Charity.

They walked back down to the main boulevard, crossed the street dodging a very noisy steamer, and down another block. This time they spotted two hotels. Flipping a coin, literally, they turned left. This one, The Concordia, was less busy and had room. Their room was up four flights of stairs, but it was large, had two beds, a wardrobe fit for big dresses along with a full length mirror, a vanity with lanterns, and a window they could open that looked down on the street in front. Suddenly Kay wished she had her trunk back.

Charity just stood there looking in the wardrobe and said, "We finally get fixed up for the wilderness and we`re back in civilization."

Kay flopped backwards on to her bed and laughed.

The hotel had baths, glorious baths with hot water that came out of a faucet, and they both took long ones. That evening when they went out in search of dinner, they saw women and men passing through the lobby in finery, dressed up for fun. Which left them a little melancholy, but after dinner they were so tired that the town lost all of its allure and nothing looked better than bed.

Missing breakfast the next morning, they managed to crawl out of their room for lunch. Kay felt like she was made of lead. She wished she still had *Wives and Daughters.* She had to give it back before she had finished it, and it was a good day to sit and read. They had been through a lot and even young bodies suffer wear and tear. So they rested. Kay got a newspaper from the front desk, read it, and then passed it on to Charity. Half the paper was advertisements. Kay had seen an ad for a printer and wrote down the address.

Denver back then was a town people came to for fun when they had extra time and money. They came in from back east, from the west all the way from California, as well as entertaining the local miners, ranchers, and railroad workers working on the new line over the Rockies to Sacramento, which at that time was carrying trains, but wasn`t quite finished. Kay realized that her poor father could have saved himself a trek over the mountains if only he had come ten years later.

CHAPTER 16

Deke began to wonder if anybody was actually chasing him. He hadn`t seen a soul since he left town. So he doubled back, then snuck up on a hill and waited all day, but there was nothing. Just flat prairie, wind, and grass. Ned didn`t mind. He and the other horses had been on the run for a lot longer than they liked, and standing around eating grass was just what they wanted.

In the morning Deke decided to take a chance and set out for the railroad. His still shiny compass told him which way to go, and by the bend of the day he had found the train tracks. Where he was on the line was another problem. But he decided that it was better to head west, since that was the way he was planning on going anyway, and why cover distance twice? They sped down the tracks at a trot because, although he didn`t want to admit to himself directly, he didn't want to miss Kay in Denver.

It was midday when he came up on the tiny town and station of McFarland. There was the town, seven buildings, the rail stretching in a line from horizon to horizon, a road stretching to horizon again in the other, and a flat sea of grass below and sky on top. They sold train tickets at the general store, but out of the twelve passenger trains that went by each day, only one stopped there and it had already gone. The next town was Geary, 18 miles away, and the store owner didn't know which train stopped there so Deke was stuck for the night. He bought a ticket for himself and three for the horses and a can of peaches to soothe his heartache. The trains were noisy so he camped away from the track that night, just to get a little quiet.

The next morning the train stopped like it was supposed to, they loaded the horses and Deke himself, and they were on their way to Denver. He sat in coach in a padded seat, a nice change after squatting on the ground for days and nights. The problem with the plains is that there are no trees and even damn few rocks to sit on. Just dirt and tall grass and the occasional Buffalo flop. Even those you have to fight the prairie dogs over. Deke was looking forward to the next two days.

He slept in his seat mostly and ate in the diner and had an uneventful ride, at least as uneventful as a person who has never been on a train before can have. He discovered the toilets, sinks, and mirrors. He hopped back to the horse car to keep Ned company and watched the ground roll by at an unnatural speed through the windows. In passing by things quickly, he found that he could see them from different sides, near and far, all in a matter of minutes. He actually climbed up on top of one of the cars and sat on the edge of the roof for a while out of sheer boredom, until a porter saw him and told him to get down.

On the second day they ran into a herd of buffalo. They were brown and shaggy and looked like half the fur was ready to fall off them. Deke couldn`t see an end to them, just buffalo wherever he looked, as far as he could see. They were kind of like the plains themselves in that regard. The train slowed to a walk and spent a lot of time blowing its whistle. It took Deke an hour, but he finally managed to stop listening to it. The buffalo, having had more practice listening to train whistles, got the hang of not listening right off. It took three hours to get by them. He finally pulled in to Denver only three days behind Kay. Deke promised himself that he was going to have to ride on a train again sometime.

That afternoon Kay pulled herself from her funk and said out loud, "I`ve got to go to the printers."

Charity just grunted. "There is no peace for the wicked."

Kay stood up, "Come on you lump," and pulled Charity by her ankle off the bed.

Charity lying on the floor amongst the covers said, "It`s true. I am a lump."

They dressed and picked up their bags with a great moaning and set out, two lumps who could barely walk. The hotel manager gave them directions and they trudged through the streets in the afternoon sun. The printer was not in the entertainment district, for which they were thankful, and his large shop was also the newspaper office which probably helped with his advertising costs. The office was filled with desks and file cabinets, as well as several presses. They had talked about it on the way there and decided on something simple: "Deke, we are at the Hotel Concordia".

When they presented this to the printer, he said, "You want me to print this? Only 100 copies? Be cheaper to mimeograph it. The copies aren`t as nice, they`ll be hand lettered, but they`re readable, at half the cost, and they`ll be ready first thing in the morning." They decided that was the way to go. They paid him and on the way back Kay saw a gun store.

"You need a gun," Kay said.

"I have one," Charity replied.

"It`s too big, too heavy, and you can`t draw it, at least not quickly."

"It will be too expensive," Charity said, as they stood in front of a gun store.

"It`s my money," she said, and walked in.

"And my job to make sure you don`t throw it away for no good reason," Charity said, following.

"It`s a matter of protection. You watch my back."

"You have your whole . . . Oh wow, look at that one," she said, suddenly captivated by the display case.

Kay saw it too and pressed her nose to the glass. "It`s for formal occasions I think," Kay said. "At the opera."

"It`s almost cute."

"That`s a double shot over under derringer," the shop keeper said, suddenly appearing. "Polished nickel plated, pearl handled."

Kay lifted her head up from the glass and looked at the owner. "Hello. We`re looking for a gun, something along the line of this," and she lifted out her pistol.

The owner bent close. "Oh, very nice, a short barreled Webley I think," he said picking it up and looking closely with a contented smile. "Yes, see here.

Lovely."

Kay thought he might start drooling.

"We don`t carry these. Women usually carry one of the pocket pistols like that derringer you seem to like, if they`re inclined to carry something. They`re next to useless really. Mostly just for show," he trailed off thinking. "The way you carry yours in your bag though, this makes sense. Men around here like the longer barreled pistols for their range, accuracy, and frankly fashion. The Webley is a city weapon, or for English officers. Interesting . . . this is a .38. I`ve only seen the .45 up close. A Pinkerton had it. Just last month," he said looking up at them. "That`s why I ordered the ammunition."

"It`s saved my life. Several times."

"I bet it did," he said with emphasis. "You`re so small. A .38 is perfect. I have cartridges for this, smokeless rim edged long center fire. You should probably buy some. They`re a new type and may be difficult to find out here. I can give you some leads as to where to look too."

Kay bought a box of ammunition. They risked dinner from a stand, walked back to the hotel, climbed the steps to their room, and then fell gratefully back into their beds, two lumps together to the end.

The next morning they went to the printer, then to a general store to buy light hammers and a box of tacks. Since he would be coming in by train they decided to start there. As they approached the entrance of the station, Charity spotted a tall lanky boy in a much used pilgrim hat sporting a feather, coming out the station door. She practically fainted right there. Gathering herself, she grabbed Kay and started pulling her towards the station.

"What are you doing?" Kay cried. But then she stopped and a small, "Oh," escaped. Then they were both running. "Deke!" they yelled. He looked around and then he saw them and stood there with a stupid smile. They leapt on him and hugged him. "You made it!"

"You didn`t get hanged!" Kay cried.

"No. I didn`t. They didn`t seem to be that interested." He hugged Kay and then Charity. "They put Ned in the station corral and I need to bust him out. What`s all this?" he said looking at the flyers.

They both held them up and Deke broke out in a laugh. "I wouldn`t have thought of that."

"It was Charity`s idea," Kay said.

Deke stopped for an awkward moment trying to think of what to say and then looked off into the distance, "Flowers that think. What will the prairie sprout next?" Then before the women could react, "I`ve got to go get Ned, and my things. Place like this someone might run off with the saddles."

The women sat at the corral and watched the horses and tack while Deke fetched his bags. When he came back, he said, "They`ve been locked up for a couple of days. They need exercise. Want to go out for a ride?"

"We`re not dressed for it," Kay said, looking down at her dress.

"Then let`s get your clothes."

They walked back to the hotel leading the horses, trying hard to avoid the traffic. Ned wasn`t pleased with some of the things that rolled by, hissing steam and trailing smoke. Deke had a tendency to rubberneck too, which didn`t help. Then they all stopped to stare when a lady rolled by on a two wheeled contraption that was driven forward with a foot crank.

"Damn!" Deke said.

"Why doesn`t it fall over?" Charity asked, half to herself.

They tied the horses up to the hitching bar in front the hotel and Deke got himself a room while the women changed. He was sitting on the boardwalk leaning against a post peeling apart a piece of straw when they came down. He looked up and smiled and Kay felt like a warm spring breeze after a cold winter. She was glad he had made it back.

They made their saddles with little trouble and headed for the edge of town. Even though they had ridden from the Missouri River to Kansas City, Kay still felt unsure. It had been awhile since they had ridden. She could feel her horse under her wanting to speed up.

"So do you remember how to trot?"

"Nooo," they both moaned.

"My back still isn`t right from the last time," Charity cried.

They practiced, and the horses exercised, and when the women cried "Enough!" they stopped and Deke decided to take a look at Charity`s new gun.

"Colt single action. A genuine piece of history. Not well cared for. Wonder if it shoots."

They found the side of a hill and Deke pulled back the hammer and let go a round. The noise and smoke made everyone, horses included, except Deke, jump.

"You sure know you shot something. Any more cartridges for this? That was the last round."

Apparently the other five rounds had been used by its previous owner and Charity never thought to look. She didn`t have any more cartridges, so they decided to see what they could do about it. Kay had her list and they had horses so getting there was easy.

The first store owner had nothing like what Kay wanted except sympathy for her search. The second though, struck pay dirt. He didn`t have a Webley, but he did have a short barrel Colt double action, which was practically the same thing, and frankly a fair bit cheaper.

The women, with the careful help of Deke, shot a box of cartridges each on the shop practice range. Charity didn`t take to guns like Kay, perhaps because she didn`t have three older brothers to egg her on like Kay had growing up. She couldn`t stop wincing when she fired, but she was a trooper, knowing that they couldn`t have gotten through the dangers they had faced without Kay`s gun. Then they sat down and worked on learning to disassemble and clean them.

Charity sold her old gun to the store owner for $30. As soon as he had it, he set about cleaning and working it over, tut tutting and tisking the whole time. It kind of made Charity feel bad for being negligent even though she had never actually fired it herself.

For dinner that night they decided to try Chinese. The restaurant had more of that furniture. They had beautiful lacquered inlayed panels on the wall. The food all seemed to be fried, even the vegetables, which was a nice change. Their waiter was a real Chinaman, with the oddest eyes and a narrow ponytail pulled tight on the back of his head. He spoke English with only a slight accent, and he explained everything on the menu with practiced patience born from long trainloads of out-of-town visitors.

Kay had decided that the time had come that she should be getting around to what she came to Denver to do, so she said, "Now that we`re all here, I think it`s time I started looking for my Papa." She still had the letters and map, having carried them in one bag or another all the way from Philadelphia and she pulled them out for the others to read.

"He found a gold mine!" Charity said, who`s ears were still ringing from the shooting range.

"Shhhhhh!" Deke said. "You don`t say things like that out loud in a place like this." Deke looked around and thought that perhaps some of the diners looked a little more attentive.

"That`s not important," Kay said.

"Yes it is," Charity said.

"It`s probably gone or taken or who knows what. That was 10 years ago. My Papa is what`s important!"

"We don`t know where he wrote this last letter from or if he even got to Denver," Charity said.

"I wish I had the envelope, the postmark might have helped, but I figure that the place to start is here since this is where he was headed and the only place we`re sure about. I was thinking that since he thinks he found a mine, he might have gone to somebody to see if he really found gold."

"We need to know more about mining. We ought to learn how to be miners. Maybe someone can teach us," Deke added.

"Why would we do that?" Charity asked.

"Because then we would know more about where he had had to have been and where he had to go."

Kay laughed, "Deke, you are the best."

Deke looking embarrassed, and Charity rolled her eyes.

They decided to ask at the front desk. "Don`t know," the clerk said. "Never been a miner. You might want to ask at an assay office though."

"And where is that?" Deke asked.

"You have to be careful. There are a fair number of places around here that do assaying and give mining assistance, but most I`m told are swindles. There`s an official government assay office, but I`d be careful there too. Most of the government around here is in the pay of somebody or other. It`s kind of the way business gets done."

She got the general location of the official assay office from the desk clerk and then they went to bed. It took a while for Kay to fall asleep. She wanted to start the chase. But the sun and the moon have no mercy, morning comes when it comes and waiting doesn`t help, so eventually she gave up and fell asleep.

They woke early and dressed for riding. Knocking on Deke`s door brought no answer, so they went down to the lobby. There slumped in a chair, staring at the toes of his boots, sat Deke.

"Hello," Kay said.

Deke looked up and smiled. "Morning," and touched the edge of the brim of his hat with the tips of his first two fingers.

Kay sat down next to him and Charity leaned over them on the back of the seat. "Been up for a while?" Kay asked.

"A bit," He looked over at her from his reclining slouch with a half-smile. "Been watching people."

That seemed to Kay as a bit unusual until she realized that Deke probably didn`t get in to large towns like this often and that they were probably a bit of a mystery to him. She looked out in the street through the windows and door at the people moving back and forth.

"They are an odd bunch," she said. "You feel like breakfast?"

"Yup."

They found eggs, bacon, and bread in a saloon, on the way to the stables. They`d smelled it as they passed the door. Five other people sat at tables eating too. They all looked like they had jobs and probably ate there every day and drank there every night.

At the stables Ned tried to search Deke for apples, but Deke had none. The stables were too close to downtown, the markets were all around the edges of the city where the normal people lived. Deke had to promise Ned they`d get some.

Riding around town on her own horse was about the finest way Kay could think to spend a sunny morning, it actually felt kind of nice. Maybe she was getting used to it. She thought about going to the Opera with Deke, about him dressed up, giving his hat to the doorman, and started to laugh, which brought questioning looks from her compatriots.

"It`s nothing," she said. "I was thinking about the opera."

"It`d be great to go, but what would we wear?" Charity asked.

"And what would we do with it after?" Kay added.

"Wear`em of course! I can see you ladies riding through the mountains in your dresses." It was Deke`s turn to chuckle. "The Indians would write songs about you. They`d probably capture you just so they could prove they weren`t telling tales. Trappers would think they`d seen fairies or something."

"We could be mountain sprites! They would invite us down to bless their fields," Kay said, getting in the spirit.

"Or trap us and try to skin us," Charity said, with a mock frown.

The assay office had a front counter. Behind it were two desks, some counters, and shelves. There was a door to a back room that looked like it had some kind of laboratory in it.

"Oh!" Charity cried, and pointed.

One wall`s shelves were filled with assorted crystals and rocks. The slanting morning sun raked across some of the lower shelves and they glittered with color. That pulled an "Oh!" from Kay and a "Whoa!" from Deke as well.

There was a thin young man with golden brown hair, sideburns, and a moustache sitting behind one of the desks writing something down at a furious pace on a piece of paper. His desk was littered with paper. "Hello!" he piped, trying to finish his paragraph. "Yes, they`re nice aren`t they? People bring them in and sometimes we give them a little money. It`s a good collection. All local." He kept on writing while the others strained to see the rocks from the counter. "Be with you in a moment," he added. He was clearly coming to an end and then with a flourish he landed a period and said, "Yes!"

He stood up in triumph and walked over to the counter. "Want to see them?" They all nodded. "It`s ten cents." And then he laughed at their wide eyes. "It`s free! In fact I love to look at them myself. Wouldn`t have become a geologist if I didn`t." He started pulling some of them down and setting them on the counter. "Most of these are from before I started working here. Lloyd can tell you more. He`s been here since the office opened. I can tell you, the ones he keeps for himself put these to shame."

"Is this gold?" Kay asked.

"Ha, everyone makes that mistake at least once. That`s pyrite. Nice crystals too. You can get gold mixed in with them though. We`ve had gold crystals in here, but everyone always melts them down. Too bad really. They`re rare."

Charity stared at a swath of pink crystals.

He saw her and put his face down at the same level as her`s and looked across the crystals at her and said, "Amethyst. Makes pretty jewelry, although it can fade in the sun eventually."

There was a clear crystal as big has his thumb. He saw Kay looking at it, smiled and said "Quartz. Fairly common, but still a nice one."

Deke began to get the idea that he was being ignored.

"What makes them pink?" Charity asked.

"Iron, but it has to form just right. Most times iron just stains things brown."

"Could it stain this one?" Kay asked, pointing at the large quartz crystal.

"Sure, that`s what amethyst is. Some people feel the best ones are purple, but frankly I like the pink, especially if there`s variation of color in the crystal itself."

"What`s this?" Deke asked.

The man glanced at it, "It`s an agate."

Yup, Deke thought, I`m being ignored. Deke turned his eyes to the man`s desk. There were at least two dozen hand written pages.

"Is quartz always clear or pink?"

"Heck no," he said with new enthusiasm and pulled down some new rocks. "There`s citrine and prasiolite, neither of which we get around here, which is a pretty clear yellow and the other's green. Then you get these solid blocks of crystal with no form at all, usually white, which we call milky quartz. Sometimes it can be brown, grey, or pink too, just like the crystals."

"What are you writing?" Deke asked.

The man frowned at him, clearly embarrassed. "A story." He moved quickly to his desk and started stacking his papers.

"You write?" Charity asked.

"Yes. At least I`m trying to."

"Can we read it?" Kay asked.

He pushed the paper stack in a drawer. "No. It isn`t ready."

"You know," Charity said, with a smile. "We don`t know your name."

He laughed, "That's true! Joseph Jukes, U.S. Geological Survey. And you?"

"Charity."

"And Kay."

"And Deke," Deke added.

"We want to learn how to mine," Charity said.

Jukes looked sideways at Deke for a moment. "For a moment with you ladies, I`d teach you how to dig tunnels to China."

CHAPTER 17

Jukes was every bit the flirt he seemed he seemed and very secretive about his writing. His attention for the women never wavered. When Deke asked him about it in a rare moment where they were alone, Jukes said, "Honest single women may be as common as apples on trees back east, but out here they`re a rare event and I don`t intend to let two gems like these just walk by."

That left Deke a little worried. This man had a university education and a job with the government. He`d be tough competition.

Joe had asked them out for a horse ride picnic the next day, his official day off. They met, at Joe's suggestion, for breakfast at a bakery that had a little shop with tables. It smelled like heaven. The shop sold tea, which pleased Kay a lot.

"It comes over the mountains from San Francisco. They ship it compressed into black bricks. We should ask. It`s an interesting process to see. The bricks get broken up into chunks and get put it in a grinder. Then they put some in a tin cup filled with holes, pour hot water over it until it`s submerged. Then it steeps," Jukes said.

The baker himself was behind the counter and Kay heard an accent when he talked that kind of rang a bell. When she asked it turned out the baker was Italian! Kay asked if he knew how to make spaghetti and the baker smiled and said yes, he made it for his family.

"I make it in big batches. We dry the noodles and can the sauce so we can store them at home. Tomatoes are hard to find, so we make a lot of it when we can. Shipments have to come over the mountains. I could make some for you sometime, but not today. We're a bit busy."

She instead had bun with a spicy sausage and gravy inside it. It was heaven too.

"Bread strings?" Joe said. "Sounds interesting. We`ll have to have dinner together."

Deke was quiet through the meal while Joe expounded on the wonders of the local mountains.

"We`re going to see the Forest Queen mine. It`s close by and owned by a local, Lou Blonger," he said. "It`s a large established operation, both placer and hard rock, so you should be able to see just about all the facets of mining."

Before they left they bought more meat buns for lunch and apples at a market on the way out. Deke handed both the women apples. "Give them to your horses. Let them know you`re friends."

"Nonsense. Horses come and go. Spoil them and they`ll give you trouble," Joe said. Deke just shook his head and said nothing.

They rode out of town and up a rutted road that wound through stream filled grey rock canyons. The sun was hot and the air dry and there was no shade. Kay could see patches of color speckling the rocks and even on some of the scrubby little trees that worked their way out of cracks in the rock.

She asked Deke what the colored patches were, but he shook his head. "I don`t know an English word for it. Most Indians around here would call it, in the general sense, <u>utsaleta</u>."

"It`s lichen," Joe said.

"It pulls rocks apart and deer will eat some kinds," Deke continued. Then to himself, "Lichen." Deke rolled the word around in his mouth and seemed satisfied.

They crested a rise and the road dipped again into a valley. It's floor was a mess, with piles of rubble everywhere. The stream meandered between the debris mounds, dirty and dead, filled with silt. At the back end of the valley there stood a town of wood shacks.

"Now keep in mind that these are miners. Some of them aren`t bright. Most of them are a bit coarse, so please try to ignore their language. It`s apt to be fairly vulgar, although with you women here it might be different."

"Did all this come out of the mine?" Charity asked.

"Yes, from the riffle tables to be precise. The ore is crushed as fine as possible then mixed with mercury and water, then run down the riffle tables. The mercury sticks to the gold and is heavy and easy to separate. It will make sense when you see it. The crusher isn`t running right now or you`d hear it. This operation is big enough that they have their own. Smaller mines send their ore out to be processed, often to a larger mine like this. There`s only one other mine nearby, the Independence Mine, and they`re bigger than this, but there`s a lot of placer operations and they sometimes send their work here for processing. Over in Cripple Creek, they share a processing plant."

"Placer?" Charity asked.

"Oh, it`s a different kind of mine. It`s the same thing only you`re digging up dirt, not rock. You don`t generally have to crush it. And because they use mercury to process the ore, don`t touch the water in the stream. It`s poison."

The mine consisted of several door-sized openings in the side of the hill, each framed with wood. There were railroad tracks coming out the holes and over to a cliff above a large building. As they approached, they saw three men push a metal box on wheels out of the mine, rolling on the tracks. It was filled with rock. Two men came out of a house near the road with rifles resting across their arms and walked slowly towards the them. One of the men called in a wary voice, "Howdy Joe. Who`re your friends?"

"Vacationers. They want to see a mine."

As they got closer, the man who had hailed them snorted and said, "I see why you brought them up."

"He knows you," Deke said.

Joe yelled back, "Is Beauchamp in a capable mood?"

"He was last I looked."

"He in his office?" Joe asked.

"Was, don`t know now."

They rode by the men with rifles towards the shack village.

"Why are they so tense?" Kay asked.

"They`re mining gold. There`s probably a third rifle here someplace we can`t see."

"Behind them in the window," Deke said. Deke

had spotted his movement in the window as they had approached.

Joe turned in his saddle and peered up at the window, "Oh yes, there he is."

They tied their horses to a rail in front of a shack and Joe banged on the door. Inside they heard a growl. "Who is it?"

"Joe Jukes, with visitors."

"Come." Joe opened the door. Inside, sitting at a desk piled with paper, sat an unshaven, unbathed man with a hard round face and receding hair. He was sitting there with no shirt, just his suspenders and union suit. There was an open bottle of whiskey sitting amongst the paper. When he saw the women he picked up the bottle and put it on the floor, but they could still smell it.

"What's up Joe?" he said, with a frown. "Who is this?"

Kay was tired of being "referred to" so she decided to take the bull by the horns.

"Kay Mapleton, and this is Charity Carmichael and Deke Hayden."

"Mapleton? I heard vacationers." His eyes seemed to acquire focus.

"Actually we're here looking for my Papa. He was a miner when he disappeared, so we thought that maybe learning a little about mining might help us to know where to look."

"Did he have a name?"

"Nathan Mapleton."

Beau sat there stiffly for a second looking at his desk and then said, "Nope. Can't remember any Nathan Mapleton's. You can look at the mine though. You know this Joe, ask the foreman before going in the tunnel." He paused and then said, "Oh, and don't take anything. No samples unless the foreman looks at it first."

So Joe showed them the crusher and the riffle boxes, where the tailings came out, how the ore was rolled over and dumped in the ore bin. He explained the rock formation, pointing out the surrounding layers in the rock face, and then took them to look at the tunnels. The foreman was coming out the closest entrance. When he heard that they had been given permission, his eyebrows went up and he said, "Beau gave you permission? He must either be sober or drunker than usual. I`ll be happy to show you a little bit, but it`s dangerous in there. There`s some crystals we want to take out, as soon as we can figure out how, which I think you will want to see. The problem is to do it without breaking them," he said nodding at Joe.

Inside, they had carved a little room that held boots, coats, gloves, and such. Above the coats they saw a shelf lined with helmets, each with little can on top. "You know what to do, Joe," said the foreman. He and Joe took down helmets and twisted open the cans on top. The foreman took down a larger can which he opened. Inside they could see grey powder. He scooped some into the helmet can on the helmet he was holding. "Carbide," he said to Kay with a smile. He passed the powder can to Joe, then picked up something that looked like an oil can. It turned out to have water in it, which he dashed onto the grey powder in the helmet can. The powder immediately began to bubble. Screwing the top on quickly, he struck a match and held it to a little shiny dish on the front. A bright white flame popped out the center of the dish shining light from the front of the helmet. He put it on Charity with a grin and said, "Strap it on."

When they all had their helmets on, in they went. The foreman explained that ore mines try to tunnel over, under, and around the vein, eating into it from around the edges until the vein is used up. He showed them different grades of ore, the seam of quartz with thin streaks.

Charity asked, "Is that gold?"

"Mostly pyrite, but there`s gold in it. We blast the quartz out in pieces with dynamite."

Then he showed them a side tunnel. At its entrance he pointed to strips of small purple crystals in the wall. "There was an air cavity here so we thought there might be more." They had to stoop to go in, but low to the floor, in the back of the tunnel there was a long crevice filled with thumb sized amethyst crystals. "If we can get it out, it`ll be worth more than week`s worth of product back east at auction." He shook his head and sighed. Then he took off his helmet, reached in and set it inside the cavity. The crystals glowed purple pink. They sat there entranced until Kay`s light went out.

"Oops, time to go back," the foreman said. As they left the side tunnel, he stopped and wacked off two chunks of the small crystals and gave them to the women. They thanked him profusely.

"I`ve never had anything so pretty," Kay said.

"That`s a shame," then cocked his eyebrow at the men.

"They`re so beautiful," Charity said, rocking her piece back and forth in the lamplight.

At the top, the men all shook hands and they all thanked the foreman. Then it was back on the horses and back to town.

When they had gone, Beauchamp walked out of his office wearing a shirt. He walked over to the foreman and asked, "They gone?"

"Yup."

"Good. I`ll be going in to town tonight, won`t be back until tomorrow."

"Sure thing, Boss."

The foreman watched him meander towards the stables and then said to himself, "Now what`s gotten into him?"

Lou Blonger sat bare chested in his carved and padded desk chair, leaning forward over his carved mahogany desk, in his mahogany paneled office while a young woman wearing a corset and little else worked his shoulders. His eyes were closed in bliss.

"Closer to the center. Yesss. That`s it," he moaned.

His cigar sat in its dish sending up a golden ribbon of uninhaled smoke in the lamp light. Next to it sat a decanter and a single small glass of golden liquid. The woman rubbing Blonger`s shoulders could see the lights of the room reflected in its contents. She thought of home and how much she wished she could be there.

There was knock on the door and Blonger`s eyes opened and he frowned.

"This had better be good!" he called.

"Boss," called a voice. "Beau is downstairs. Says he has some ace news for you."

"Tell him to wait. I`ll be down in a bit," Blonger growled back.

He tried to regain that bliss, the woman worked his shoulders, but he just couldn`t get there. He was curious. So he shooed the woman away, downed his drink without tasting it, pulled on his shirt, picked up his cigar and headed downstairs.

Beau watched Lou come down. He admired his affable stance, the friendly crinkle of his eyes, his harmless paunch. He wasn't called the king of the confidence men for nothing. Lou was a man you wanted to trust. Those who knew him knew better.

"This better be good," he said, pointing his cigar at Beau. Beau smirked unafraid, which peaked Blonger`s interest.

"You remember The Rose," he said.

"Yeah, that vein in rose quartz. It was sweet, but now it`s gone," he paused. "You`re telling me it isn`t gone?"

"Maybe," he said. "Mapleton had a daughter and she`s in town looking for him. She`s interested in mining. Jukes had her and some friends up at the Queen today."

That brought silence from Blonger, and then a small growing smile. Beau though he looked like Santa Clause, before he tucked into a bloody steak. Lou took a thoughtful puff of smoke from his cigar. "I wonder if she needs some help," he said, letting the smoke roll out.

Lloyd Stickney had been sitting in that same termite riddled desk in the middle of the same God forsaken hell hole of a town on the far side of nowhere doing the same job for fourteen years. He had made little from it in any form that had come to him honestly. He had learned early on the simple facts of life. The government paid its employees what it considered a living wage. A living wage perhaps, for someone willing to sit chewing cud until the day they led him into the barn.

He stared at his shiny new assistant fresh from back east, clueless and inspired. Stickney wondered how long it would take for the shine to come off. How many chumps, yahoos, and gawking bumpkins was it going to take before he wised up. At the moment he was bubbling about girls, mine trips, and Italian dinners, which at least was a change from the stupid stories he was always writing. Lloyd sighed. It was 11:08 and he was fed up. "Joe, I`m going to lunch. Watch the desk."

"Yeah Boss?"

Lloyd pushed back his seat, lifted the board that got him past the counter, and ambled out into the street, the wood of the sidewalk creaking under his feet as he walked. Down the street, past the barber, and into his favorite saloon. Bud the bartender was polishing a glass behind the bar and nodded to him as he entered.

"Beer?" the bartender called.

"Yup," Lloyd replied.

He sat down in his favorite seat and waited for the glare from the street to clear from his eyes. Bud brought him over his beer. He slurped the warm suds from the top and enjoyed the taste. A shadow passed through the door and walked over to his table and sat down. There was Louie the Louse or sometimes Little Lou, actually Louis Worter, but among his acquaintances, when he wasn`t in the room, he was just known as "The Louse".

"Hi Louie. Why`d they let you out so early?" Lloyd said.

"Lou wants to see you. Has work for you." Louie nodded at the bartender and who started to pull another glass of beer. Bartenders hated Louie. They all paid Lou protection and Louie being so close to him, didn`t have to pay.

"When," Lloyd asked.

"Now," Louie replied.

"Can I finish my beer?"

Louie smiled. "Probably."

Lloyd looked down at his beer and sighed the sigh of the damned. He tipped it back and managed about a third of the glass and then rose. "Hurry up and die Louie," he said.

Louie smiled. "You first, Lloyd."

Lloyd left the nickel on the bar so Louie couldn`t steal it and headed back out into the sun. Lou Blonger lived, when he was in town, in the town's best dance hall, the La Femme Peinte, dead center downtown. Naturally, he owned it, like he owned most everything else in one way or another. He kept an apartment upstairs in the back amongst the harem of dancers who worked the hall. The main hall had a fresco, which is what Lou called it, a painting on the ceiling full of angels and little angels called cherubs. The angles were all women of course and most of them seemed to have clothing problems. The cherubs wore nothing at all. He had to admit, it was a nice show.

The hall was closed, since it was the middle of the day. The latest debt slave was spiritlessly sweeping the floor. Backstage there were two seamstresses working on the costumes. He went up the steps two at a time. Down the hall, the guard at the door nodded to him, got up and knocked lightly on the door. Another man, Ian Gleeson, opened and peered out. Lloyd could smell the cigar smoke. "Finally here," Gleeson said.

"If anyone took his time, it was the Louse."

"Just let him in," called Lou from inside.

Blonger was sitting behind his big desk. He didn`t invite Lloyd to sit, so Lloyd just stood. Lou made him wait, as was his custom with everyone. Finally, "Lloyd, I have a little job for you."

"Name it," Lloyd replied

"That assistant of yours is seeing a girl by the name of Kay Mapleton. I need information about her. Who her friends are, where they're going, where they're staying, although that last one I`ll probably know soon."

"Sure," he said. There really wasn`t any other answer for Lou.

"Be interested, listen, report."

"Sure."

"Daily," Blonger said.

"Sure."

"I`m fairly sure we'll have more for you to do later."

"Sure."

"See Gleeson, that`s what I like. No wasted talk," Lou said, looking over at Gleeson with a smug smile.

"Anything else?" Lloyd asked.

"No, you can go."

And so he went.

Grace crept between shadows down the dark corridor. Lou the Bastard liked carpeting, the thickest most expensive kind, and she was grateful for the help it gave her with the creaks and pops in the wood floor. It didn`t help though with the sound of the building settling as she moved. She just took it slow.

She had made it all the way down to the end of corridor, where she could see the moonlight glinting from the kitchen knife in her hand, before she heard anyone stir. The floor creaked before the knob turned on Gisella`s door. Grace leaned back into the dark corner. The door opened showing a middle aged woman in a long night dress holding a single candle in a pewter candle holder. She turned away from Grace and headed down the corridor. Where could she be going?

Gisella was the assistant madam. She kept watch on the girls and made sure they had what they needed, like new stockings, makeup, or abortions. She locked the doors at night and opened them in the morning. Her being awake and moving meant no good. When she had gone down the stairs and her candlelight had gone, Grace eased the window at the end of the hallway open and slipped out on the roof. The split wood shingles were rough on her feet and she was certain she would have splinters, but she had no shoes that were functional. Even those were left downstairs backstage because they belonged to the company. She carefully closed the window back the way it had been.

Lou`s bedroom was across and up the silver lit roof, on the third story, its windows in shadow. She crept upwards along the edge of the roof, where the third story wall abutted it in the hopes that it would better hold her weight. Up to the corner and then across to the windows. There were two, both looking in on Lou`s bedroom. The night was warm so they were both open a bit. She edged along to the first window and tried to lift it, holding her breath as if that would make it quieter, but the thing was stuck. She`d pulled on one side and now it was crooked in its frame. She thought about standing in front of it to lift it like a person normally would, but she would be silhouetted in the window. So she tried to push it from below. There really was no choice. Creeping under the window, she lifted it with both hands pushing from beneath.

She never knew what it was, perhaps the clumsiness of her position crouched low, trying to push up from below, or perhaps it was just that claptrap roof and it`s dry shingles, but her foot went out from under her and she was down and sliding towards the two story drop at the end, making a racket all the way. She tried for the gutter at the edge but it came loose in her hands and followed her down.

Lou followed the guards down to see what the noise had been. There broken on the ground was Grace, kitchen knife on the ground beside her. "Looks like

Jessie was a bit unhappy about Nakota," Jessie being Grace`s hall name. Nakota was the name for a breed of horse, bred and sold by the Dakota Indians. They are known for their even ride and endurance. It was also the hall name of Grace`s best friend Amanda who had died of fever. She had been turned out by Lou so she wouldn`t infect any of the other girls and had been found dead in an alley. She had been too sick to make it to a flop house.

Lou looked down at Grace`s broken form. He slowly shook his head at the waste. "Dump her outside of town. Oh, and don`t worry about any marks," which meant that the guards could do anything they wanted. She`d be found in a few days, another mystery death, and a warning to others.

So the guards got a wagon and rode her through the dark early morning streets. Then when they hit the empty field they pulled her out the back into the dirt and had their way. In the end, she looked bad enough that the job seemed done. Piling back on the wagon, they rode back into town to drink until dawn.

CHAPTER 18

When they were out of earshot of the mine, Deke said, "There`s something wrong there."

"You think so?" Joe said. "Beau is a mean drunkard, but he`s always seemed straight to me."

"He was lying. I think he knew Kay`s Papa."

"Why would he lie?" Kay asked.

"Knowing Beau," Joe said. "If he was lying, it was probably out of pure cussed laziness."

"I would say, maybe we could get him drunk, but it`s already too late," Deke said, which got a laugh.

"So you`re looking for your Papa?" Joe asked.

"Yes," Kay said, and she told him the story about his last letter, leaving out the part about striking it rich.

"Finding him out here will be hard. People go missing a lot. You figure that learning a little about mining will help you to know where to look?"

"That was the general idea," Kay said.

"I can help you there a bit. If Beau did know something, others will too. You need some introductions I think. Maybe we should go visit the Independence next."

Joe left them at the hotel, but not before bowing and kissing the women`s hands.

As they were walking upstairs, Deke stopped, "Should I kiss your hands too?"

Both women laughed, took his arms at the elbow, and escorted him upstairs.

Deke really enjoyed their warmth next to him, but when Kay gave him a little kiss on the cheek before they left for their rooms, Deke nearly fainted.

Deke woke in the early dawn, as was his habit and stretched. He really enjoyed this bed. Good beds were something he could get used to. He could see his room in the dim blue morning light. It was a quiet room with a window that opened and let in the breeze. He could get used to that too. Kay wouldn`t be up for an hour at least, more likely two, so he had to decide what he wanted to do with himself. He thought for a bit and decided the horses could use a run, so he dressed, pulled on his boots and went out in the dim streets to the stables.

They were awake and starting their morning chores. He called to the stable boy up in the loft shoveling down hay.

"I`m taking our horses out for a run."

The boy took a close look at him and felt satisfied he was who he seemed, and nodded his head. That was enough for Deke and he went to the rack and found his tack. Ned, the greedy thing he was, immediately began a search for apples, of which Deke had none.

"If you`re good, I`ll bring you some later," Deke promised.

Ned wanted out. Deke had to be firm to keep him still while he saddled him. Next he pulled out the mares and then, mounting Ned, led them to the street. It was cool but not cold, which promised another day of heat. The street was mostly empty so he left at a trot.

Down the street, towards the river, past the edge of town he could see one of the great zeppelins leaving the city aerodrome, huge and grey in the distance, too far away to hear its engines. Painted on the side were the words "Trans-America". Someday maybe he could ride in one of those too, he thought. He made the edge of town and turned off the road into a field of grass.

He had tied the mares up to an old tree and was going to run Ned when Ned stopped instead, all by himself. Deke looked around. He hadn`t brought his guns being as he was in town. He didn`t want to find out what this was so he tried to turn Ned, but Ned wouldn`t go. Deke watched Ned`s ears, as he was clearly listening. Then he heard it too – a cough. Off to the right, he could see that someone had ridden a wagon through there recently. Then he caught a whiff of blood.

There she was, a bloody and battered woman, laying heaped in the trampled grass. Deke leapt down from Ned and knelt beside her. She was a mess. Whatever wasn`t cut was bruised. By its bend, she had at least a broken leg and maybe more. Her head turned slowly and she looked at him with one eye.

"You need more help than I can give you. I`ll be back. Just hold on and you`ll be all right," he told her. He didn`t know if she understood. She just closed her eye.

Deke leapt up on Ned and they took off like a bullet for town. He was back in the streets in less than three minutes, but once there he stopped. He had no idea who to ask for help.

Down the block there was a bread wagon making slow progress down the street. Deke galloped towards it. Inside sitting on the bench was an old man. Deke could smell the bread.

"There`s someone hurt, I need a doctor and a wagon!"

"Dr. Balderson, two blocks that way," and the man pointed. "Something wrong?"

"No time!" He took off down the street until he saw the doctor`s name on a small swinging sign over the street, Dr. Nathan Balderson, General Practice. He left Ned to trust and banged on the doctor`s door. After a moment a man in a robe came and opened it. He was holding a mug of something steaming.

"There`s a woman hurt. Hurt bad!"

"A woman eh? Where is she?"

"In a field just outside of town."

"Oh," he said in a dead monotone. He shook himself just a little, then pointed himself in the right direction and said, "Let me pull on some clothes." He called inside, "Zeb! Zeb!"

Deke heard a young voice inside, "I'll go hitch up the carriage."

"Go around the back and I'll meet you there. You'll have to go down to the end of the street and come around," he said to Deke.

"Thanks!"

Deke and Ned took off down the street and around towards the alley. Deke could see a barefoot boy hitching up a mare to a light wagon in back of the Doctors house. He had to pull off a feedbag before he could get the harness over the horse's head. Ned skipped nervously back and forth while the doctor piled some bags in the carriage and Zeb tossed in some shoes, and then they were off.

Deke led them out of town and across the field. The mares were still tied to the tree and she was still where he left her. Hopping down from Ned, Deke knelt down by the woman. She was still breathing. There was so much damage, he didn't know what to do, where to start.

Dr. Balderson's carriage pulled up and he hopped down and knelt next to Deke.

"Damnation!" he said. "This is Blonger's work. It's good you found her in the morning. We've got to get her back into town before anyone sees. I've got to set these bones before we move her though. Be ready to hold her down." He went back to the carriage and brought down a satchel.

Opening it up, he pulled out a black leather case. Inside was an evil looking contraption, almost as bad as the horse doctor's bone saw. It was a glass tube with a vicious looking needle attached. The doctor took out a bottle of liquid and poured some into the glass tube, then stuck in a plunger. He tipped the thing back, squeezed the air out, and then stuck it in her thigh. Deke was horrified and fascinated. The doctor squeezed the fluid into her leg!

"We`ll give it a minute." He went back to the wagon and pulled out splints and bandages, these at least Deke recognized. The Doctor looked up at Deke and said, "Get ready, I`m going to straighten her leg. There's no telling if the anesthetic will take." And then to Zeb, "Zeb go and get the stretcher."

The doctor pulled her leg straight and squeezed her leg with his other hand trying to make sure the bones went back together in the right way. Then he set to binding it. Zeb showed Deke how to pull open the stretcher. Together they carried it over and set it down next to the woman. The doctor, as he finished wrapping the splints, said "Zeb, show him where to lift."

Working together, they lifted her onto the stretcher, and then the stretcher onto the wagon.

"We better cover her," the doctor said, and Zeb pulled a big tarp over the back of the wagon.

"Why cover her?"

"She`s one of Blonger`s. She was probably meant to die. If he finds out we helped, then we`ll all be in a world of trouble and she`ll be dead. Go. Meet us at the house."

Phillip Van Cise, an ex-army colonel, was the new first governor of the new State of Colorado. He'd been elected by popular vote, without the support of Lou Blonger. Lou offered, but Van Cise had turned him down and despite the stuffed ballet boxes, overwhelming advertising, and intimidation, the people of Colorado had elected him.

Now he was governor of a state that had still to raise a militia and taxes, in a city where the police force was owned by Blonger. Van Cise was a brave man, but he was alone. Half his cabinet was in Blonger`s pocket. He didn't expect to live through the day. There were people who supported him, a lot of them, the very ones who had elected him, but they were as yet unorganized and Van Cise, if he wanted to live to see the state born right, had to think of some solutions quick.

His first act as governor was to avoid his new office altogether and to instead send an appeal to the President directly from the telegraph office itself at the rail station. Then he boarded a zeppelin heading east, watching for snipers all the way. Now he was in Washington D.C., waiting to see Abraham Lincoln himself, to see if he could get federal troops to guard his administration until he could get things organized. This was a final judgment. Without them, he might as well not go back.

Pacing back and forth across the reception room, Lincoln`s secretary politely ignoring him, he strained to make out the voices behind the thick oak door to Lincoln's office.

The secretary sniffed as he endured shape shuffling back and forth. People did this often while waiting for the president. Pacing. The secretary, when he had had the room appointed, had provided every comfort he could think of. It was studiously and meticulously equipped with functional seats, shelves of books, electric lights, and ashtrays. And yet most still chose to pace.

Finally, with a rattle of the doorknob and then a thump as the door opened, that made Van Cise jump, two generals came out trailing cigar smoke. They shook their heads with apparent dissatisfaction. One handled his cigar like it could be a weapon, leaving a trail of smoke as he gestured and pointed. "There`s nothing!" he declared. "There can be no changes. We are completely committed!"

"Then we will make do some other way," said a

voice inside. "Good day gentlemen."

They grunted out their goodbyes as the door was closed behind them. Van Cise was not yet invited in, so he resumed pacing. The generals marched down the hallway.

Finally one of the lights on the panel on the secretary`s desk lit. The secretary stood, bowed, and said to Van Cise, "You may enter now."

After all the waiting, Van Cise was strangely reluctant. But he steeled himself. He could not go back. He must have courage. Approaching the door, he turned the handle and entered.

And there he was, stacking papers on a table, tossing out the contents of an ash tray with clear distaste. His office was filled with books, many in small stacks on top of tables or on the floor. There were papers everywhere and a cold teapot next to a stained empty cup.

"You don`t smoke do you?" the President asked.

"No. No sir."

"Good. A vile habit. Good men my generals. The killer spirit we need in these horrible times. But I detest cigars."

"Yes sir."

He started rolling up maps and stacking them. "I am to understand from your letter that you need troops to pacify the remnants of the original territorial government."

Van Cise nodded. "Yes sir."

"I brought that up with my generals. There are not many who would laugh in my face, which is why I respect them, but they have been very clear that they have no troops, no garrisons, no militia, and no reserves."

"Yes sir."

"We are locked at this moment in a great battle which may decide the war. There are no resources that have not been mobilized and committed. Both we and the Rebels are putting everything into this. The fighting stretches across a thousand miles. It`s our grand gamble."

"Yes sir, of course sir."

"But that`s not what you're concerned about is it?" He smiled at Van Cise. "We have a new state to give birth to and if I`m to expect its support in the future, then we need to make sure it gets started out on the right path." He picked up the pile of maps and carried them to an umbrella stand and tipped them in. "I know things that the generals don`t think I know. I know for instance that there are two companies of cavalry at Fort Laramie, which is near you. They are supposed to be resting. Since we are gambling, then why not gamble a little more? The Miners and the Shoshoni may not notice that we've ceased patrols, for little while at least. If I were to lend you one of the cavalry companies I think we could get by, but it could only be for a two weeks. Do you have a way to accommodate them?"

Van Cise felt the knot in his stomach let go.

"Not yet sir, but it will be found," he said, almost in tears.

"Then you must hurry back. I`ll give you access to our telegraph office so you can prepare."

"Thank you. Thank you sir." He was practically bowing.

"Yes, yes, act quickly, decisively! Now wait outside and tell that scarecrow secretary out there to come in."

Kay awoke thinking of Deke. Charity lay in her

bed, a pillow over her head with nothing but her mouth showing. She was a quiet sleeper, for which Kay was grateful. The first rays of dawn leaked between the curtains, crossing over her head lighting motes of dust gold. How could they live? Deke was a ranch hand, which is fine for a loner. If they were together then they would need more. She was at a loss as to how to proceed. These were issues that were supposed to be dealt with by her Father.

Then she started counting the days, but it was hard. These had been the longest days of her life, although there were still longer ones to come. She reckoned she had been on the road for almost a month. She would have to check the newspaper to make sure of the day, but if she had counted right then her birthday was in ten days, July 17th, 18 years old. How old was Deke? That, at least, was something she could ask him.

Pulled herself out of bed and quietly opening the door to the hallway, she made her way down the hall towards the WC.When she made it back, Charity was awake.

"Morning sleepyhead," Kay said.

Charity groaned.

Kay wanted tea. She also needed some idea as to what to do next. They couldn`t sit there in that hotel forever. For one thing, it was expensive. She began to dress. Charity always rose like a corpse from a grave and this morning was no different. She moaned, pulled off her covers, and then slowly willed her limbs to function, eventually sitting up on the edge of the bed, blinking at Kay.

"How do you manage to be so cheerful in the morning?" Charity asked. "I could just fall over and go back to sleep."

"I want tea," Kay said.

"I should try to like it," Charity mumbled.

"Maybe we could find some coffee."

"That coffee we had was nice."

"I want to go to the Bakery. I want spaghetti tonight." And then to herself, "and I wonder if I should show the map to Joe."

"We hardly know him," Charity replied.

"He seemed nice," Kay added slyly.

"He was . . . eager," Charity said, with a smile.

Which brought a laugh from Kay. "That`s him exactly. We`re going to have to find this place and for that we`re going to need maps and maybe someone who knows the area. Joe`s the only one we know, at least so far."

"True, but we don't really know him very well yet."

"I want tea. Get dressed! We can talk about it all at breakfast."

"I should," Charity moaned.

"You could come to breakfast as Lady Godiva!" Kay added brightly.

"The horse wouldn`t fit," Charity sighed.

"I`m going down."

"I`ll be down soon."

Kay left the room and thumped down the stairs, which was nice since no one was near. You can`t thump in a really satisfying way in heels, she thought. Deke was nowhere to be seen and Kay wondered where he was. She sat down in his seat and, thinking of him, stared at the toes of her boots and the people in the street.

CHAPTER 19

Zeb stoked the potbelly stove that set out the back door on the porch outside of the operating area as Deke and the doctor lifted the stretcher onto the table. The doctor began scrubbing his hands and bobbed his head at Deke. "Boy, roll up your shirt sleeves and then scrub your hands and arms." He stepped away from the sink and just shook his hands to get rid of the drops. Picking up a cup from the drainer by the sink and a gallon bottle from the shelf above, he poured a cup full of some kind of foul vinegar smelling potion. Deke looked at it with distrust.

"Zeb, get down a bowl full of bandages. I`m going

to need the needles and silk." Zeb came in carrying two buckets of water and then it was Zeb`s turn to wash.

"Oven`s still warm. Water`ll be hot in ten minutes," Zeb said, over his shoulder as he was scrubbing.

Deke just stood there trying to stay out of the way as they rushed about.

Dr. Balderson pulled down a tray, picked a towel from a roll–top box, laid it flat on top; then he opened a tall square jar with a metal lid and started pulling tools out dripping of what smelled like whiskey. "Young man, get that long–nosed pitcher and fill it from one of the buckets."

Deke picked the pitcher out of the drainer and started to reach for the bucket. "Stop," he said. "Dip it. Don`t touch the bucket."

The doctor laid out his tools in a row on the towel in the tray. He turned to face Grace and said to Deke, "Go around the other side. If she wakes, we may need you."

So Deke stood there and watched as the doctor peeled off the scraps of her clothes, cleaning the blood and dirt off, and then cleaning her wounds, scrubbing them with bandage cloth dipped in the cup of potion. When the wounds were clean, he stitched them closed with the silk thread.

They took her to a small bedroom by lifting the sheet off the table and sliding her back onto the stretcher and then off again onto the bed.

By then half the morning was half over. Deke was ready to call it a day then and there, but then he smelled food. Mrs. Balderson had cooked breakfast! But the big shock was when he stumbled over Kay and Charity in the living room.

"How did you find me?" he asked.

"There aren`t many horses like Ned. We just kept asking," Charity said.

"You were only three blocks away," Kay added. "So I hear you found yourself a new girl?"

Deke stopped, unable to speak.

"I`m teasing you!" Kay said with a smile.

The doctor came out of the workroom and plunked down in a chair with a sigh. "We may all be in a lot of trouble," he said, which got everyone`s attention. "She`s young and pretty, and considering the remnants of her dress she worked in a dance hall, almost certainly for Lou. We have a dilemma."

"Lou?" Deke asked.

"Didn`t think you all were from here," replied Dr. Balderson. "Lou Blonger, he controls everything that goes on here and indirectly half the territory. No, state. We`re a state now." He dropped his head back on the chair and rubbed his eyes with his palms. "Sorry, I`m tired."

"And . . . ?" Kay asked.

"Oh yes." He lifted his head again. "Either she was abducted from Lou, in which case he`ll be interested in knowing her whereabouts, or he did this himself, in which case he`ll want her finished off quietly."

"That`s awful!" Charity said.

"Yes, it is," the doctor said. "There`s worse. She was probably Blonger`s prisoner, either through debt, blackmail, or drugs. Looking at this one, I don`t think it was drugs. He buys orphans and runaways too."

Mrs. Balderson came in, "It`s too early for this kind of talk. Breakfast is getting cold."

"Yes it is," the doctor said. "Sorry Madge."

They all retired to the dining room, where Mrs. Balderson had a big table full of food. Apparently the Baldersons entertained patients and loved ones often.

She brought pancakes, apples, Mormon honey, butter, milk, and happily for Kay – tea from China! They ate and swapped stories about where they came from until they had a better measure of each other. The doctor had come from back east and had been in Denver for 22 years, back when it was just starting out as a little mining town. He knew everybody and everybody knew him.

"So let`s get back to our problem before somebody calls me away. What are we going to do with her?" he said. "She can`t stay here. Somebody will see her and tell somebody else, or even sell us out."

"We`re in a hotel. We can`t keep her there," Kay replied. "But then again we can`t stay there. We`ll run out of money, it`s just too expensive. I wanted to discuss that this morning. I`ve been trying to think about what to do. Maybe we could rent a house or something? Maybe for a month? Then she could stay with us."

"In town or out of town?" Dr. Balderson said. "In town you might get help if he finds her and I`ll be close so I can keep an eye on her. Out of town he might not find her, but I`ll be far away and you`ll be on your own."

"There`s the Widow Hollender`s place," his wife said, as she came in wiping her hands on a towel.

"Yes, I guess that`s a compromise," Dr. Balderson said.

"It has a small stable too, although I`m sure it hasn`t seen any horses in years," Mrs. Balderson added.

"And it doesn`t belong to Blonger. We should ask Ruby. Zeb, after breakfast go find Ruby, ask about boarders and how much she wants. Don`t tell her about the girl, but tell her she needs to talk to me before agreeing."

They heard a knock on the door and Dr. Balderson heaved a deep sigh.

"Doctor! The midwife says there are problems. She says there's bleeding."

"That's important," he said, and he pulled himself up, grabbing his bag as he headed towards the door.

After he left, they all helped clean up and Kay asked Mrs. Balderson how much he charged.

"I don't know what to say," Mrs. Balderson said. "She isn't yours, and I think Nathan has something in mind, but I'm not sure what." She looked worried. "Things are changing here. I think there's going to be a fight. And I think that fool man wants to be in the middle of it."

"We knew he would do something like this. Lincoln might even see him. But there's nothing he can do," Lou said. They were sitting in Lou's lounge, drinks and cigars all around. The cigars, though all lit, lay untouched, and the drinks sat undrunk. The men attending all listened anxiously to Lou's every word.

The girls had been dismissed, and it was time for business. Behind Blonger stood Gleeson and Louie.

"Lou," the sheriff of Denver said. "We tried to get a bead on him. He moved so quickly, like he knew were there." He gripped the arms of his seat. "And we couldn't shoot the ship. It could have caught fire or something and Trans-America would be hacked off."

"No one's blaming you, Duffy," Lou said, with his best reasonable face.

"Thank you, Lou."

"Course your wife needs to show up as agreed to make amends."

"No! Lou. Please."

"We have an agreement and those are the rules."

The sheriff started to sob quietly to himself.

"We need a plan just in case this governor succeeds and gets help. We need to lean on the new House members. I want a majority in my pocket. Micky, that`s your job. Take the old gang out and work the list. Look for levers we can use to move them. Make a list of easy targets in case we have to kill some."

"What could Lincoln do?" he said, half to himself. "There`s Laramie just over in the pass. How many troops does he have? What can he send from Tulsa and Kansas City?"

"Nothing I think," the Mayor replied. "Everything is stripped bare."

"We need to check. I need a count of available soldiers and equipment. Duffy, that`s your job. Send out deputies."

"Yes, Lou."

"Lunney," he said to the mayor. "Make sure that the telegraph office is extra vigilant. I want to know everything that comes through. Oh, and Duffy. Work with Dodds," he said, nodding at the head of the Miner`s Union. "I want to know how many deputies we can raise and how long it will take. We will need arms for them and ammunition, and those old cannon too. Make an inventory. I want to know the cards I can play." Lou was clearly getting excited about the prospects. "And Lunney. I want a plan for seizing the airships at the aerodrome. We could use them to drop dynamite." He burst out laughing.

Joe`s boss asked him about his new girlfriend at work the next day. Lloyd seemed to be in a better mood lately, and Joe welcomed the talk in an otherwise boring office.

"Oh! Lloyd, you`ve got to see them. There`s a tall blonde and a shorter one with wavy red brown hair. Both bright. And they can ride as good as any man I`ve seen."

"Don`t need bright. Riding sounds promising," Lloyd said.

"I bet even you would be impressed."

"When they`re bright, they want to talk. I don`t need talk from a woman."

"I don`t know. I like talking."

"You`ll get tired of it. Trust me."

A customer with a mining claim came in. It was a placer deposit. Stickney eyed it with distaste. It was almost certainly worthless, but he would pass it on to Lou none-the-less. The man had samples to assay, tiring work, but that`s what assistants were for. If it turned out that the man was on to something, Lou would make sure he was herded into the "assistance" system and that he hired Lou`s chosen, bought equipment through Lou`s suppliers, and refined his product through Lou`s refinery. If the deposit turned out to have legs, Lou might even force the man into debt in order to take his stake.

Joe eyed the dubious samples, thinking about how long it would take to fire up the furnace. It was late in the day. "That reminds me. Can I show them your collection?"

"Sure. The key`s in my drawer here."

"Oh, and can I leave early today?"

"Leave early?" They had lab work to do, Lloyd thought.

Joe had been wincing when he asked, expecting a rebuke, but instead he got, "No problem. Where you going?"

Joe was more than a little bit surprised. Why was Lloyd being so nice? "I told you, spaghetti dinner. With the girls."

"Oh yeah. Get lucky."

They closed up the office early and Joe hurried off. Stickney waited a bit and then followed. The kid took off like a bee towards a flower, straight to The Concordia Hotel. Stickney found a saloon across the street with windows, bought a beer, and sat looking at the hotel door. It took awhile for them to come out. Women always did. Besides Joe and the two girls, there was a guy. He looked young, but there was something odd about him. Lloyd couldn`t place him. He was wearing guns. They looked well used and carefully cared for. Lloyd could spot a mark a mile away and this wasn`t one. There was no greed or laziness to take advantage of. And again, once he looked carefully, he didn`t feel easy about the girls either. They were too sure, walked too easy. Their clothes were all function, no frill. These were an odd bunch. Lou would want to know.

"Oh, the week we`ve had," Charity said, spinning as she walked, arms spread, looking up at the sky. But then she stopped and looked at Joe. "Joe." She was dead serious. "It was awful what they did to her!"

"So we`re getting a house for awhile. The hotel is too expensive. Eating out is too," Kay said.

"So we`re staying," Charity added, smiling at Joe.

Joe smiled back and then tripped over a rut. He righted himself quickly though, clearly embarrassed.

They arrived at the bakery, the window lit. They had spaghetti and red wine. The cook brought his family down to the shop and some of the employees brought theirs too. One of the employees played the violin and another played the harmonica. Now you might think this a strange combination, but after enough spaghetti and red wine it seemed that the music flowed like a river. The men danced with the women and the children just jumped on the tables until Kay felt over-heated and had to step outside. She felt someone behind her. She turned around and there was Deke. He put his arms around her and with the care one uses when handling royal china, kissed her in the moonlight, with the music and laughter flowing from inside. She put her arms around him and held him and they stood there with their heads on each other`s shoulders enjoying the smell of each other`s hair.

Joe walked in the office the next morning late and practically floating, if Stickney could have measured it, at least six inches off the floor. "She is wonderful, Lloyd"

"Which one?" Lloyd asked.

"Charity," Joe said.

"The blonde? She`s a girl, kid."

"She is."

"Hmmm. . ." Lloyd said, with a frown. "You`ve got it bad."

"Hum?"

"Yup, it`s bad." Lloyd frowned at him. Despite his callous nature, he was a little worried about his assistant. Even great men had been brought down by this. And though it went against his mercenary nature, the fall of a man disturbed him, especially since Blonger probably had plans to have them killed eventually.

"This will pass, kid. So they`re getting a house?" Lloyd asked.

"Yup."

"Know where?"

"No, not yet."
"Do that lab work."
"Oh! That`s right. I`ll get right to it."

Kay rose from her sleep as if she were riding on a fountain of bubbling laughter. The sunshine never looked better as it leaked in between the curtains. The bed was warm and soft, and her feet sat down there below her just wagging back and forth. She`d never noticed before just how far they had grown away from her. Somehow, just yesterday, they had seemed so much closer. She watched them with amazement as they did what she told them.

She needed to see Dr. Balderson. They had to hide that woman. And what was she going to do with Deke? He couldn`t live with them. It wasn`t proper. But then again, if there was trouble, if that Lou Blonger sent killers, then Deke might be handy to have around.

"Really," she said to herself, "there`s nowhere to go but forward. There`s no choice." So she flipped back the covers and let in the cool air.

Charity heard Kay`s bed springs squeak as Kay sat up on the edge of the bed. She took her first deep breath of the morning, letting out a moan.

"It`s morning," Charity said, pushing back the pillow that was covering her face and blinking at the sunlight. "I dreamt about your bread string last night."

"Was it bad?" Kay asked.

"No. But it was strange."

Kay laughed. "Spaghetti in your dreams. I think it would be."

"Last night was fun." She looked at Kay and smiled. "I saw you kissing Deke."

"Shame on you," Kay said, with mock severity. And then wistfully, "It was fun, wasn`t it?" And then accusingly, "I saw you dancing with Joe."

"I danced with Mr. Benelli too."

"So you did." Kay got up and started dressing. "We should get started. Dr. Balderson is in danger as long as she`s in his house."

"Yes." Charity steeled herself, took a deep breath, then rolled over and put her feet on the cold floor. "We need to hurry. It`s late already."

They dressed, packed, and clomped down the stairs. Deke was sitting in the lobby staring at the street. But when he heard them coming down the stairs he got up and went over to the potbelly stove near the desk and picked up a tin pot, using a rag to hold the handle. Carrying it back to the couch seat, he poured the hot water into a teapot that was sitting on tray beside three tea cups, and two little cups with sugar and milk. He looked up at the women with a smile. "Tea?" he asked.

Kay laughed and hugged him.

Charity said, "Where did you get that?"

"From the restaurant three doors down. I`ll have to take it back when we`re done."

They sat and let it steep for a bit before they poured. A patron walked by, stopped, then turned towards the desk. "Can I have that too?" he asked.

"Sorry, sir, but we don`t serve food. They brought it themselves."

"Dash it. Hotels serving tea in the morning is a great idea." Then he walked on shaking his head.

Serving tea in hotels would be a great idea, Kay thought. Maybe she should open a hotel.

As always, the tea disappeared too quickly and then they were walking, Deke dropping off the tray on the way. When they arrived, the doctor was out. Mrs.

Balderson was there though.

"He`s almost always gone in the morning," she said as she let them in. "People wake up with problems."

"Is Zeb here?" Kay asked.

"I'm afraid he`s asleep. They were up late."

"Is she awake? Can we see her?" Charity asked.

"Not yet. You`ll have to wait for Nathan and ask him."

"Then we`ll go out and come back," Kay said. When Charity eyed her questioningly, she said, "I`m hungry!"

"You will not!" bellowed Mrs. Balderson "I will not hear of it!" and she forced them to sit down in the dining room to eat breakfast.

After about twenty minutes, the doctor himself sat down with them. "Just checked. She`s not awake yet, which is a blessing. She`ll be in a plenty hurt when she does."

Mrs. Balderson proved to be a cornucopia of food, and they rolled back full into the living room. The doctor sat down in his seat as if expecting to have a conversation, but fell asleep immediately. Mrs. Balderson saw him and shook her head. "The poor dear had a long night." But then maybe it was the meal, because Kay dozed off too.

Deke touched her shoulder and said, "Wake up." She looked around. Zeb was there, the doctor was awake, and there was a new man. Deke squatted down next to her and said, "This here is Pete Jarvis. His mother owns the house."

Kay blinked her eyes clear and looked up at him. "Hello Mr. Jarvis, it`s a pleasure." She tried to stand up.

"No no." He waved her down. "The pleasures mine." He had an easy smile. "Nathan tells me we have several problems which might all fit together. I`ve got an empty old house, you need a place, that girl needs a place too, and Blonger needs a poke in the eye. So when you feel up to it, maybe we can take a ride."

They all three rode with Mr. Jarvis around the edge of town for a ways until they came to a two story wood house with a big front porch. It had a yard with a picket fence out front that used to be white and was just about ready to let go of the ground. The windows had glass, which is not always a given out towards the frontier, and a split wood shingle roof that from the outside looked to be sound. As they walked up the front steps the wood creaked but held, and the door lock was simple, but sturdy. Inside it was dark, with dusty curtains covering the windows. Pete pulled them back, which let in light, but also raised a lot of dust.

"The house has been closed up since Ma came to live with me, about six months ago."

Inside they saw that it still had the woman`s furniture, books on the shelves. Kay wondered if there was a copy of *Wives and Daughters*. Upstairs, the bed linen was still on the beds, towels still in the cupboard on the back porch.

"We cleaned out the stuff that had memories, and, of course, the food. But everything is pretty much the way she left it."

They were walking through a bedroom upstairs when Pete pointed at the bed. "I was born on that bed." Kay wondered if it really was that old and what condition the springs were in. She lay down on it carefully. It creaked, but it held. The cover left dust on her clothes. *Maybe he meant the frame*, she thought.

Out in the fenced backyard there was a stable. The stalls had a roof and there was a small shed for tack, but the rest was open air. It looked like there had once been a garden in back, but it had long since dried up and blown away. The outhouse was sturdy. Someone had rebuilt it and the pit was dry, even the flies had long since given up on it and moved on. Lastly they tried the pump, which took a bit of coaxing to get started. The priming bucket was dry so it was brute force until the first rusty slosh of water burped out. It took another five minutes of pumping before the water came out clear.

Altogether it wasn`t the halls of Montezuma, but it was more than enough for their purposes. They agreed on a price that seemed ridiculously low to Kay, especially considering the risk to his property harboring a fugitive from crime would bring, but he seemed pleased to just have someone there to look after things. She was pleased too that he was willing to talk to her instead of Deke.

They shook hands, she paid him, and he gave her the key. Before Pete left, Kay asked about a wash tub and clothes line. The tub was on the back porch and the line and soap in the cupboard above. The soap was in a tin and still good. He showed where the line hooked, both inside and in back. They were going to need clean linen that night.

The rest of the day was spent moving and cleaning. Charity pulled apart beds and started washing while Deke and Kay walked to the stables to get the horses and feed. She needed to talk to him.

"Are you going to stay with us at the house?" Kay asked.

That was a stumper for poor Deke. He didn`t know what to say.

"You have to, " Kay said. "We need you there for protection. If it`s just us alone, they`ll just walk in and take her, and somebody will get hurt. Probably us."

They walked for a bit while Deke mulled this over.

"I promise, I`ll keep my distance," Kay said, seriously.

That brought a snort from Deke, "You`ll promise! It`s me that I`m worried about."

"You know I`ve got feelings for you," she replied, quietly.

"You`re the most beautiful thing I`ve ever seen. Which is a good reason to sleep somewhere else."

Kay smiled at that. "You worried about people talking?"

"No, not really. " Deke paused for a moment and then added, "Except maybe Ned. He`s bad with secrets."

"I know, he told me a couple of things."

Deke turned and gave Kay a look. "When did you talk to Ned?"

Kay laughed at the joke.

"I swear though," Deke said, with a smile. "it`s almost sometimes like he can. You two still haven`t picked names for your horses."

"We should, we will tomorrow. It will be an occasion!"

"As it should be. Naming things is important to the Indians. It`s serious business."

"So are going to stay?"

"Yes."

"Downstairs," she added.

CHAPTER 20

Grace woke up that afternoon in a strange bed, adrift in a sea of pain. She tried to move which hurt so bad she cried out, but that hurt too, just taking that breath. A dark–haired boy rushed into her room, cooing to her and asking her sit still.

"Sit still, sit still," he said. "Or you`ll pull your

stitches. You`re safe. You`re safe. Please sit still.”

She tried, but the pain just kept bouncing all over her. She did her best, but it hurt so.

“Water will help.” He picked up a cup with a metal straw, which he put to her mouth, but her lips felt thick and were stuck to her teeth. She couldn`t get a grip on the straw, so the boy dribbled water in with a rag until she could get it all working. Once the muck was out of her mouth, the water tasted like ambrosia. She never knew water to be so good. He brought her another cup and then a cup of chicken broth that was just warm. It was wonderful.

“We fished you out of a field. You`re at the doctor`s house, but we`re going to move you someplace safe tonight, late.”

A field? Then it came back to her, and she started to panic.

“Stop, stop!” he held her down. “I`m the only one here. You`ll make yourself bleed again.” There was already blood on the sheet.

She saw he was panicking too, and that helped her to calm down, for his sake. “Please stay still. I`ve got to check what you did.” He lifted the sheet and looked at her leg. “That`s nothing. It will need washing again though. I`m sorry, but you`re going to have a scar there.” She could see that he was genuinely sorry, like he had let her down. “There are some things we can`t help. Can you try to talk? It would help if we knew your name.”

“greef.” It came out all wrong. Her face wouldn`t work right. “Grass. Gr-ace.”

“Grace?” He smiled. “Don`t worry. They hit you a lot. That bruising will go away. You`re kind of swollen up a bit. Hey, and you still have your teeth. You have no idea how many people lose them in a fight. People wouldn`t do it if they stopped to think about that."

Grace liked this kid. She wondered where they were going to take her.

He got up and came back with a basin, and some rags, and pulled back the sheet and started washing her. It hurt, it hurt, but not as much as before, and she stayed still. He rewrapped some bandages and then brought a new sheet that didn`t have blood on it.

Where`d he learn to do all that? she thought. Doctor`s son I guess.

She drifted off, and when she opened her eyes it was evening and she could hear voices in the next room. The kid walked by, glanced in and saw she was awake. He called in to the house, "She`s awake!"

There was the thump thump of shoes walking, and then there was a man`s face above. She started to cower away from him, but he just shushed her like he was talking to a skittish horse. "It`s OK, it`s OK. Just sit. You`re safe, you`re safe." He looked at her eyes and then started looking her over. "I`m Dr. Balderson. You are amazing," he said shaking his head. "They tried so hard to kill you, and you know what?" He looked at her eyebrows raised. "I think you`re going to pull through fine. While you`re awake, let`s get more water and broth into you."

He fetched a cup and straw and while she was drinking, he continued. "We`re going to move you tonight to a different place. Too many people come here. Some of them are the wrong kind of people." He looked her in the face and said, "Blink twice if you want to stay away from Blonger." She almost spit out her water, but she managed to blink twice. "Thought so," he smiled.

She must have blacked out again because there were a bunch of people in the room, two new young men, and two young women, and the doctor and his son.

She was lying on the bed and they were all watching as a blonde woman washed her.

"Her name is Grace?" said the short redhead. "That`s the same as my aunt."

"I was always partial to it myself," the doctor said. "Now, you can`t be squeamish around the stitches. That`s the most important part. If it bleeds a little, that isn`t bad," he said, pointing. "At least not at this stage. " They all took turns and she just lay there and watched. She had woken up in a lot of strange places, but this was the strangest. She guessed these were her future keepers.

They wrapped her in sheets and moved her onto a stretcher, put her in a wagon and took her for a painful trip to a big old wood house. When she finally landed, it was in a soft squeaky bed in a pleasant room with a window. The doctor left a bowl, a paper–wrapped bundle of bandages, and some bottles on the dresser. He said good night and that he would be back tomorrow, and there she was. He said she was going to spend at least two months, maybe more, here before she could move on her own.

They moved in and tried to settle as quickly as they could, but there were so many things they needed. It seemed they never stopped going from one store to another.

Kay wrote her aunt about her adventures and gave her the address. She told her about Grace, Blonger and the Baldersons, and how they had found the location of the mine.

Kay, Deke, and Charity, stood around Joe and swore him to secrecy. No one, no one, ever, was to know where they lived, even if they already knew, and no one was to know about Grace, or Blonger would kill them all! And since they were trusting him with Grace, Kay decided that he should know about the map. She was sure he could help.

It`s hard to cook when you don`t have time to keep the stove stoked. It takes a long time to build a fire and heat a big iron stove, so they tended to eat out fairly often. Joe often came along, as he did the night Kay fished out her letters. When he had finished them, she showed him the map piece. He looked at it and sighed.

"It`s a geological survey map. We produced hundreds for Colorado alone."

"We may not need to see them all. Some have to be more likely than others."

"True. We could go look tonight. It has to be after hours, the later the better, or Lloyd will know."

"Too late and they`ll think we`re robbing the place. Then you`ll have to explain."

He frowned. "Also true."

It was midsummer, looking at fall, and the light was waning, but it still stayed light late. That first night Deke stayed with Grace because Joe wanted to show Charity Lloyd`s rock collection, and Kay had to be there for the map. When they got to the office, Joe lit a lamp and pulled out the first map drawer.

"Let`s start with this area since we think he may have been at the Forest Queen."

It was like looking for a single piece in a jigsaw puzzle. Joe took out ten maps and then Kay started going over them, trying to match the piece.

"Come, I want to show you Lloyd`s collection, " Joe said to Charity. "We`ll be back in a minute," he said to Kay.

"I need to stay and help Kay," Charity said.

"No, just go," Kay replied. "There`s only once

piece and extra eyes won`t help much. At least they won`t help until I get tired."

So Joe got the key from Lloyd`s desk and they went into the lab. Lloyd`s collection was spread over several drawers of his map cabinet. Lloyd didn`t go for big, he went for quality and his collection was amazing. They were going from drawer to drawer when Charity`s eyes fell on a particular stone.

"Kay," she called.

"What?"

"Come here."

Kay`s chair moved in the next room and then Charity could hear her walking.

"What?" Kay asked.

"Look at this," Charity pointed.

There in its own little compartment was a candy pink piece of milky quartz striped with gold.

Kay reached down and picked it up. Her father had once held this.

She looked at Joe. "How did he get this?"

Joe looked worried. "He sometimes buys them off people who come in. Others he just brings in."

She rolled it over in her hands. The yellow lamplight made it look a little orange. On the bottom, in the cracks in the stone, were specks that came loose like flecks of paint. Some of them had fallen on the table top. Kay waved to Joe to bring the lamp closer. Under the direct light they looked dark red. They looked like dried blood.

Van Cise had requested body guards from the secretary, whom the president had given instructions to provide every requested resource possible. He had received one. Captain Beauregard Jennings.

Jennings was clearly the bottom of the barrel, in his 50s, sun wizened like a raisin, and five-foot-six. But he held himself with poise and dignity.

Van Cise`s plan was to ride by zeppelin only so far as Kansas City. To fly directly into Denver would be suicide. Instead he planned to sneak past Denver by train and get off directly at Fort Laramie station. They were almost certainly watching, waiting for Van Cise to do just this, since there were really only two ways to get there, but he could hide on the train, he could disguise himself and perhaps sneak past. To this end, his first step was to shave off his mustache, a mustache he had proudly worn and cultivated for 25 years.

Van Cise had thought about all sorts of disguises: ministers, Indians, ranchers, and even a woman. They all had two problems. First, they all stood out from the crowd in one way or another. Second, he wasn`t any of them. He just wouldn`t look natural. Instead he chose the path of least resistance. There were piles of empty uniforms in Washington, just waiting to be filled. He`d go as Jennings` sergeant. He picked a care worn uniform and half used boots from the stacks retrieved from the dead and wounded that more or less fit. They`d be just two tired soldiers among the many.

He met Jennings for the first time at the Fort Stevens Aerodrome, just prior to take off. Van Cise had been given a description and there was no mistaking the man standing in the grass field. He had marched straight up to him and saluted. Jennings had returned the salute, but was obviously confused, which pleased the governor.

"Van Cise?"

"Reporting for duty, sir!"

"You`re travelling in disguise." Jennings was not pleased.

"We'll be attacked if we are detected. Worse yet, attacked by Denver City Deputies. They'll certainly search the train at some point claiming to be looking for fugitives."

"It can't be that bad in Denver."

Van Cise just chuckled and waved him towards the airship ladder. The courier ship dropped them off at Washington Aerodrome, where they waited in the terminal lounge until their flight was ready to board. Van Cise's disguise didn't work well here. Their faded blue uniforms stood out amongst the rich elite waiting with drinks and finger food. But he really didn't care at this point. He wondered how many of their privileged sons were wearing uniforms in any place that might actually be dangerous.

When their flight was announced, everyone stood and filed through the double doors and took seats in the steam carriages that were waiting to take them out to their zeppelin.

The airship loomed huge and grey, unreal in its size, beyond human scale. The ground crew were spread out down its length awaiting the command to release the mooring lines. Painted across its length was the immense TransAmerica logo. They were met at the top of the ramp by a pair of crewmen. Like all air crewmembers, they were small and thin. Weight was paramount to profit, and since women tended to be smaller, crews were dominated by them. They wore TransAmerica uniforms, spartan tan, unadorned suits, close cut, topped with hard round kepi hats of European design. At the top of the boarding ramp, one of them took their bags and said, "Follow me, please," and led them to their cabin.

The cabin was smaller than a jail cell. There were two narrow beds that folded down from the wall, one above the other, leaving just room enough to stand and dress. No other furniture. You kept your things in your bags and there was only a single porthole window that they could open for air.

Van Cise pushed his bag under the bottom bunk, followed by his boots, and lay down with a sigh. He`d been running non-stop since he hit Washington.

"I`m going to look around," Jennings said, and he left quietly, closing the balsa–light door with a click.

Van Cise grunted that he had heard and then stared up at the pieces that made up the bunk above him. He had noticed in his last trip that every part on these ships had cast into them or stamped onto them a short description in German and a number. There could be no doubt which piece went where or how to ask for a replacement. Even the sheets and plates had them. On his last trip he had passed the time, when he had gotten tired of looking down, by looking for things unlabelled. He`d found three. The vases on the tables at dinner, the paper in the WC, and the crewmen themselves, of which there were seven. He loved the WC. When you pulled the lever, the bottom opened up to the air below. He wished it had a bomb sight.

The ship shifted under him with the drifting air. They were held down by cables, but some of them had probably been undone in preparation for departure. There would be seasick passengers, just like the last trip. He was grateful that he had not been one of them. Coffee would be nice. He rose and, without bothering to put his boots on, opened the thin door, and shut it behind him with its simple precise click. He made his way down the narrow corridor to the "Aufenthalts - speiseraum," which was what was engraved above the entryway to the lounge. *There is no explaining German*, he thought.

The open lounge, where they would spend most of

their time during the voyage, had four large windows, folding tables, couches, and chairs, precisely one spot for each passenger to sit so they could all be called together, as they would be before they took off.

Sitting at a table was Jennings, surrendering his pipe, tobacco, and matches. Van Cise chuckled to himself. The fool had tried to have one last smoke before they took off. He hoped they both wouldn`t end up dead fools before this trip was over.

CHAPTER 21

Old Man Webster was not old, not by his reckoning at least. He just looked old. Opium did that to you. It was because you didn`t want to eat. He was just thin.

He used to be a foreman of a railroad tunnel team until he had an accident. Some of his boys used to smoke in the evenings around the fire, and finally he had tried it. He`d be damned if it wasn`t fun. Eventually, with practice, he learned how to go places no white man had seen. Oh, the things he had seen! But after the accident he had no job and no access to opium. It had hurt, and his life had turned grey and sick, at least until he found Lou.

He was sweeping floors for food when he smelled his opium from down in the basement. He went down and there he saw men and women sitting smoking. They laughed when they saw him, but he didn`t care. What he cared about was that pipe. That was the gateway to life. With that he could do anything.

Lou knew. He knew what opium could do for you. *Work for me he said and I will give you opium. Do things for me.* And so here he was, watching them girls.

They were in the assay office looking at maps and walking around and talking. He would tell Lou and Lou would smile and give him opium. He loved Lou.

Inside the office Kay looked through map after map as Webster looked on from across the street. She was frowning. It was going to take time to find the spot. Looking for the right map with the right shapes on it was maddening. She thought she had found it several times, but Joe looked and just shook his head. Webster kept count of the maps and drawers.

Kay had wanted to take the stone, but Joe said no. Lloyd would miss it. It had to be her father's blood on it, it was hers!

Finally Joe had to say they had to quit for the evening. The clock said eleven. They had been at it for over two hours and had finished only the first drawer. There were eleven more drawers to go, although most of them were highly unlikely. For instance, she doubted her father had made it all the way to Utah.

They walked back down dark dirt streets toward their house, a shadow following from alley to doorway. When Charity kissed Joe goodbye on the cheek, which raised Joe's spirits considerably, the shadow scribbled a note intently.

Inside their new home it was still dark and dusty. Kay struck a match and took one of the candles by the door. They hadn't gotten to cleaning the living room yet, concentrating instead on bedrooms and the kitchen, so they had to walk carefully as to not raise dust. There was a candle, still tall, in Grace's room. Going quietly to the door, they looked in. Her face was all the colors of the rainbow. Kay thought she looked like a potato doll. They could see no sign of bleeding and so they left her sleeping.

Deke's room was downstairs and there was no light

under the door. Kay knew, though, that Deke had heard them come in. She knew from experience just how much he listened, even when he was asleep. Upstairs Charity got a candle from her room and lit it from Kay`s. "Don`t worry, we`ll find it tomorrow," she said before she shut the door. Kay thought it unlikely, but she knew they would find it eventually.

She had left her window open a bit so her room was cold, which was fine by her. It meant that her covers would be just that much warmer. Closing the curtains, she took off her clothes, and pulled on her night dress. On her dresser was her pitcher. Pouring water from it into her cup and then into her basin, she scrubbed her face and hands with cold water, shivering from the chill. Then taking her toothbrush, she dipped the bristles in her water cup, then touched it in the tin of tooth powder. Scrubbing her teeth, she spit in the basin. After rinsing her mouth with water from her cup, she picked up the bowl and threw its contents out the window into the silver moonlight out in the backyard. In the next window, lit by the yellow light of the candle beside her bed, Charity was doing the same thing. They giggled and then said goodnight again. Lastly, Kay blew out her candle, then snuggled into her new creaky bed and was asleep before she knew it.

Old Man Webster knew though. He stood out back in the alley, watching the windows, scrawling notes.

Over the next two days they cleaned and searched the cupboards for the utensils and things they needed and knew had to be there. Grace was awake and talking. She was starting to itch, which the doctor said was good, but she shouldn`t scratch. Clean cold water might give some relief, he said. He gave her pills for the pain, which helped a little, and she ate soft easy things like eggs, bread, and soup. Her mouth was cut inside and her throat was bruised where they had tried to strangle her.

Even though it hurt, she spared no effort to tell them about Blonger, getting it out in little bits and pieces. Being in his personal harem gave her access to a lot of inside knowledge. "Don`t trust the sheriff," she said. "Blonger owns him. The mayor too." More than anything she was deathly afraid that he would get a hold of her again. They were all worried. Maybe inside town was a bad idea, maybe even inside Colorado was a bad idea.

While Kay was feeding her soup one morning, she asked her about guns. "Have you ever handled one?"

"No."

"Do you think you could? I mean if they came for you?"

"Yes." Kay got the feeling that she might enjoy that situation.

"Then I`ll see what I can do," Kay said, and then she sighed. "I wish you could go out and practice. We sure could use your help."

Kay and Deke went out that day to search for a gun for Grace. Something she could hide in the bed with her to hold off any kidnapping or murder attempts. Everywhere they went, they felt like they were being watched. Deke was sure of it. Although why they might have drawn Blonger`s or anyone else`s attention they couldn`t guess.

All they could find was a .45 Schofield. It was used and although it had been well kept, it felt odd to Kay to use someone else`s gun. At least it loaded like her Webley. She loved her Webley, but she felt that maybe Grace should use the smaller caliber gun since she was so skittish of them.

When they went to the range to try the .45, the recoil almost hit Kay in the face. The store owner and Deke helped her to brace her 110 pounds with definite concern.

"This ain`t a woman`s gun," he persisted, which only made her determined. "There`s nothing ladylike about it."

When she properly braced herself it went straight, but with two rapid shots the second was clearly in the air.

"I`ll take it," she said.

The owner was shaking his head as he took her money. They went out of town and emptied half a box of cartridges, which was about all Kay could stand. She could tell she was going to be sore. Then she and Deke lay in the grass and spooned and kissed for awhile and stared at clouds and talked.

That night Deke went with them to the assay office and got a good look at the stone.

"They want to crush that for gold?" was all he could say, and shook his head in disbelief.

While they were leaning over the table, looking at maps, Kay accidentally bumped into Deke. So he accidentally bumped her back. Laughing, she accidentally bumped him again, which sent them both laughing and ended with their holding each other and another kiss. Joe, a little embarrassed, went and found something to do in the lab.

Outside in the dark, Old Man Webster watched them through the window from across the street in the dark, just the same as he had been watching them all day. He knew Lou would want to know about this too.

They found it the next night. Charity spotted it during her shift. She was moving the map piece along looking at shapes, and then she just stopped and stared. She turned the map piece and stared a bit more.

"Joe, come look at this."

"Found something?" He walked over.

"What do you think?"

He stared at the spot too. "That looks good. Look at this Kay."

It was Kay`s turn to stare. "Where is that?"

"Coal Creek," Joe replied.

"Can we take the map?"

"No. It`s our only copy. We have extras of some, but only one of this."

"My papa must have had one. Your boss won`t notice it`s gone, and we`ll give it back after."

"Just carrying it around will ruin it."

"Can we order another copy?"

"From Washington?"

"Yes!"

"It`ll take two months to get it."

"Can we buy another map, a different map?"

"Not like these, and for this we need to be precise."

"Then we need to somehow make a copy. I wonder if the printer can do it?"

The next day they went to the town newspaper again and asked them about making a copy of a map.

"Sure," said the balding ink-stained man behind the counter. "We`ll make a blueprint. It won`t last forever, but unless you leave it sitting out in the sun it will last years."

So when Lloyd took off on his usual two and half hour lunch that day, Joe just closed up the shop, took the map over to the printers and had it copied. The printer took a sheet of yellow paper from a foil wrapped envelope in a big flat box and sandwiched it in with the map between two sheets of glass and then he and Joe hauled it out in the sun. Joe got to watch the image form from the back, the paper gradually turning from yellow to blue.

"This is incredible! We`ll never have order maps again," Joe said.

"Be grateful for the business," the printer replied.

They washed it and left it out to dry. He could pick it up later. And Lloyd was none the wiser.

That night he took it to the house and rolled it out on the kitchen table. The map piece still matched perfectly. Now they had to decide what to do. They had Grace to look after.

"Maybe we could bring her in a wagon?" Kay said.

"Absolutely not. The doctor said she wasn`t to move. If she starts pulling on those stitches she`ll scar, they might pop, and possibly infect. It will be at least a month before she can even go to the outhouse with help," Charity said.

"This is so maddening! I bet he left a note there or something. Why else send me the map piece?" Kay asked.

"Patience," Charity replied.

"We can talk to Dr. Balderson," Joe said.

"Oh. Good idea!" Charity said. Joe grinned at her and she kicked him gently. He looked surprised so she said, "Really! He might know someone who could stay with her."

"Yes, I suppose we could move her again to another house until we got back," Kay suggested. "But it would all depend on what Dr. Balderson says. I guess if he says no, then it`s no."

Old Man Webster stood in front of Lou`s desk, having just given him his morning report. Lou never made Webster wait. When he did, Webster`s mind wandered and that really got Lou`s goat. The point was for Lou to forget about the man standing in front of him, not the other way around. "Damn," Lou cursed to himself. "They shoot, they ride; if it wasn`t for that mine I could put them in a show and make money!"

The Louse, leaning on the wall next to Lou, chuckled. "They could do it naked. Then you`d really make money."

They both laughed. Webster just looked fretful. He wanted his opium.

"So they didn`t show at the office last night. They must have found what they were looking for." He worried the end off his cigar with the blunt blade of his cigar knife. "Hellfire! I told them to sharpen this." He waved Webster away towards the door with an annoyed frown.

Webster backed out bowing and muttering, "Thank you, thank you."

"I bet they found what they wanted at the assay office," Louie said, making kissing noises, which got a sideways smile from Lou.

He struck a match and puffed his cigar alight. Taking it from his mouth and contemplating its curling ribbon of smoke in the lamplight, he said, "Then I think it`s time we reeled them in. That boyfriend might be the key that unlocks her." He looked at Louie, "Get Duffy and that judge in here, what`s his name? Winslow. Get him."

"Sure thing, Lou," he said, nodding before he left.

Lou leaned back in his chair and smiled a mean smile. He wanted that Mapleton girl in the basement by tonight. He was in the mood for some fun. He`d make a party of it, invite the old gang, with her as the entertainment, and at the climax of the party she`d break. He could almost taste her tears, and as the final bonus he would get The Rose.

CHAPTER 22

It was full dark when they heard the knock on the door. He and Kay were sitting on the sofa, cuddling and talking about the future, when Deke heard footsteps on the porch and knew there were at least three.

It took another second for Kay to understand. She had felt Deke tense, and her eyes immediately darted towards the door. Before she knew it, Deke had shoved her on the floor and followed her down.

"Who`s there?" he called.

"We`re from the sheriff. Got some questions for you."

From the corner of his eye he saw Grace`s room go dark. Charity was out with Joe who knows where, so it was just the three of them.

"OK, give us minute. We need to get some clothes," Deke called back.

There was one looking in the window next to the door. *Why hadn't they closed those curtains?* he thought.

"Open up now or we`re comin in!"

Deke could hear sounds from all over the house.

He tried to pick out the ones that mattered. There was a window opening in back in the bedrooms and maybe someone trying the kitchen door. He drew his pistol from his holster on the table.

Then there was a bang and flash of light from Grace`s room followed by breaking glass. Deke picked up a cushion and threw it at the candle as they kicked in the door.

They were there, silhouetted in the doorway, rushing in. Deke fired, causing the first man to fall. The next two fell over him in the dark. Something rattled in the kitchen as someone bumped into it. Deke had no time to waste. He shot the other two on the floor and turned towards the kitchen. Blinking through the after images from the muzzle flash, Deke saw a dark shape moving through the kitchen doorway. He shot again.

Then they sat listening. It was quiet, the crickets slowly returning..

"Grace?" Deke called.

"Here," she called from the bedroom.

He went to the front door and counted five horses out front. Then he checked the three bodies in the doorway. They were dead. He could see blood soaking into rug in the moonlight. Deke had liked that rug.

"We are in a heap of trouble," he said.

"They dead?" Kay asked, a little shaky.

"Haven`t checked the one in back." He thought fast. What were their priorities? "Kay, I need you to take one of their horses and get over to the doc`s house and tell him what happened. He`s got to come right now and get Grace. There`ll be more coming when these don`t come back. Stay there. I have to do a few things."

"I`m not dressed for riding," Kay said.

That sounded a little rattled to Deke. He helped her up and looked her in the face, "The dress doesn`t matter." Then he smiled. "It`s dark and no one can see you. Just go. Take your bag and your gun. Hell, go get your pants first, but hurry," and he kissed her lightly.

He saw her to the door, then turned away and walked carefully towards Grace`s room. "Grace? It`s Deke. I`m coming in."

"OK," he heard.

Deke could see that she had had to twist a bit to get her shot and some of her stitches were bleeding. She was lying there on the bed, clearly spent.

"You got one," Deke said, sitting down in the chair next to her, trying to smile.

She smiled back, though he thought it must certainly hurt. "I did," she said.

"Kay`s going to go for the Doctor and he`s going to take you out of here, so you`re going to have to be careful about who you shoot at. I won`t lie. I don`t know who`ll get here first."

"OK."

"We`re going to have to ride, but we`ll try to make sure you get clear. There`ll be a posse after us for sure." He risked a quick look out the broken window. The body was lying in the dirt with no movement. He checked again when he got out back. She had hit him square in the chest. *They were as bad as the Yavapai the way they had tried to sneak up*, he thought. He grabbed their saddlebags and saddled the horses. With all the noise, Ned was ready to go. He even stood still while Deke legged up.

Deke didn`t want to come straight out into the street from around the back of the house, but he had to hurry. Anything could be waiting out in the dark and there he would be, up in the air on top of Ned. But nobody shot him. Deke supposed they thought five was plenty and that maybe they had gotten them all.

There, tied to their hitching post next to the front walk, were the deputy`s horses. Spare horses would be a big help when they were on the run. So, since he was already a murderer, he might as well be a horse thief as well, and he took the four remaining horses reins and pulled them along behind Ned and women`s horses. Kay and Charity had yet to name their horses, he thought. There never seemed to be time.

The noise had woken people all over. Lanterns were being lit in windows, houses were creaking as people moved about, and doors were opening as some folks come out to look around. Some of them had guns. He looked for Charity and Joe, but they were nowhere to be found. Then down the street clattered Zeb and Mrs. Balderson in their wagon in the silver moonlight.

"That you Deke? " called Mrs. Balderson.

"Have you seen Charity?" he replied.

"No. And get yourself over to the office, now!" bellowed Mrs. Balderson.

"Yes, ma`am," he said, because he had been well brought up.

He headed there as fast as he could leading eight half–spooked horses. As he entered the shadows in the alley, three men with rifles drawn looking for all the world like more deputies on horseback galloped by heading towards the house. They were too intent on their destination to notice Deke and his herd.

Mrs. Balderson was going to get caught! Deke thought. Since he was up for hanging already he drew his rifle, aimed carefully, and dropped all three.

The rifle shots unsettled the horses, and they tried to scatter, but he caught their reins before they pulled loose from his saddle horn. Cooing and shushing, he tryed to calm them and regain order. *Perhaps they thougth Ned was forming a new herd!* Deke thought.

Hell, maybe he was. Deke smiled.

Leaving them to Ned, he slid from his saddle and chased down the three new horses, recently vacated, the last horse being brought to by a man in a nightshirt.

"What's going on?" the man asked.

"Blonger`s after the Baldersons," Deke replied.

"Damn! "

Deke bent down and picked up one of the deputy's rifles.

"What is it Nate?" called a woman from an upstairs window.

"It`s finally comin`" he called back. "This`ll be the last straw for sure," he said.

"Well sir, I don`t know about that, but I do know that we all have to hide so I`ve got to go," Deke said.

"You sure do," the man said. "Now you better git."

Deke led the herd down the alley to the Balderson`s backyard and tied them up, eleven saddled horses. Better than two spares each!

He grabbed a saddle blanket from the shed, ran down the alley back to the street and brushed out the tracks from the street, then down the alley, and in through the gate. It wouldn`t fool anybody come morning unless they had wind or rain, and there were too many witnesses if they asked, but it might keep them off the Baldersons` backs for awhile. When he came back, Kay was waiting for him.

She jumped into his arms and said, "You`re alive!"

"So I am. We all are, so far."

They went in through the backdoor and there, coming in the front door was Dr. Balderson, Charity, and Joe. Charity and Kay hugged, tears shining in their eyes.

"What happened, we heard shots?" Charity said.

"They tried to arrest us," Deke replied.

"Arrest?" Joe asked.

"That's what they would call it," Deke said. "I'd call it an ambush."

Joe was clearly stunned. "Why?"

"I sure would like to ask, but they keep trying to kill us," Deke said. Then he turned to Kay. "You have the map?"

"In my bag, like always."

"Then we need to ride. Joe, you don't have to come with us. It's us they want."

"It might be the map. It has to be the map they want. I have to go too. I know where the mine is," and then to himself. "It must have been Lloyd. That stone." Then he turned to Charity, "Besides, I can't leave you like this."

Charity smiled and reached out for his hand.

"We're going to need supplies, especially cartridges," Deke said. "Half those saddles out there have rifles, but we're going to need ammunition, to hunt if nothing else."

"McMillian's store down the street. Wake him up. No, I'll come with you," said Dr. Balderson.

"You have to take care of Grace, keep her safe and your family too," Deke replied.

"You're right. We have friends where we can stay. We've got to pack fast."

Deke could hear the wagon coming up the alley. "Don't pack, just get on that wagon and go." He grabbed Kay's hand and said, "Let's go," and they stumbled into the back with the others following.

Grace was lying in the wagon. She was bleeding.

"She's been moving," the doctor said.

"I'm OK," Grace mumbled.

"Of course you are dear, " Mrs. Balderson said to her. "Deke, was that you shooting?"

"Yes ma'am. They were coming for you."

"We're much obliged. Nathan, get in the wagon."

"Yes ma'am," Dr. Balderson said.

"Zeb, you should come with us," Deke said. "You're mom and pop will either be fine or they won't, but you can't do any good for them by staying."

"He's right. Zebadiah, go with them, get your horse," Mrs. Balderson said grimly. "Three's easier to hide."

"Mom."

"She's right son," added Dr. Balderson. "Three in the Joule's attic will be plenty enough. We're old. We can sit all day. Hell, it's a day off for me, but it'd be hell for you."

"Come on, Zeb!" Deke said, as he headed for the back. Zeb left with clear reluctance, but they mounted up together and rode down to the store with people looking out their windows, recognizing the Baldersons in their wagon and calling, "What's going on?"

Dr. Balderson yelled back, "Go to bed! You'll find out tomorrow."

At McMillian's, the Baldersons' wagon with the Baldersons and Grace left them heading for their friends' house to hide. The gang pushed open the door of the McMillian's store before he could open it properly and barged right in.

"Mr. McMillian, I'm sorry but we're going to rob your store, if you get my drift," Deke said. "We'll pay you later, but we can't stop. Blonger's men are after us, and there'll be a posse for sure."

"I understand," he said. Then to Zeb, "How's your mom and pop."

"They have to hide."

"I understand that too. I'll do what I can."

"In the meantime it would help if you two put your hands up so we can look like we're doing this the proper way," Deke said grimly. "Joe, can you kind of sort of point a gun at em? Now where`s those cartridges?"

"Behind the register on the shelf," Mr. McMillian replied.

"Matches?" asked Zeb.

"Drawer under the cigars."

They loaded burlap feed bags because they didn`t have but two saddlebags and tied them in pairs with rope to hang over the saddle horn. Then they mounted up in the dark street, lit by shine from town windows and rode out of town, a gang of five desperados with a posse on their tail and a trail of eight dead deputies. It was the first flight of the Hayden Gang from the law, a foreshadow of their trials in the long years yet to come.

CHAPTER 23

The train was pulling in to the Denver station when Van Cise pulled out half a bottle of whiskey. He had poured half out in the street just after he bought it, to the horror of the bartender he bought it from just to make it look used. He took a sip and passed the bottle to Jennings. Jennings looked at it like it had just been passed to him in church.

"For your breath. Take a sip." Jennings took the sip

then passed it back. Van Cise then slouched down in his seat with the bottle in his hand as if asleep. "Get down, fool," he whispered to Jennings. Then they waited.

Sure enough, two toughs came walking down the aisle with rifles over their arms, hammers cocked. They were questioning passengers.

Poking Van Cise with a rifle butt, one asked, "You two. Where`d you get on?"

Van Cise looked up slowly with what he hoped were blurry eyes. "What`s it to you?"

"Deputies. We`re looking for a fugitive."

"No fugitives in here. We got on in Kansas City."

"Let`s see your ticket."

Now Van Cise looked up at him with anger, but he fished their tickets from his pocket and showed them to the men.

"Sorry," the deputy said without any attempt at sincerity, and moved on down the aisle.

After they passed on to the next car, Jennings said, "Well I`ll be damned."

"You`ll be dead if they catch us. Now here, have a pull on this whiskey, just for show."

"They got away!" Blonger yelled, his evening spoiled. He pounded the desk with his fist, "They got away!"

"Eight dead deputies," the new sheriff, Corrigan, said. Duffy had packed up his family and headed for the hills. "The posse is forming up outside. We`re leaving as soon as I report. I`ve sent scouts on ahead to pick up the start of their trail."

Lou was disappointed. He wanted to hurt someone, but he couldn`t fault Corrigan.

"No sign of Van Cise yet either?"

"No, sir."

Lou sat back in his chair and thought for a minute. "Leave some of your people, and you stay too. We`re going to start swearing in deputies. Dodds knows the plan."

"How many?"

"Six hundred."

Corrigan took a step back and then rallied. "May I ask why?"

"We`re going to need them. Most are already hired and all they need is swearing in. The hills around here are full of men down on their luck, looking for a stake to get them to the next gold strike. Hell, we`ve been turning men away. To be frank Sheriff, I`m expecting an attack." Then Lou looked up at Corrigan and smiled. "It`s the whole pot now or nothing, all cards down on the table."

"Why six hundred?"

"We`re going for the whole territory."

"That`s impossible!"

"Nonsense. The Union is overstretched, it may even fall. There`s only two companies of soldiers, maybe 250, in the whole territory. Sure we can`t hold it forever, but a year or two`s take will make us kings in South America or any other place. What would you like to rule? Argentina, Peru? Senoritas begging at your knees?"

"I built this town. It's mine!" Lou brought his fist down on the desktop. "But if some skinny hairy bastard squatting on the east coast is going to take it away from me, then I'm damn well going to get proper recompense or he`ll at least bleed for the effort. You get it now? I wanted more men, but six hundred are all we could supply."

Corrigan was staggered by the magnitude of the

plan. But if it worked, if Lou was right, then they would be rich, kings even. But then what if he was wrong? If he was wrong, then he`d just follow Duffy up into the hills. Corrigan nodded.

Lou watched him. He knew what Corrigan was thinking and knew how far he would go. He could trust Corrigan only as long as things went according to plan. Lou was going to have to send somebody along, just as greedy, to be ready to kill Corrigan and step in.

"Take Gleeson with you. Go find Dodds and do it!" and he pointed at the door.

"Yes sir," Corrigan replied, picking up his hat and heading for the door.

"Louie, go find that idiot mayor."

"Sure, boss."

Twelve horses leave quite a trail. Deke did his best to obscure it. They rode up streams, made side trails, rode single file, took travelled trails, and doubled back. But Deke didn`t doubt for a second that they could cause any more than momentary confusion. There were just too many horses, and this posse would be a lot more motivated than the Kansas City one. So he switched again to distance.

"This is why you learn to trot," he said to the women, smugly.

Rather than getting them caught boxed in a canyon, he took them back out towards the plains and its endless sea of tall grass. They changed horses every two hours with Deke checking his compass at every stop. When they finally stopped for the night, Deke figured they were 30 miles northeast of Denver.

They slept on piles of cut grass, with no blankets,

not even a toothbrush, and they woke hungry. Deke slipped away before dawn to watch their trail, but he saw no one. Eating a meager breakfast dug out of tin cans from the store, they headed south towards the railroad.

Come mid–morning they ran into the Indians. Their teepees were sticking up above the tall grass in the distance, Arapaho, or Inuna-Ina as they called themselves. Deke didn`t know their language precisely, but they shared enough languages with him, a small bit of English included, that they could get their meaning across. These were families out on their summer buffalo hunt. It was the time when they taught their children about being Arapaho.

Normally most of them worked in the machine belt factory in Namaqua, but in the summer the factory closed up and they all went out to wander the plains. Arapaho Patented Annealed Belts were used in machinery and factories all over the East, each made from rubberized non-skid non-stretch buffalo hide. Factories in those days needed a lot of belts for their pulleys and clutches so business was good.

Their teepees and wagons were arranged in a half circle around the central fire so they could watch the sun set. Being good folk, they invited the gang to sit, and had coffee with goat`s milk and sugar around the fire.

Deke watched one of the wives crank a coffee grinder.

"They ambushed us," Deke said. "Tried to sneak in the back and windows, trying to come at us from every direction." Deke didn't call them Yavapai. He wasn't sure how Arapaho felt about them.

"Tell them about Grace," Kay said.

"I'm getting to that," Deke said to her. Then to the elder, "All because we tried to help a girl they tried to murder."

"That's Bonger." The elder nodded. He turned to his wife, Deke thought he was asking about phrasing. "We lose a few every year. Mostly kids too foolish to listen. Stay out of Denver we say." He sighed. "Kids don't listen. Go to Kansas City we say, but kids, they have no common sense yet."

"They disappear?"

"Some. Some get a trial. It`s the same thing."

"More coffee?" A woman offered to fill their cups.

"Thanks. They could get pressed in Kansas City."

"A little time in one army or another would do them good. Teach them to listen."

Deke tried a little more goat's milk in his coffee, still a bit unsure as to whether it was a good idea or not. When he asked about it, because coming from the southern plains, he`d never seen Indians with goats. The elder tucked his arm under one pants suspender and leaned back in his chair and explained, "It`s milk on the hoof and fits in a wagon. I like milk in my coffee. I admit cow`s milk is better, but you have to make do with what is possible," he said.

Deke looked around at all the grass around them, devoid of any cows. He had to agree.

They ate corn flatbread, buffalo, and beans seasoned with red peppers and onions fried on a big iron griddle that they pulled off one of their wagons. It took a bit of the edge off all they`d been through.

While they rested, they talked over their situation and decided rather than just wandering the plains living off of buffalo until the end of their days, that they would go to Coal Creek to see if they could find the mine. Of course, that would mean crossing past Denver again, which Zeb liked because he wanted check up on his parents.

Once it was decided, off they rode again, eating up

the ground at a trot, regularly changing horses. By nightfall they were back on the outskirts of Denver. They had covered 70 miles in two days. What they didn`t know was that the posse was only eight miles away, still stumbling around the beginning of their trail on the other side of town, still sorting out the confusion of trails Deke left two nights before.

Van Cise and Jennings exited the train at Fort Laramie, Van Cise carrying the bags like a good sergeant. The station was empty. Not many people lived there in those days. There was just the fort and the town. The territory under them belonged to the Indians. So it was pretty easy to spot the two thugs in the station, and the four more waiting outside. They were leaving the station and Van Cise had just begun to think they had made it through when someone yelled, "Hey, you two, halt!"

Van Cise dropped the bags and they ran for it down the street. A shot rang out, a bullet buzzing by on his upper right like an angry bee. He pushed Jennings left through a saloon door as two more shots whizzed past, knocking splinters out of the wall above their heads.

In the dim light inside they tried to see some place where they could barricade themselves, but they were blind for the moment as they stumbled towards the back of the bar.

"Captain, Sergeant, are you in need of assistance?"

"Criminals, Rebels, we`re on a mission," he gasped.

"Then I think, gentlemen, we have a position to defend," the voice said.

Van Cise, as his vision cleared, saw that the saloon

was full of men in blue. He had found the cavalry.

Four men ran into the saloon after them, but were tripped or kicked. Then the two that came in the back met the same fate. All six were hoisted up off the floor and into chairs, some still doubled over trying to catch their breath.

"Have a seat, gentlemen, and we can sort this out without gunplay," the major said.

"We`re deputy marshals and these men are criminals, fugitives disguised as soldiers," gasped one of the deputies, through gritted teeth. He was holding his shin rocking back and forth trying to ride out the pain.

"Is that true, Captain?"

"No sir, I`m Captain Beauregard Jennings, appointed by the Office of the President of the United States to escort this man, Governor Phillip Van Cise of the State of Colorado to this outpost, where he is to receive assistance. I have orders here signed by Abraham Lincoln himself and sealed orders for the commander of the base."

"Which would be me, and whose birthday party you have joined."

"Congratulations, sir."

"Thank you." Then he addressed the deputies. "And what authority do you claim?"

"We`re deputy marshals of the city of Denver appointed by Chief Marshal Patrick Duffy."

"Are you aware that Duffy is no longer Chief Marshal."

"No, sir."

"It was in the paper today. You work for Waldo Corrigan now."

"Wald got promoted? What happened to Duffy?"

"Resigned apparently. Left town."

That seemed to leave the deputies a little

bewildered.

"Gentlemen, I respect your desire to perform your duty, but I`ve been expecting these gentlemen. The secretary to the president sent me a telegram telling me to render every assistance. If you would be so kind as to lay down your arms? Sergeant Patterson, could you collect them?"

"Sir."

The deputies were clearly out of their depth and did as instructed, handing their guns over to be collected and stacked.

Turning to Van Cise the major said, "The 3rd and 4th companies, 65th regiment of the US Army, Heavy Air Cavalry, and Fort Laramie, Major Douglas Birchnill commanding, are at your disposal, sir," and he saluted, which Van Cise returned with a military snap.

"Gentleman, there is an open bar. And now," the major said. "I believe we were about to sing happy birthday."

After the party, the now just a bit drunk deputies were ensconced in the fort brig. Birchnill, Van Cise, and Jennings sat in Birchnill`s office in the fort. The office walls were of log construction, as was the fort itself, it having been continuously occupied, guarding the pass and now the railroad, for almost 40 years. They were looking at a map of Denver.

"You know, sir," said Major Birchnill. "It may be hard for us to get in to Denver. The best route in for us naturally is the aerodrome, the ground will be cleared and flat. But if they've fortified it, especially if they have aerial defenses, then we may take heavy casualties for no effect."

They were in the fort commander`s office, which

"When I received the telegram and understood the possible nature of the mission, I sent scouts into the city to gain intelligence. As of the day before yesterday, the aerodrome was clear. We are waiting for today's report. We will almost certainly see some trenching. They will in all probability have explosives, being as they are miners."

"Starting the assault at the aerodrome would be best from my point of view because we would have Main Street to take us to the government center," Van Cise replied. "It's the widest street. You would have a clearer field of fire and the objective would be in clear view." He was amazed how easily he slipped back into his old military self.

"From our reports we know they will have us significantly outnumbered. Their troops will certainly be highly irregular and should be no problem in an open fight, but if they were to ambush us, say on Main Street itself, then we could have a significant problem."

"I may have a solution to that if I can find a way to make contact with my friends in the city."

"Then we must find a way."

Since time was of the essence, they could only use the telegraph. The solution they came up with was to send innocent telegrams to friends:

"Congratulations on your birthday on the 17th of July"

"Emmy will arrive 17th of July."

"Bank xfer should arrive 17th July."

They tried to send them at irregular intervals to hide them in the normal traffic. It was ham-handed, would probably tip off the enemy, but they had very little time. Their departure time was 4AM.

Lloyd had watched the preparations going on

around the city and was appalled. Here he had thought Lou a smart operator, but what did he see? He was using force. All commitment, no bait and switch, no sucker leads, and no fake outs. The song and dance was gone and what was left was just bald-faced force. Something had gone wrong in Lou and Lloyd didn`t want to get caught in it. This job had been useful as had his association with Lou, but maybe it was time to move on. He`d heard good things about San Francisco, a booming drug and human trade and there was still big money to be made selling mining supplies. He knew when it was time to cash out, so he packed the blackmail evidence, the bank accounts, his souvenirs, and most of all – his rock collection, and off he rode.

At the edge of town though, right there on the road, he was stopped by armed men who stepped out of the brush and blocked the road.

"Hold it mister, we`ve got to check you out," the leader said.

"What`s all this?" Lloyd replied coarsely.

"We have to check everyone going in or out. Blonger`s orders."

"Hey, don`t you run the assay office?" said a voice in the rear.

Lloyd didn`t like the idea of being recognized. They were on foot and he wondered if he could make a run for it.

"What if I am," he replied. "I`m a friend of Lou`s. You need to let me through."

"If you`re a friend of Lou`s, why are you leaving?" the leader replied.

"Skip, that`s the guy who stole my claim," said the voice in the back.

Lloyd didn`t like this at all.

"I work for the government. I don`t steal anything,"

he replied.

"All I know was that my claim was gone and I was sweepin floors."

"I`ve heard stories about you too," said another.

"I think you should stick around for a bit, maybe talk to the boss," the leader said.

"Hell!" Lloyd exclaimed, and spurred his horse, trying to drag his two pack mules along. This made for a slow start. But he did take them by surprise, which was why he didn`t catch his first bullet until he was fifty feet away and that, in turn, is why, these days, you can see his rock collection still on display in the Denver City Hall.

The fort aerodrome had been abuzz with activity all night long as airships were serviced and stocked. Van Cise had tried to sleep, they had given him an officer billet, but of course with little success. He was still trying to fall asleep when the corporal knocked on his room door. He was already dressed. He had gone to bed dressed and his pack was sitting next to his bed.

He thanked the corporal, sat up in the dark, pulling on his boots. His gun belt was on the chair nearby, within easy reach. He'd been issued a helmet and jacket. The helmet was a dark blue stamped steel bowl with leather webbing inside and a buckle under the chin. It was something new since the days he had served. The coat was cut short and made of brown leather, cinched at the wrist, waist, and neck. It was too warm to wear it, but he was assured that when they made altitude he would be grateful for it.

Grabbing his pack, he left the room, hopefully for the last time. Outside, in the glare of limelight, stood ten airships tethered in the open airfield, the cool still air, unstirred yet by the sun. Their envelopes were grey blue with American flags on their back fins. Underneath, their gondolas were stacked with gear, but as yet no men. He headed for his assigned ship, handing his gear up to the loading sergeant after identifying himself. Then he turned towards the mess hall along with 122 other men. They were all going to battle. The early hour and the eminent threat lent an unreal quality to the morning. Nervousness made many over jovial and he was slapped on the back by several men in passing. He got his tray of food and sat down next to the Major, who would be in command of the expedition. They ate quietly together, saying nothing.

At last the bell was rung. A single loud clang and then men stood and began to file out and walk towards their assigned ships, leaving their trays. They climbed up wooden ladders which, when the ship was loaded, were removed. He could hear the constant sizzle from the gas generators as they attempted to compensate for the new load. Once all were on board, the bell was run twice. He heard the same order given ten times, "Engines even 90!" followed by an "Aye sir!" The crewmen manned the engine winches that lowered them from their stored position to their cruising position

When the engines were locked in place, he heard the call, "Injectors on full."

"Aye sir!" replied the chorus.

"Crank 4!" and the airmen sat with their feet in the stirrups dangling out over the edge and reaching out, grabbing the pull cables.

"Pull!" came the order, and they all pulled back with grunts. Every engine precisely tuned with its mates nudged their prop blades a bit and backfired with the report of a gunshot.

"Pull!" This time the engines turned over with their defining roar, four engines each, on ten airships, the ships pulling at their mooring lines.

"Injectors off!"

"Aye sir!"

"Cast off in order!"

One by one, first to last, the air ships lifted up into the night sky.

CHAPTER 24

Ex-private Fleetfoot Parnell, now Gunnery Sergeant Parnell for the Denver Sheriff`s Department, and enjoying every minute of it, yelled at his crews just as he had endured the yelling under his ex-sergeant ten years before. When they had called out from the skill list during recruitment, he had heard "artillery" and he'd jumped up and yelled out "gunnery sergeant!" And who was to say different? Now he was in command of three, as best as he could guess, 6-pounders. Yes, of course, they were museum pieces, but they still worked. They had no caissons and were therefore, for all practical intents and purposes, immobile, but they were, as static field artillery pieces, still effective. Besides, he couldn`t remember precisely how to limber and unlimber a caisson anyway.

As an officer, or whatever you were in the Sheriff`s Department, he had signed on for the unheard of pay rate of $40 per week! If this job lasted only a month, he would have the money to go to Alaska or anywhere else he thought he might like to go. And being the officer for a change was fun!

Where they found the powder and balls for them he didn`t know. They were fresh cast. No shells, no shot, just ball, which was good because he couldn`t precisely remember how to fuse shells either! But he knew how to yell like he meant it, and he looked good, which made his bosses happy. He aimed the guns, since that was one of his jobs, by dead reckoning because they didn`t have the appropriate artillery tables, which was fine by Parnell for reasons that should no longer need to be stated.

His first act was to take the crews out and drill them, because there was one thing he did actually remember and that was that you don`t fool around with black powder – ever. It was with this one act alone, enforcing powder discipline and proper gun usage, that Sergeant Parnell almost certainly saved more lives, notably his own crew`s, than he ever finally managed to take with his cannon.

"They could come by air, by train, or by horse. That`s the gist of it," Lou said. "That`s too many options. We need to narrow their choices."

"We could blow the tracks," Corrigan suggested.

"Do it, and keep them that way. Six men on horseback with a couple of cases of dynamite should do it. Make it as close to their side as possible." Turning to Lunney, "What about the aerodrome?"

"We plan to shell it if they try to land there."

"Not good enough," he frowned. "I want those airships too."

"Half of them have left, and the other half can`t because they`re missing parts or supplies."

"You let them go?" He stared at Lunney with unmasked fury. Lunney visibly wilted.

"They were gone before I could get there, and I went there that night. They must have heard rumors or seen the recruitment. Shooting those cannons probably didn`t help either."

His people were getting to be too efficient. He was finding it difficult to find fault. There was just no place to vent.

"So we`re back to reducing their options. Could we ruin the field somehow, block it?"

"If they`re coming by air, then they could be here anytime. We probably don`t have much time," Gleeson said. Then he stopped and looked into the distance for a second. "I remember a picture in the newspaper once. They had made things that looked like children`s jacks, only out of iron rail. They were big. They kept out airships and tanks. I wonder if we could make some of them, put them in the field, maybe in the streets too?"

"Good. Do it. Rip up some of the rail between us and them." Turning to Corrigan Lou said, "Troop deployment."

"We can`t expect our troops to maneuver. They don`t have any discipline. They might charge if we order it, but mostly we shouldn`t expect them to do more than stay where we put them and shoot at what comes their way. It`s difficult enough to keep them from looting." He paused for breath, clearly unhappy. "I plan to use them in street ambushes. Half of them are bandits and bushwhackers already so it will come naturally to them. The veterans we have know nothing more than to stand in a line in front of the enemy. They know nothing about street fighting. We`re counting a lot on our regular deputies. Losing eight the other night didn`t help. We`re planning on giving the men positioned outside of town dynamite to throw, which may help too." Corrigan didn`t look pleased, but kept further opinions to himself.

"Artillery, ambush, no air support. Good, good, not good," said Lou. "Still, I want you to know that I`m being cautious. I doubt they can bring more than a hundred men and at seven to one odds, that gives us a pretty big advantage. I expect them to take one look, then turn around and head home to wait for reinforcements. Besides, I still have an ace or two up my sleeve."

He stood looking at each of their faces and seeing no further issues to be discussed, pointed at the door and said, "get to work!"

They waited until well past dark, staring at the town lights in the distance. It was decided that Deke and Zeb would go in since Deke was the best at sneaking and Zeb knew the way and wanted to check on his family. They would go straight in by road, without trying to hide. The posse was looking for five. Two cowhands coming into town for fun was just business as usual.

But as they approached, they realized that there was no business as usual to be found. They were met at the edge of town by men with guns, black shapes against the grey starlit road.

"Hold it right there!" said a man with a rifle. Deke and Zeb stopped with their hands up.

"Remember orders. No looting," said a deputy out somewhere in the dark.

"We ain`t goin to loot them," said the man with the rifle. "I just want to check their bags for weapons or bombs." It sounded to Deke like he intended to loot. The man and a friend walked up to their horses to search, but Ned stepped sideways and planted a hoof on the first one`s foot.

He let out a howl, dropped his gun and rolled on his back holding his boot, his foot broken inside it.

Everyone, even his friends laughed.

"What`s all this?" Deke asked the deputy. "We come in to town for a little fun and get met by bandits on the edge of town!"

The deputy sighed in the dark, falling back on his old job of town pimp. "Things are little tense in town right now. We have a lot of new deputies." He sounded like he didn`t approve. "You can go in if you want, but if you`re smart, you`ll turn around."

Zeb and Deke looked at each other, then Deke looked at the deputy. "We`ve been riding for four days to get here. I think we`ll go in."

"Suit yourself. But get a bath before you mess with the girls."

Deke couldn`t argue there. They did need baths.

They rode into town and around to the Joules` house. Looking down the street, they could see the house had a light in a window. There was no sign of activity or watchers, but even though the street was quiet, the town felt tense. There were too many lights in people`s windows, and they had passed an unusual number of people walking the streets. So they decided to pull in their horns and take it slow. Tying their horses in the shadows at the top of the alley, they approached carefully.

At the Joules` house itself they stopped in the shadows and Deke just sat there and watched, which was especially hard for Zeb. But he understood the need for caution. Trouble here could not only get Deke and him killed, but his family as well. So they sat and listened, but there were no coughs, telltale spitting, or any of the other giveaways that sentries usually make.

The back door was open and the house was quiet. A quick peek in the living room showed it to be empty, as was the rest of the house as well. Deke ventured a cautious, "Hello?"

Then Zeb called, "It`s Zeb!"

At that they heard a thump upstairs. "Zeb!" came his Mother`s voice, muffled through the ceiling.

A trapdoor with a folding ladder came down in the hallway and down came his mother. They hugged and laughed.

"Your fool father has gone off with the militia."

"Militia?" Deke asked.

"That`s what they call themselves. They think the Army is going to attack tomorrow, and they plan to hit the deputies from behind."

"Pa`s going to attack deputies?"

"They aren`t real deputies. Blonger has hired hundreds of mine vermin and deputized them. He`s laying an ambush for the Army."

"That explains the men on the road," Zeb said.

"We`ve got to get back and tell Joe and the women." Duke looked Zeb in the eye. "We need to make plans."

"I`ve got to go help my pa," Zeb replied.

Deke thought for moment. If there was going to be a fight, then Zeb`s place was with the wounded. Heck, he might be among them. So he nodded and said, "Fair enough."

"Take care getting back," Zeb said.

"Will do," Deke replied with a smile.

And they both took off back to the streets.

Sneaking out of town alone wasn`t hard for Deke. The guards were all looking in the wrong direction. But when he got back to where he had left his friends, they were gone. There had been a struggle and there was blood, but he couldn`t tell who it belonged to. Looking over the situation, he figured there had been eight at least on foot coming in, and just their horses riding out.

They had left a lot of stuff behind, which meant they had been in a hurry. He found Kay`s bag with the map still in it, but not her gun. She had tossed the bag in the brush before being captured which made Deke proud and meant that she had had time to react and had done so deliberately. It would be getting light soon and if he was going to get back through the lines into town and help her without being seen, then he had to hurry.

Kay sat staring at the town lights. She could hear Charity and Joe whispering behind her, but she couldn`t be bothered to listen. All she could think about was Deke. When was the world going to give them a break? The thought of settling down in town with him in that house warmed her heart. She couldn`t think of anything she wanted more. Maybe they could open up an honest hotel, one that served tea in the morning to its customers. Some hotels back east had restaurants built right in to them. People came to the hotel just to eat. There had to be people who came to this town for other reasons than sex and gambling.

She heard movement out in the brush.

"Deke?" she called carefully. Nothing.

She pulled her gun from her bag then shoved the bag in the grass.

"Deke?"

She stood up and began to back towards the horses. She could see Charity and Joe getting up.

Then there was a voice in the brush. "Now sit still girl and you`ll live thr . . ."

She shot. The flash was brilliant and the noise thunderous.

Movement on her right and she shot again, then someone hit her from behind. She rolled and caught him in the head with her gun butt. Then her gun was pulled from her hand and she was slapped twice hard across the face.

They rolled her over and tied her hands and arms behind her. She thought she heard howling and someone else say, "He`s dead."

"Shoot her now," someone growled.

"Orders, we take em in."

"What about Clamp?"

"Leave `im."

"We can`t."

"He`s gut shot. I ain`t carrying him through the streets just so we can watch him die. If you care, then shoot him."

She heard another shot, then quiet.

She was hoisted over a saddle face down. The saddle horn dug into her side as she hit, her head and legs dangling down. Then they tied her down.

"If we had some light, I`m sure that would be a mighty appealing sight, but the boss`s orders are not to be ignored. No lights and women untouched." She heard Charity and then Joe grunt and curse in the dark.

"Is Long awake yet?" another shape in the dark asked.

"Kinda."

"Get him in a saddle or he can walk back by

himself and have to explain.”

“Come on, Long.” There was moan from Long and the nicker of a horse clearly unhappy with the situation. It sounded like they had to lift him up.

“Tie him on if you have to.”

“No, I can ride. You little bitch, I`m bleeding!” Long said in the dark. That warmed Kay`s heart despite her hurts.

“Enough. All loaded?” There was general affirmation. “Then let`s go.”

“I swear. If Blonger doesn`t kill her, I will.”

“Enough, Long!”

They rode back at a walk. Kay was thankful it wasn`t a trot. She bounced up and down against the ropes as it was, and she was sure they would draw blood before they got to wherever. She wondered what had happened to Charity and Joe. Her face was getting numb and she expected it was swelling. She was purely and down in her soul tired of men slapping her.

They hit a road and followed it towards town. At one point they were stopped. She could see the shapes of men in the dark, but whatever it was got done and they were sent on into town.

Down the streets they bounced. She saw people looking out their windows. She thought of Grace and what Blonger had done to her and she was ashamed of how angry she felt at those people for not helping.

They weren`t all bad, though, she thought. There were some good ones too.

They rode up to a big dance hall, where they hauled her off the horse and left her on the ground. She could see the dung on the road around her. The guards came up looked at the blood and bodies and said, “What in hell is this?”

“It`s that girl.”

"That little thing did all this?" He looked like was going to bust out laughing.

"I`m goin to kill her," muttered Long.

"She was carrying this," and he showed them Kay`s gun.

The guard whisled, "Big gun. She couldn`t have fired it. Look at her. It would`ve knocked her ass over tits. I suppose she hit you too, Long."

Long turned quiet.

"I`ll tell you what," the deputy said. "I`ll untie her, give her back her gun, and you can see for yourself."

Two men came out the front door of the hall and approached. The mousy one said, "That`s them, boss. That one there`s Mapleton`s daughter."

Then the big one looked up at the bleeding bodies tied to the horses and laughed. "Miss Mapleton. I am going to make so much money off of you, and I`m going to have so much fun doing it. And I get my party! This is a good omen, Louie. Have them hauled down to the party room. And tell Tex she`s here." And then he laughed, "The Rose is mine!"

CHAPTER 25

A cold wind whipped past Van Cise`s face, his head poking through the top hatch, as he stared into the distance trying to see some sign of Denver through his goggles. He lifted them for a moment to try without them, but his eyes immediately teared. Down below, sitting next to him was the major and to either side of them sat tank gunners, staring forward in the dark, alert for enemies, their hands on their Gatling gun triggers.

The engines were deafening, jets of white fire popping out the exhaust manifolds as oxygen mixed with kerosene. The flames added a teeth rattling "rak rak" over their deep droning rumble. Above was the great envelope of their airship stretched taught by the gas cells within, filled with hydrogen. The signal box light shifted from green to yellow. He strained to see, and there up ahead was a trace of light, Denver dim as stars. They had passed false dawn and behind the city`s lights was the grey of true dawn on the horizon.

Men climbed into to their seats in the tank and were running along the catwalks beneath the envelope. They were doing the same in the other airships, he was sure.

The pilot pulled a lever, and a new sound burst forth above the low pounding of the engines as shrill jets of blue hydrogen flame vented under each airship. They were going down. The tankers lit their quick fire engines in their tanks, forcing them to life with a roar as they flooded and ignited their coal boxes with acetylene and oxygen. Dropping altitude they came down on columns of blue fire and jets of excess steam from the tanks.

The light box turned red, and he could see the city now spread below.

"All engines even 45!" The men up in the catwalks began cranking the engines up so they wouldn`t make contact with the ground.

"Aye sir. All engines even 45!"

The grass and dirt of the airfield came at them frightenly fast. Bullets began pinging off their armor.

"All engines reverse!" cried the ship captain.

"Aye sir. All engines reverse!"

The engines stilled for a second as they switched gears, and then picked up their old pace, and suddenly packed dirt swung by under them. The .30 caliber heavy

Gatling guns opened up with hammer blows of sound, their silver tracers arcing out over the field, cutting through the overturned wagons and barriers that protected the sources of the gun flashes in the distance.

Dawn lit the tops of the airships orange and grey, their undersides still deep hydrogen blue strobing white as their guns rattled. They touched down hard, the springs in the tank wheels cushioning the impact, sliding forward across the dirt until the docking clamps released and the airships, one by one shot back up into the sky with ear popping speed, their guns still blazing away at the remaining targets too foolish to run. Then the rumble of their own tank`s motor took over, blocking out everything else, and they rolled forward opening up with the hammer beat of their own guns.

The 3rd Company, 65th regiment of the US Army Heavy Air Cavalry had arrived.

Eli didn`t mind his job as messenger. It was better than cleaning brick molds at the brick factory or mucking stalls. As far as jobs a kid could expect to get, messenger was ace. And, when the tips were good, it really helped to put food on the family table too. Since his Pa had died, things had been tough. Ma had to go back to bar tending, and his older brother was three days out of town working as a ranch hand.

Though the job was normally ace, like he said, today it was aces and spades! Today there were deliveries, more than they had kids to deliver and most of them carried a secret message. It had something to do with the number 17.

Eli stood at the side door in the alley back of Heinkleson`s Fine Suits. That`s where the Heinklesons lived. Eli knew Leroy, the Heinkleson`s son. They were generally on the same side in dirt clod fights.

"This makes no sense," said Mr. Heinkleson. "It must be a mistake. It`s not my birthday and I don`t have a brother."

"I was told that you might want to talk to Mr. Jenkins or Mr. Maler." There was Leroy coming up to the door. Eli nodded.

"Who told you that?"

"Mr. Fletcher the key operator."

"This is paid for?"

"Yup. He said it was important."

"Hi Eli," Leroy said.

"Hi Leroy. You want to walk with me back to the station? I`ve got news."

"What kind of news," Mr. Heinkleson said. He looked a little worried.

"That was all I was supposed to tell you," Eli said.

"Look son. If you know something important then you better say it."

"I don`t know anything important. It`s just that there`s a lot of messages and they all have 17 in them."

"Today's the 17th," Leroy said.

That raised Heinkleson`s eyebrows.

"Can I go with Eli Pa?"

Mr. Heinkleson fished around in his pocket and pulled out a whole nickel and gave it to Eli. Aces and spades! "No. It`s too dangerous with Blonger`s men all over."

"They don`t care about us," Leroy whined.

"There`s been shooting. You might catch a stray."

"Sorry Leroy. I`ve got to hurry," Eli turned to go, but then turned back. "Thank you Mr. Heinkleson." And then he ran back to the station. He wasn`t about to pass up more tips like that.

Outside in the streets Blonger`s troops marched, breaking into houses, stealing and sometimes worse. Once in awhile there was gunfire when they picked the wrong house to break in to, but mostly it was quiet. They took up their perches in windows, eating food from kitchens of the homes and stores they robbed, preparing to commit the greatest dry gulching the world had ever seen.

Those Army boys would march down the street like army boys do and they would be waiting. Some of the old-timers remembered the old days of muskets, some carbines and pistols, and all what army boys did when they made war back when they were army boys too. They stood in line, marched in formation, and played by rules. Blonger`s men had no intention of doing the same. They sat behind their barracades and perched in windows and on rooftops, watching and waiting.

Behind them, looking down at them from dark windows, around corners, and from a distance through empty streets and alleys, others watched and waiting too, carrying guns pulled down from above fireplaces and out of closets, many cleaned for the first time in years. They were waiting for the army to arrive too.

When they were picked up by their shoulders and feet, Kay couldn`t help but yelp. She was sure her arms would come out of their sockets, and the ropes bit hard on her sore and bleeding arms. Charity cried out, and Joe was cursing until someone slugged him and he could only choke for breath. Gritting her teeth, Kay tried to endure every bounce, but couldn`t stop the tears.

Down the stairs they went. It smelled down there, something sweetish, not cigar or tobacco, and there was urine and bodies. People were lying about on pillows and chairs, just smoking. They stopped at a door and were hauled upright. It opened into what must have once been a storeroom. Inside there were chairs, some cushions and a long table, but no light. They were tossed into a dark hard bare corner. Kay could hear Charity crying quietly to herself.

They waited in the dark, with just the light from the hallway. Perhaps it wasn`t long, but time can go slow when you`re hurting and scared. Finally a thin clean shaven man came in, silhouetted in the doorway, with a box under his arm, and addressed them with a cheerful Southern accent.

"Sorry for the wait. We have a lot goin` on upstairs." He struck a match and lit a lantern. "Allow me to introduce myself, Miriam McAllister, but everyone calls me Tex. Honestly, I don`t care if you call me Miriam. I used to get teased about it, but these days I really don't care." He lit two more lamps. "I have no clue as to why they call me Tex. It could be because I`m from Texas." He let out a small chuckle at his own joke.

Pulling a towel out of the box, he started arranging metal instruments on it. Then he pulled out a dozen hanks of different types of rope.

"Be right back," he said, pushing the empty box under the table.

When he returned he had two more boxes, one on top of the other, and from these he pulled various bottles, cups, a box of cigars, mirrors, and things best left unidentified. Then he set about rearranging the furniture.

"The place is a mess," he said, with his friendly smile. "We don`t use it much. Don`t need to!"

Then he was out the door again and came back with a victrola, balancing the horn on top. This he sat it on the table, opening it up, and dropping the horn into its bracket.

"Lou loves music," he explained.

His next trip brought a box of records, which he set on the table behind the Victrola. Then he moved three sturdy chairs to the middle of the room in a triangle, each facing the others. The chairs had holes cut out of the seats.

"Now I know he wanted to know about that mine location from you," he said, nodding at Kay. "But if I`m to understand right, he`s expecting more than that, so don`t bother telling me." Then he looked at Charity. "I know he wants you broken in for work, but he didn`t say anything about a blonde. Can`t see as how he`d waste you though. You`re pretty enough. It`s just a matter of the right leverage. Maybe one of you has feelings for this boy over here?"

He looked back and forth between their tear-streaked faces.

"Well. If not, you will before we`re through." He opened the door to the hall and called, "Sykes, get in here."

"Yes sir," Sykes said, eagerly.

"Help me get them up on the chairs. Those ropes have got to be hurting."

They hauled them up on the chairs and handcuffed them to the chair backs, then tied their legs to the chair legs in front.

"That will be all Sykes."

"Yes, sir," Sykes said, a little disappointed he wasn't asked to stay.

Tex picked up a knife from his towel. Kay felt a rush of dread, but he walked behind each of them and cut the ropes on their arms. They could hear booms from upstairs. Tex seemed a little distracted by it.

"Let`s take a moment to appreciate the feeling returning to your hands." He stepped back and sat on the table, holding his knee.

Her arms had grown numb, but as the blood leaked back into them it grew to be excruciating, getting worse and worse, her hands and arms burning with fire. Kay couldn't stop a sob. She could even see tears in Joe`s eyes.

"I actually didn`t plan this, your hands and all, but we can be grateful for life`s little bonuses. You know little girl, I actually entertained your Daddy for a bit. Did you know that?"

"You didn`t."

"Someone can talk!" He smiled pleasantly. "I did. he was in that seat you`re in! It was the only time I ever failed."

"You bastard!"

"True! But that`s not important," Tex replied. "He`d taken a slug in his left lung. Still, I had him for six hours. You all are young and healthy, so I expect we won`t be leaving here for a couple of days at least. We`re in no hurry." He looked around with a confused look. "Now where`s Lou? He`ll want to gloat before we start. He likes to be here for the beginnings and the ends."

He got up and checked the handcuffs, then paced for a minute.

"Be back shortly. Don`t try to break the chairs. They`re California oak. You`ll break yourselves before you break them. Trust me, many have tried."

Then he left, closing the door behind him. The

quiet sank over them.

Finally, Kay said, "I`m so sorry. I led you into this."

"It`s not your fault," Charity said. "I didn`t watch your back."

"You couldn`t. They were on top of us before we even stood up." Joe squirmed and pulled at the ropes on his legs.

"Maybe if we told them where the mine was, we`d have to at least be able to ride so we could show them," Kay said.

"Maybe. He said he didn`t care about it though," Charity said. "Oh Joe, stop pulling at those ropes. You`re bleeding."

"Blonger might say different," Joe said, continuing to struggle.

"Somehow I don`t think so. I think he wants us," Charity said.

"Well I`ll be damned if I going to let him get with away this!" Kay growled, and she began inching and bouncing her chair towards the table. It took forever, but finally she was close enough that she could lean forward, her neck straining, pulling the towel of tools down into her lap with her mouth. They spilled across her lap, some onto the floor.

"Damn!" Kay said.

"What`s wrong?" Charity asked.

"Didn`t get the one I wanted. We`ll have to make do with this. Joe, bounce over here. I don`t want to drop this stuff."

"Which way?" Joe asked.

"I want your hands."

Joe bounced over and turned his back to Kay and then she began directing his reach.

"Left, no left! That`s it. Oh Joe, your arms are bleeding too."

"Ow!" Joe said, as he grabbed the wrong end of the scalpel.

"That's the one. Now your finger's bleeding too."

Joe picked it up and turned it around. Kay bounced around until her leg rope knot was near the knife.

"Joe, the blades pointing up. Turn it over. Good. Down, down, feel it?"

Joe sawed at the knot and the scalpel cut through quickly. Kay's leg came loose.

"Yes! Now the other." She bounced around again. "Charity, you better start bouncing over here."

When the other rope parted, she stood up arms still handcuffed to the chair, waddled over to the door and wedged her chair under the handle and sat on top, her weight wedging the chair in tight. "That ought to stump them for a bit!" Then to Joe, "Joe, we've got to get off these chairs. Try to look for something."

Charity chimed in, "I'm looking at the ring on the back of Joe's chair. Careful, Joe, left. They're held on with screws. We need something flat we can turn. You got anything like that in that lap of yours?"

"Maybe," she said, looking frantically.

Charity stood up, turned around and took the knife from Joe and began working on his legs.

"I've got some kind of clamp thing with kind of rounded edges that might work."

"Keep looking," Joe said. "I see something, but it's on the floor."

"Kick off your shoes and pick it up with your toes," Kay said.

"I get cramps in my feet," Joe said.

"I'll get it," Charity replied. She finished cutting Joe loose and then pulled her boots off with her toes, and then her socks. "Joe which one do you mean? This?"

"Yes, that's it. Lift it up to my hands. Now

where`re the screws?"

They worked on those screws, and upstairs they heard the booming replaced by explosions, and then more explosions near and far. Time just kept on going by with no one coming to check on them.

"Where are they?" Kay worried. "Why aren`t they at the door?"

"Don`t say that," Charity said. "You`ll curse us."

Then Joe was free. He rolled on his back and pulled his feet through the handcuff chain and went to work on Charity and then Kay. They heard three quick shots upstairs. They looked at each other, but Joe just shrugged and went back to work.

When they were all free, Kay opened the doorway as quietly as she could and took a quick peek. The hallway was empty. Down the hall, where the guard had sat, on the table next to his chair, was their stuff. Kay guessed it had been left there for Blonger to look over. She picked up her gun. It was still loaded, four shots left.

Deke and Ned wandered down an alley, just a bit lost. He saw two of Blonger`s toughs crossing a street and decided he might as well ask.

"Hey!" They looked up. "I need to find Blonger."

"Downtown, at the big dance hall, La Femme Peinte."

"Much obliged," he replied. He tipped his hat.

"No problem," one said.

Deke smiled as he rode on. He didn`t know where this dance hall was, but he did know where downtown was. He rode on at a trot past gangs of men being led to one place or another. Everything seemed to be in confusion. He asked a lone man leading a horse where the La Femme Peinte was, but got a shrug. The next, though, pointed towards a large building down towards the train station. As he drew close to the dance hall, he heard gunfire in the distance, but it was like no kind he`d ever heard before. This was rapid, deep, and steady.

In the growing morning light, between two buildings, he could see airships out towards the aerodrome with lines of white fire pouring down from them.

Blonger was using the street in front of the dance hall as a place to get men organized and it was pretty crowded, so he decided to try around back. Sure enough, there were only two guards standing in back in the well-lit alley next to a car. Judging by the steam leaking from it, the car was ready to go. Two guards were better than a hundred, but it they were still a problem. There was no way to get close without be seen or raising a fuss.

Then there were booms from over by City Hall. They sounded like cannon, and gunfire broke out all over town. Deke`s problem was solved. He figured with all that gunfire, two more shots wouldn`t be noticed. He got down from Ned, pulled out his rifle, and dropped both the guards. It took two shots for one because, as he later found out, one of the men`s badges had stopped the slug and only knocked him down.

Deke tied Ned to the hitching post next to the back door under the light of two lanterns hanging at its sides. The car was all fired up to go, but there was nobody there except the two guards, who were dead, so Deke figured the owner must be inside. That's where he had to go too, so he pulled open the door and walked in like he owned the place.

Three tanks rolled to the edge of town followed by a scrambling wave of blue. The tanks had swapped out their tracers for solid slugs, first because they didn`t want to set fire to the town, and second because tracer shells cost three times as much and the Army, back in those hard times was, if nothing else, cost-conscious. Behind them were one hundred and ten infantry out looking for fun.

"We were due replacements for these," the major said to Van Cise as they sat in their perches inside the lead tank. He nodded toward the guns as one of them tore a splintering hole in the front of a building. "But we keep being deployed. We should have Maxims. They`ll be far lighter."

"Yes, but they overheat," replied the gunner, and then added, "Sir."

"True, but I saw these water contraptions they had for the barrels," continued the major. "Like a canteen cover." The tank tipped a little as it rolled over and crushed several bodies.

"I`m not climbing out on the front of the tank to change a barrel during a firefight," the gunner said, as he punched a line of splintering holes through a wagon that had been upended across the street and was rewarded as he saw the lifeless arm of a new corpse flop down in the street behind it.

"These seem to do fine," Van Cise yelled over the racket.

The tank, venting jets of high pressure steam, pushed over the wagon, slowly climbed up and then crushed it under its wheels

Van Cise squinted through the observation slit. "Are those cannon at the end of the street?"

"Six pounders. Left over from the Mexican war I

think," replied the major. They could hear the shells flying over their heads, still aimed at the aerodrome. Ahead, half a dozen deputies broke cover to run, only to be gunned down in the street.

Van Cise listened and swore he could hear shooting in the next street over, but there was so much racket that he couldn`t be sure. "Do you hear shooting?" he asked the major.

"Maybe," the major replied. "They`re probably those friends of yours," he said. And then to the driver, "Take it around on the right."

Up in the sky Van Cise could see three airships as they slid towards city hall in a line. A bullet pinged off their armor and he ducked down and lost sight of them, but when he looked out again they were immediately over City Hall. They drifted over it, and past without anything happening, until suddenly the ground below began to boil with dozens of explosions as the bombs finally reached the ground.

The major laughed and slapped the bulkhead. "That`s what I like, complete air superiority!"

The artillery was quiet after that. However, it should be noted, that Gunnery Sergeant Parnell and his crews largely survived the bombardment. As far as airships go, these were military and fast, but you can still see them coming and when they did, the gunners wisely ran.

The cavalry swept the deputies back until they surrendered en masse in front of their wrecked artillery position. There were maybe thirty left from Main Street. None of them was Blonger, but Van Cise didn`t expect him to be actually in the line himself.

"We`ve got to take Blonger`s dance hall. That`s where he`ll be holed up."

"Point the way," said the major, with a smile. He

was clearly having fun. He detached 30 men to watch prisoners and hold City Hall. Then the column turned towards the railroad station.

When he looked around the stage and hall, the only place Deke could see to go was upstairs. It had the kind of carpet and luxury that he expected would lead to the boss, and the boss would lead to Kay. He crept into the main hall. Upstairs he could hear voices, but they were distant and faint. Edging along the wall, he could see men out front but none in sight inside. The hall was dark, but the stairs were lit from above. Hugging the wall at the base of the stairs and looking up, he could see that the balcony above was empty as well.

Taking a deep breath, he slipped up the stairs. Leading back from the main hall was a hallway. Taking a quick glance around the corner he saw nothing, not a soul. Where were the guards? He could hear voices from down the hall but couldn`t see anyone.

Edging down the corridor, he saw doors on each side, sometimes hearing movement inside. They were plain doors. None of them were Blongers, he thought. They just weren`t luxurious enough. Whoever was inside was probably safer with the doors shut and locked.

The corridor branched. Down the branch there were stairs and the corridor ended in a window looking out on the roof, but there were paintings in the corridor straight ahead and none down the branch. He kept going forward. It was quiet now.

Light spilled from an open door. Looking around the edge, there was a big man loading money in a bag from a safe behind a desk. He cocked the hammer of his pistol to let the man know he was there. Blonger froze, hand in the safe. There had been voices so Deke knew there had to be someone else. Ducking across to the other side of the door gave him a better view, but he saw no one. Behind the door then, he thought.

He kicked the door to slam it against the wall and stepped in only to watch the door swing through empty air. Instead he got sapped from behind. Whoever it was, he had been flat against the wall.

Kay edged up the stairway. The carpet was thick, and for that she was grateful. The balcony was clear and she could see a corridor leading back. Behind her came Charity and Joe, trying their best to be quiet, but she still winced at every creak of the steps. Stepping as quickly and as lightly as she could across the lit balcony she came to the corridor and stuck her head around and glanced down.

Way down the corridor, standing by a doorway, was Deke!

She was about to dance for joy, when she saw him step across to the other side of the doorway, gun held out. He kicked in the door, stepped in and then she heard him yelp. She ran and ran and there, gun drawn was Tex. He was about to put a bullet in Deke.

"Hey, Tex!" she called.

He looked up and she pulled hard on the trigger and with a bang that could burst windows she put a bullet in him. It hit his shoulder blade sending him spinning. His arm ripped loose from his body and hit the carpet before he did. The spray of blood washed across Blonger, standing behind his desk.

"Come out from around there, Mr. Blonger. We have some business to discuss."

Blonger looked at her with pure hate, but he put up his hands and came out.

"Why don`t you just lay on the floor for a bit," she said.

Joe and Charity came up the corridor behind her.

"Deke!" Charity cried, and she rushed over to him.

Kay`s pistol didn`t waver, though she loved Deke so. Blonger was too dangerous, and so she just stared that snake down until he was flat and spread on the floor, right next to Tex`s arm.

Joe rolled Deke over and got a moan out of him. "How`s my hat" Deke said.

Kay stooped down next to him still pointing her gun at Blonger. "It`s kinda bloody," she said. "I think we`re going to need a new one."

They searched Blonger, but they found the keys to the handcuffs in Tex`s pocket. Kay squeezed the handcuffs extra tight with all her anger on Blonger's wrists.

Charity and Joe held their guns on him while Kay cradled Deke and kissed his head, rocking him.

"You know what?" she said.

"What."

"Today`s my birthday."

"Marry me."

And she hugged him until his poor hurt head was about to fall off.

"I love you so much Deke Hayden, you bet I`ll marry you. Just you try and stop me."

The Hayden Gang Rides Again, #21, Hollywood Comics, ©1932

EPILOG

It took another half an hour before a soldier in blue ducked in the doorway and held them all at gunpoint. When Van Cise found out what they had done, he had them let go and promised to visit them later.

They returned home and fell down on their beds - - dirt grime and all – and slept until the next day. That afternoon found them hobbling around like cripples. Deke`s head had a great huge knot and he took one of Grace`s pain pills just so he could eat breakfast.

Dr. Balderson came by with Zeb and they looked at their wounds. Grace was doing fine. She and Mrs. Balderson had ridden out the battle in the attic. The doctor hadn`t done any fighting at all. Instead he and Zeb had taken care of the wounded as best they could. Their house had patients sitting on the porch and in every room. The Union soldiers had not lost a single man.

When Van Cise dropped in, he said he would try to get them a reward for the capture of Blonger, who was languishing in the jail, now staffed by Union soldiers. There was certainly money enough in his safe and they deserved a share. When Blonger finally did hang, the hangman let him down easy so the official count was 23 kicks, won by three of Blonger's ex-dance hall women.

The newspaper, when it reopened, changed its name from "The Rocky Mountain News" to the "Colorado Times," and its first headline read "The First Meeting of Our State Legislature." They were going to meet in one week. Barely time for folks to get there, but Van Cise wanted it done while he still had the troops nearby. He had to clean house.

When a reporter came by the old brown house to take down their story, they turned him away. Unfortunately, the story leaked out anyway and pretty soon people were coming by to discuss business, offering to help them mine, and to set up stock holding companies for them. It got so bad that they packed up and left.

They had collected, over the course of their

adventures, quite a number of state–owned horses. Governor Van Cise did his best to make sure they got to keep them, however they didn`t precisely get exactly their horses back. They got the same number back, all good ones too, so it was probably for the best that Charity and Kay had never gotten around to naming theirs. Ned had his own herd.

Hounded by reporters, entrepreneurs, and other scallywags, they rode up into the hills, Zeb with them, this time well provisioned and rested. They rode up streams, made side trails, rode single file, took travelled trails, and doubled back until the multitude that followed them were thoroughly lost, and then they headed up Coal Creek Canyon. When they came to the spot on the map, all they found was a rock fall. But they dug, pushed and cleared away the loose rock, until three days later they caught sight of a hard wall of pink, which was quickly covered over again as new debris fell down.

Kay had thought a lot about the future over the preceding days and right then and there she asked her friends if they wanted to be partners and with none of them being fools, they all agreed. So she got her mine and her friends together. To be sure, and we should be clear about this, every one of those kids could pull his or her weight. Kay was no fool. Logs were cut and buried sticking up at the corners of their stake and when they got back, Joe as the new head of the local USGS office made sure that the claim was solid, legal, and properly filed in Washington.

They hired that foreman and his family at the Forest Queen when he was put out of work with Blonger`s fall. He stayed with them until the end and retired happy. Eventually Joe and Charity married and had four kids that lived.

And that`s it. You know the rest. Read the dime

novels.

Kay`s aunt published her story from her letters that Kay had sent her, in the newspapers and made a killing, and then later Joe, always an aspiring writer, published that series of dime novels about their later adventures that were popular sellers.

They worked that mine for 23 years. Almost none of the pink got crushed. Andrew Carnegie had his wife`s bathroom trimmed in the stuff and a big piece still stands in the Smithsonian. And when it and the ore were gone, and their five kids had grown, Deke and Kay finally took that trip on a train to see the big cities back east.

ABOUT THE AUTHOR

Mark Bondurant, a chronic student with too many degrees to count, and an SF/fantasy fan practically since birth, recently discovered that he had rated over 3,600 titles on Netflix. Having emptied every library he ever encountered of SF and a goodly amount of history and mysteries as well, he found himself surprisingly at loose ends. On one hand, there were the chores, which loomed about him, and which he doggedly attempted to deal with fearsome ferocity, and then there was his computer which could be filled with the stories he wished he could find in those now empty libraries and desolate Netflix queue. Really and truly he tried to do his chores, but his need to escape was undeniable. And so they started popping out. He has written two novels so far, which he is lavishly illustrating, and many short stories. You can listen to the clatter of his keys and his grunting with effort at markbondurant.com on Facebook.

If you liked the story, and want to help the author, then please rate it, or even better - review it - on Amazon.com

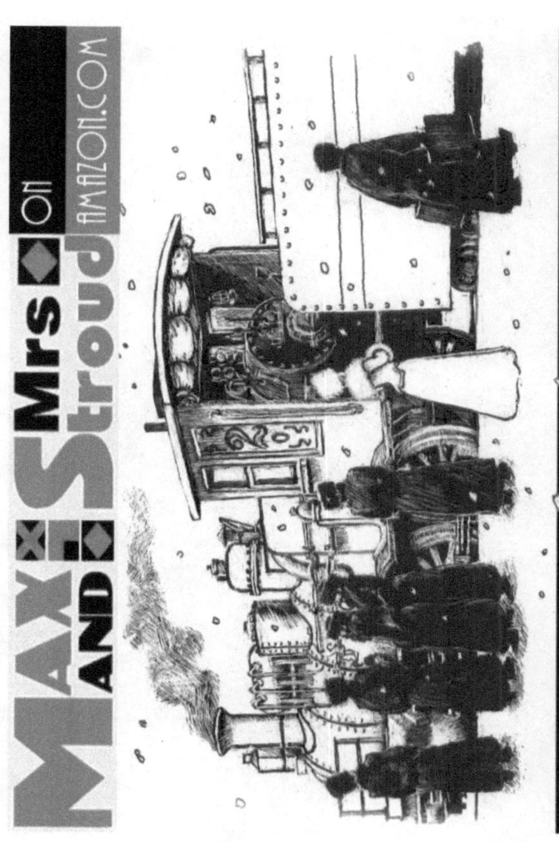
MAXIS AND Mrs Stroud ON AMAZON.COM
Dig It!
From Mark Bondurant and Bongo Books

Red
Jacket
Mark Bondurant
The New American Steampunk
Dig It!